Rainsongs
of Kotli

Tariq Malik

We acknowledge the support of the Canada Council for the Arts for our publishing program. We also acknowledge support from the Ontario Arts Council.

Canada Council **Conseil des Arts**
for the Arts **du Canada**

ONTARIO ARTS COUNCIL
CONSEIL DES ARTS DE L'ONTARIO

Cover design by David Drummond

Edited by Charles Anthony Stuart

National Library of Canada Cataloguing in Publication

Malik, Tariq, 1951-
    Rainsongs of Kotli / Tariq Malik. – Lohars Fiction

ISBN 1-894770-15-3

    1. Lohars--Fiction. I. Title.

PS8626.A44R33 2004   C813'.6   C2004-905367-1

Printed in Canada by Coach House Printing

TSAR Publications
P. O. Box 6996, Station A
Toronto, Ontario M5W 1X7
Canada

www.tsarbooks.com

for Abbaji and Ammiji

whose generosity of spirit informs each word on these pages

Contents

. . . Paani

Everyone lives downstream

By midsummer, waters from the rapidly melting winter snows of the mountains have begun to pool inside the gorges and valleys, and acquire a critical mass that resonates with a singleness of purpose. The river Chenab, in its spirited descent to the plains of Punjab, can already taste the salt of the distant sea.

So can its four siblings, the Jhelum, Ravi, Sutlej and Beas, all emerging from their shared sources in the Karakoram Mountains, each torrent tracing a separate southwesterly route through the plains for an eventual union with the mighty Indus and the waiting sea.

Encountering the gently sloping land that offers little resistance to its heedless plunge, the Chenab hesitates in the pursuit of its destiny. It begins to meander. Even this early in its incarnation, the river has already acquired a splintered mind. Bifurcating endlessly, it splits itself up into a web of eddies and rivulets; a weaving snake reclaiming its discarded coils amongst the transient dissolving banks.

Over the millennia, the Himalayas have thus been transported piecemeal into the open arms of the waiting plains, ladled out over vast swaths of land. Forests of bulrushes, reeds and sedge grasses line the river's transient multiple beds, thrive amidst these seasonal and diverse wetlands. Finicky marsh hens twitch from stem to stem; nervous bee catchers and migrant swallows skim open-beaked mouthfuls from the surface; and a bounty of carp-like mahseer and rau, saul, catfish and

1

trout churn its nutrient-rich murky depth.

At the same time the monsoon clouds, having risen from the distant Bay of Bengal in the east, migrated north and encountered the Himalayas, are now being nudged steadily west by the trade winds. Soon the monsoon will encounter the land of the legendary five rivers of the Punjab and lash it with rain.

At such times of mountain snowmelt and monsoon rainstorm it seems there is only one reality in this world, that of water: Paani! It is this reality that has shaped all the dreams and all the aspirations of the inhabitants of this lush land. It has made the existence of life itself possible, and impossible.

Once the seasonal floods have wreaked their havoc, crested and receded, they offer up the gift of a transformed land, whose legendary fecundity was already known to yield two harvests per year a millennium ago. The soil can instantly clothe itself with vegetation, even if left exposed for a single day of the monsoon. During harvest time the vast land unravels into endless ocean waves of amber wheat and drooping stalks of pearl rice. Its fertility has made this land the most coveted of all regions, by not only its sedate inhabitants, but also its frequent invaders. The flamboyant Punjabis are barely able to contain their pride in their land; boasting often and loudly that they need only to toss the seed onto the ground and then leap to safety.

Set amidst the folds of this bounty is a tiny dwelling where humans seem to have turned their backs on both the ancestral and traditional arts of warfare and agriculture. This is Kotli Loharan, the home of the ironsmiths and metal craftsmen, who almost four centuries ago forged their sickles and ploughs into hammers and anvils. Confident that their future welfare lay in their skill at the manufacture of articles of iron and steel and ornaments of iron, gold and silver. Their lives transformed by the affluence these professions afforded them. During the wars they thrived as manufacturers of weapons and shields of superior workmanship; in times of peace they used their skills in the manufacture of damascene artifacts.

In our journey down the Chenab, we encounter this border town and its people in the 1950s, almost a decade after the cataclysm labelled "the twentieth century's first successful postwar experiment in ethnic cleansing," i.e. the partition of India. We are witness today to the web of cross-pollinated dreams of its inhabitants. Standing on the cusp of this critical moment in history, the town seems destined to shrug off the heavy burden of its four-century heritage, to belatedly encounter the insecurity and anonymity of the modern age.

Within the lifetime of a single generation, more than two thirds of Kotli's inhabitants will have deserted their hometown and settled overseas. Most of them will relocate to fill the need for skilled labourers, in the newly awakening Arabian Gulf states or the recently opened up East African coast. Lamentably, this exodus will sap their hometown of all its essential vitality, gradually transforming a vibrant and productive community into a generic backcountry Punjabi town with nothing to distinguish it from countless others, except for the myth of a very special people and a very distinct history.

At dusk on this opening day, an itinerant fakir, fondly called Malhaara in acknowledgment of his beguiling rainsongs, has stumbled upon Kotli in his single-minded pursuit of an ancient riverbed that has vanished and reemerged several times before his eyes. On the banks of a ghost river, the town appears to him to be larger than most villages and hamlets he has encountered on his journey. He is intrigued by the discovery that the seemingly prosperous inhabitants here own none of the bounty of the surrounding land.

Homesickness and Other Fevers

"Nanak dukhiya sab sansar"

Nanak, the whole world is grieving

Hafeez Tarkhan, the village carpenter, dreams, and in his dream
two brothers stand side by side at dusk in a field of thrice-har-
vested bajra. They scan the parched and fading horizon for a
missing landmark tree, dust devils swirling around them like dervishes.
A handful of tawny eagles, having ridden all afternoon the warm cur-
rents rising off the gently undulating plains, trim their wings and begin
a languorous plunge to earth. Their descent goes unnoticed, the land
below appears to have been deserted.

Balwinder, the taller and elder of the two men, stretches an unsteady
left hand to trace the wavering outline, in the far distance, of a village he
presumes to be Kotli Loharan. In turning to his pensive brother to point
out a salient feature in the landscape, the tone of his voice seems to tease
rather than inquire: "Oy Sukhi, tukk! Can you see that winding row of
trees by the horizon where the road turns to the right? Can you make
out a mosque anywhere near that spot?"

Not receiving a response, he continues to follow the chain of his own
probing thought: I can distinctly remember there once having been a
massive pipal tree next to that mosque. It was always the first landmark
you saw on approaching Kotli from any direction. Now, all you can see
are the minarets of the jamiya masjid and that tree is nowhere in sight.

His hesitation, however, does not last long: "I am absolutely sure I recognize the natural features of this land but the buildings all seem to have been misplaced. Somehow, it feels like such a long time ago that we were actually here, back then, blissfully unaware of the world closing in around us."

Desperate for signs of anything even remotely familiar in the altered world before him, Balwinder continues his search, mesmerized by this first sighting of their destination, his confident recollections of the layout of the land suddenly tossed into disarray. He wonders how the span of a mere ten years could have altered this thoroughly familiar land in such a drastic manner. With the level of his animation and excitement rising, he once again turns towards his companion in bitterness: "Just look at all those shiny new brick houses! Tukk Sukhi, tukk! See how indulgent and fat these Muslaas have grown in our absence. Where do you think all this sudden newfound wealth has come from? Could it be that with the Hindu banyas gone and all the debts written off, the Muslaas have finally learned to save and prosper?"

He looks up to his brother once again as if seeking the comfort of a familiar response, knowing full well in his heart that there is no logical answer to the bitter and lingering questions in his mind: What was it within us that had triggered such extreme animosity? What had we ever done personally to deserve such treatment? Unable now to trust his voice or contain the sudden emotion, he falls silent, willing the rising bile inside him to subside. An imperceptible tremor that has crept up his left arm is now threatening to become more pronounced with his every effort to contain it.

The unpredictable yet gentle undulation of the wind is once again picking up dust, and the men are barely able to distinguish a number of kites bobbing from the distant rooftops. The plaintive call of the evening adhan washes over them from the minarets of the distant mosque, its flow rising and ebbing on the wind.

The younger of the two brothers, Sukhinder, who has been making an even more determined effort to decipher the landmarks in the fading light, has also been dwelling on the unsettling reality before them of the missing pipal tree. In his alarm over the intensity of his brother's agita-

5

tion, he turns away while asking: "Do you think they might have burnt the pipal down, too, like they did Babay di Beri at the temple of Gurudwara Nanaksar?"

The question remains unanswered, for in squinting ahead of him against the abrasive dust carried by the wind, Balwinder's consciousness has already disassociated itself from their current predicament and is exploring the other images beginning to stir from his own past.

The long shadows of that behemoth tree have towered over the span of his entire youth. Its shaggy branches have continued to arch ever higher, the roots sinking deeper, the longer he has stayed away from this, his birthplace. The pipal's massed bulk of trunks and branches had stood like a tight crowd of humans with upraised arms, anchoring the sky to Balwinder's earth. And now here he is, confronting the reality that this personal icon that had flourished for so long in his mind has been erased from the face of the earth. Shaken and bewildered, he turns slowly to his brother, to ask with his silence: Is it not enough that men own the land and everything on it; do they have to own the sky above it too?

They stand speechless for several more minutes, caught up in the grip of their reflections, forced by the wind to squint at the dissolving, dust-choked horizon. As all colour and light begins to fade around them, they realize that the proximity of Kotli has somehow chastened their brash spirit of enterprise. Feeling vulnerable, they wish they had come better armed for their mission.

It is the younger, Sukhinder, who again expresses the thought foremost in their mind: "Balway, I told you; we should have come better prepared for this. Have you any idea what fate might await us once we venture in there? Have you so easily forgotten what it was like the last time you were here?"

All Balwinder can do is stare back witheringly at him, absentmindedly tracing the reassuring and familiar outline of the kirpan tucked under his kurta. He draws out a sigh, muttering under his breath, more to himself than anyone else: When we left here ten years ago, we never stood a chance of getting out of here alive; and who could have foreseen the severity of the ensuing storm . . . and yet with Guruji's blessings, here we are now. Sukhi, I am never again going to be caught out under similar circumstances! It has to be different this time, with you by my side and everyone else unaware of our presence here.

As they become aware of the increasing chill and moisture in the air, and unable to distinguish the distant village any longer, they decide to set up camp inside a deserted mausoleum. They had stumbled upon it earlier. They have come here fully prepared for these shrines, seeking them out wherever they are, tucked away into the folds of the country-side; solemnly observing which one is in favour with the locals and which one neglected. The brothers have chosen this season of late spring for their journey, as the days have warmed and lengthened, and one can again sleep out in the open without concern for the rains.

Sukhinder, still wary of the fresh smear of ash he has discovered around a discarded earthen oil lamp, is too weary to be cautious any longer and falls asleep the minute he lays down his head. His ability to sleep so soundly under even the most trying of circumstances amazes his brother, who, alone and adrift, stares vacuously at the familiar river of stars beginning to spill out above them, then once more at the land around. This landscape of drought and smothering dust is very different from the one they had waded through during the lush monsoon of their last departure, ten years before. The rivers and streams may be drier now, he muses, but they still etch the same routes over the land. This is my land and I know I can find my way back home. But where is home?

How will I ever reconcile within myself the impossible experiences and sights of that first journey from here to Gurdaspur? How is it that even after the passage of so many years, the experience still rips through me like a stifling blast from a tandoor in full heat? I am already begin-ning to forget on which side of these lines demarcated by the rivers I am. Were the turmoil and bloodshed real or a dream, with the images so vivid and fresh in my mind? I have been doomed to eternally live through the same fevered, recurring dream, in which I keep losing myself; every time I stand at the beginning, I am already tumbling and looping down towards the end; an endless series of jumbled images gets tossed repeatedly onto the insides of my eyelids. And I sit transfixed and immobile, captive to the delirium, the drama beginning once again to unravel before me.

Here I am, stumbling once again on a field similar to this one, shrouded in the early morning mists, as I find a severed human head. A short while later I discover three more strewn along the railway tracks. It is as if a train had passed randomly sowing death in the dark of the night. I find myself discovering only a few yards further up in the same field the bloodied ends of a severed rope, secured around two telegraph poles just high enough to decapitate passengers crowding the rooftop.

Amidst this carnage is the body of an infant, lovingly bundled, tight. During my journeys, how many such infants there would be held high over their parents' heads, or thrust into my arms by desperate grandparents, with the call to save what was left of their dwindling family: He is all we have. Our sons and daughters have all gone on ahead, and we have been left to fend for ourselves. Take him with you and our family will continue to live on.

How could they possibly have known from which side of the divide I had come, where I was headed? How profound was their desperation that they could delude themselves with the belief that I, of all people, or anyone else given these circumstances, could ever miraculously restore to wholeness their fractured families?

I was to learn that the infrequent structures of road bridges were always the worst places to stop at. As these were the only sites of seclusion, in this flat open land that will keep nothing secret for long, we were to discover here with shocking frequency the discarded or ripped clothing of women, and never to find a single chunni or chuddar among the mute remnants of past violence. I wondered how anyone could possibly survive these nightmarish landscapes with their sanity still intact. Sukhi, my poor brother, then only a boy of eight, an unblinking witness to all this carnage, was already acquiring the brittle, impassive adult shell of detachment; filing away all that he saw, in recesses he would never be able to fathom. How could I possibly have shielded him from that world?

It had all begun a few months before the day of the partition in mid-August of 1947, a date that would split our Punjab forever into "ours" and "theirs." Upon hearing for the first time of this scheduled demarcation of his beloved land, my father, who belonged to a different age and time, had openly proclaimed that he would believe the reality of this imposed political decision only on the day he saw a corresponding line dividing the sky above him into "ours" and "theirs." Mercifully, he himself would not survive these times long enough to witness the final reality of the partition, along the lines of its waterways, of the land that he had tilled with his own hands.

Amid the news of mounting attacks on Sikhs and Hindus in the areas surrounding Kotli, he had finally reluctantly sat down with the other elders of the Minhas clan to plot out a strategy for dealing with the deteriorating situation. It was becoming increasingly obvious with each passing day that if we continued to live on complacently the way we had till now, our homes, lands and temples would all soon be snatched away from us. But of all those who were gathered at these meetings, no one could have imagined or comprehended the scale of the movement that would eventually relocate so many lakhs of our people from their homeland. Nowhere, in the entire four centuries of the existence of Sikhism, were there such upheavals as those we were now witnessing.

What finally precipitated our decision to leave was the lynching in broad daylight of our relatives, Mukhand Singh and his young nephew, near the deserted brick kilns north of Kotli. This was followed a few days later by the kidnapping by the local nambardar of a Sikh girl out working in the fields. She was held captive for two days before the local elders prevailed to secure her release. There were daily rumours of similar killings and abductions in the area, in an emerging pattern of daily mounting belligerence towards us. For days the maulvi in the local jamiya masjid had been ratcheting up his rhetoric of hate against the enemies within. One Friday afternoon, his venom spilled out onto the streets as the congregation was leaving the mosque after prayer, and three of the local Hindu cloth merchants' shops were attacked and looted. With this incident, an unmarked line had been crossed for the first time; from then on the targets would be anything and anyone associated with non-Muslims. The Sikhs elders reluctantly decided that the sanest thing to do under these circumstances was to abandon our adopted hometown and join the others of our clan in Amritsar, on the other side.

We had lived here for almost five generations.

The other side, or paar, as it was referred to in all our conversations, was a vague entity that lay far to the east across the river Ravi. For the Hindus and Sikhs, who faced the plight of being trapped in predominantly Muslim regions like Kotli, paar could just as well have been on the other side of the moon.

By then also steady streams of Muslim refugees from the Bajawat area near the proposed border were beginning to pour into Kotli with their entire households crammed on their backs or on bullock carts. Some of these people were housed inside the mosques, while others were settled into the houses hastily vacated by the wealthier Hindus who had correctly anticipated the turmoil. A deserted Hindu temple was by now being used to house their cattle, and a day-and-night vigil was kept in all the surrounding villages. People were learning to defend themselves when attacked. Rumours spread like wildfires and would bring entire villages out looking for trouble.

It was the crusty and seasoned retired subedar Gurdeep Singh whose opinions finally prevailed. Relying heavily on his personal experiences in the military, he single-handedly ironed out most of the finer details of our escape. It was he who decided that we would travel in separate and manageable groups of about eight each, in order to avoid attention. In light of what later transpired, I will lay the blame squarely on him, even though he was only carrying out a very difficult responsibility. It was also he who decided that all families would be split up so that there would be greater odds of at least some members surviving from each. What is done is done now, yet in hindsight this policy was to cost our family dearly. Perhaps if I could have had only my immediate family in my charge, matters would have turned out differently. But then what of others, like my fiancé Manjit, who had no elder men in her family except for her old parents. Would any of them have made it out alive any other way?

During the early part of my youth, I had acquired an extensive knowledge of the marshlands between the rivers Chenab and Ravi while fishing and hunting for wild boar. Therefore I was chosen to escort the first batch across them. The original plan was for me to see my charges safe across the border and then return to the temple of Gurudwara Nanaksar to pick up the next batch. Since the Mussalmans were the only people not being targeted, it was thought practical that we as Sikhs would try to look like them as closely as possible. The men would leave their beards untied if they could not bring themselves to shave them off; our easily identifiable turbans would be abandoned in favour of the smaller pugris, and everyone would have to wear kurtas and salwars. The women would cover their heads with chuddars or chunnis at all times.

No one had a precise map of the region, so a rough route was traced using all the known villages to the east of Kotli. Although the state of Jammu was close, it was rejected as a destination for being too far north of our ancestral home. This, in hindsight, proved to have been a wise decision. From Kotli we would make our way east by southeast on foot following the meandering streams of the Aik and the Palkhu, and then head for the temple of Gurudwara Nanaksar at Babay di Beri. I would head for the railway bridge near Narowal by traveling alongside the Sialkot-Narowal road through Pasrur, and than attempt the crossing from there. The established checkpoint of Wagah near Lahore was too far to reach on foot. Once safely across this point, we would head east for Gurdaspur and then later regroup south at Amritsar. We would also avoid all public roads and large cities or towns.

Accompanying me on my very first trip were my mother, my younger sister Nitu, my elderly maternal uncle and aunt and their daughter Manjit, and her younger brother Navjot. I reluctantly agreed to let my elder sister Sardar, and brother Sukhi, to follow with the next group. How I now wish I could go back and undo this one fatal decision.

On the appointed day we left Kotli late in the afternoon, hoping to arrive by nightfall at the Gurudwara on the outskirts of Sialkot. Making our way eastwards, we followed the noisy meandering flow of the Aik, the stream fleetingly visible through the dense vegetation, and were able to reach our first resting place at the ancient Gurudwara at Babay di Beri. I can still feel the thrill of that moment as that blessed tree beside the fluted dome loomed out of the darkness to greet us. Sadly, this was also to be the last time I would behold that spiritually moving scene.

We were blessed that day at the gurudwara, Balwinder now murmurs, grinding his teeth in half-sleep, while his brother continues to snore loudly beside him. Who could have foreseen then that an Indian train full of mutilated Mussalman bodies, arriving at the Sialkot railway station from Wazirabad the very next week, would ignite this whole region? Our beloved tree, the Babay di Beri, would be burnt to the ground in the events that would follow, the gurudwara set on fire, the inmates all slaughtered. This was the gurudwara that our leader, Guru Nanak, himself had once blessed by staying under the Beri tree and bathing in its pond.

We were blessed that day.

Upon returning for the second batch of refugees I stumbled onto the smouldering ashes that had consumed my cousin and neighbour Rattan's entire family. They had been sheltering there with Sukhi and Sardar. My sister Sardar was lost here to us forever in an attack by a mob while Sukhi ran screaming from body to body, desperately searching for her. How could subedar Gurdeep have anticipated this when he was devising the plan to split up each family before the journey?

We were to learn later from his family in Amristar, of his eventual martyrdom, how he succumbed to the Mussala's knives upon refusing to abandon the home he had built with his own hands.

During that first flight, when we thought we were still this side of the imagined line called the new border, we learned to shout out loudly Pakistan zindabad and Allah O Akbar at any signs of human approach. Our Muslim friends had taught us these slogans. I still recall my friend Ismail showing me how to raise my right fist while belting out these slogans: You have to make it believable, he had advised, it has to come from the pit of your belly to be convincing.

Once we were across the line delineated by whitewashed drums marking the beginning of Indian territory, we switched to the more familiar slogan of jai guru ki, sat sari akaal or jai jai sate, hari ka naam sate and jai Hind! It was sheer luck that we were never challenged by either the vigilante mobs called jathas, waves of armed men roving the countryside on both sides of the fast flooding rivers and paddy fields, or the men from the hamlets that had been invaded on the offensive and seeking revenge. Nor did we encounter any of the feared and unscrupulous opportunists thriving on easy pickings in the confusion of bloodshed and divided loyalties.

The place where the Ravi crooks an arm around the northeast corner of the Punjab had been identified to me as the location of the border between the two new nations. Passing through the dreaded marshes and restricted to a diet to boiled water, baked tubers, dry fruits, achar and thick, dried wheat cakes, it had taken us over a week to reach it from Kotli, but weak with exhaustion, we were all still alive.

Getting across the river would now be the next great challenge for us, because none of us could swim well enough to make it across the stretch of water before us. Since this was mid-monsoon season, the Ravi was just beginning to flood. We could also see other refugees like us wading into the water with their meager belongings, attempting to swim or float across. For once, there was complete calm and quiet around us, no fires or screams or the stench of decomposing bodies, just the vastness of the flat water stretching to the faint distant shore. Once we had all bathed in the bracing cold water, I set off to look for a barge or boat to take us across. That first crossing by boat was comparatively easy and uneventful, even though I had had to pay dearly to convince the boatman to risk taking us across.

Upon my return, the waters had already begun to rise swiftly and flood more of the marshes we had threaded our way across before. However, nothing I had experienced till then could have prepared me for the scene that awaited me at the Babay di Beri. Through the cloud of intervening years, I have tried to sort the sequence of events of that day, but that one incident remains the hardest for me to wrestle with, and lay to rest. Perhaps this madness we are now embarked upon is our final effort to address the lingering sorrow over that day's loss.

The brothers wake early at dawn and discover that they have slept in close proximity to a small graveyard. The dozen or so unmarked graves are untended and overgrown with weeds. What draws their attention is a toppled gravestone on which someone has painted in white the words of a universal eulogy: Nanak dukhiya sab sansar, Nanak, the whole world is grieving. The words are familiar and a godsend this far into their journey, and Sukhinder, mistakenly thinking that he is in the presence of kin that have been erroneously buried instead of being cremated, hastily begins tidying up the graves. But Balwinder impatiently drags him away, pointing out that they have dead of their own to attend to.

"We have no way of knowing who is buried here," Sukhinder protests. "What if these are the remains of someone close to us?"

Quietly they venture closer to Kotli. By now they have defined a comfortable middle ground where there is no need for further dialogue on the matter of their quest, having searched diligently and unsuccessfully in their own peculiar ways, for the tenuous thread of logic or madness that has brought them so far.

Balwinder, whose experiences and recollections of the events of the recent past are in sharper focus than those of his precocious sibling, has tried to impress upon him, unsuccessfully as it turns out, the similarities between the tribulations and aspirations of the side where they have now prospered and of this, the land their father had trodden so fondly. He has pointed out how the violence on one side was matched equally by the madness on the other. There are no heroes or villains, he tells him, only ordinary folks like you and me, who were transformed into something far greater and far more evil than what we had previously been. Just look how the land itself has no memory or history of what happened here. Look how it has shrugged off the cataclysmic nightmares that ran out their course here, and how the rains have washed the blood away, and how all remaining traces of destruction have been eroded away by wind and dust. It is only in us humans, the survivors and the witnesses, that history lives, deeper than the skin of our conscious memory. We have to teach ourselves to look beyond our own traumas and prejudices. And in quiet summation Balwinder observes that the fevers that once ran along these rivers have now subsided, and we are learning

14

to pick up the threads of our lives in a different part of this very same Punjab.

And Sukhinder, who shares none of his brother's tolerance or pacifism, has insisted with equal passion that the poison still exists deep within us, only biding its time for just the right trigger: I have known this from childhood. I have been a witness to this dark secret lurking in every schoolyard bully, in every taunt of an elder sibling, and even in the sadistic behavior of the bruised egotist who passes himself off as my schoolteacher. You have only to look at how our neighbour Jasbir comes home drunk every night, beating his wife and children. Is this not the same dichotomy of wills that drives the Punjabi folklore hero of my nanni's bedtime tales, venturing forth as the proverbial gabru, forever caught between the twin urges to ravage and to cherish? It is as if a virulent fever lurks beneath the surface of our collective skins, waiting out its time, before erupting forth unannounced. And yet, we go about our daily lives, unaware of this split within our innermost selves.

With the old and tired arguments discarded, they now set out to visit the cremation site of their father. It is located at a considerable distance from the village. Coming to a secluded spot of scorched earth Balwinder recalls as the location of the crematorium, now overrun with weeds, he squats down with one hand resting lightly on the soil. It is here that the full extent of the tragedy of the partition comes crashing down on his burdened heart, as it suddenly dawns on him that there is something extremely mournful, even perverse and unnatural, in the fact that his mother will now never know the solace of the physical remnants of her husband's life.

Do you remember your Mussalman friend Inayat Ullah explaining to us one day about his belief that in order to create you the creator had to take some soil from your homeland, and upon your death this borrowed clay will be returned to the same land? Lately I have begun to wonder in which homeland this borrowed soil of mine will finally come to rest.

By noon they have set out to reacquaint themselves with their hometown of Kotli Loharan. Approaching it from the outskirts on the northwest by first passing through the Khoja community of Bhulowal, and then crossing the bridge over the unseasonably dry canal of Nehr

15

Mardan, they find themselves lost with disconcerting frequency. In retracing their remembered paths through the redrawn alleyways and cul-de-sacs, they seize on familiar doorways and rooftop details for guidance; the slight rise of the cobbled street informs them that they are getting closer to their destination. Sleepy mongrels arise self-importantly to proclaim their territories at the openings of deserted streets. An army of crows that has followed them from the outskirts is briefly joined by a retinue of street urchins chanting: Jogi oy, jogi oy!

We are not jogis, we are fakirs, an irritated Sukhinder lashes out at them.

Fakir oy, fakir oy, they respond, before losing interest and returning to their game of guli dhanda. The crows, however, continue to hound them, tracking their progress by flapping their wings noisily from the rooftops.

The visitors do not enter or stop at the street they have come looking for, but pass by it twice, only briefly glancing at the familiar four-paneled door at the end of the gentle rise. The palpable flood of memories in these familiar corners and doorways is only tempered by the odd fact of alteration or restoration that has taken place. Theirs had been a time when each one of these mohallas was dominated by a single extended family employed in a single trade. Thus the kamyaran da malla housed potters, and the barbers had chosen to settle in the mohalla naiyan. Balwinder notes that the arrival of the refugees from the other side and opportunists with their new brick houses has shifted the status quo, and inner mohallas have now sprung up to reflect this altered reality.

They also discover from a distance that Balwinder's fondly remembered pipal has indeed been burnt to the ground, and its numerous stumps are now beginning to sprout green eruptions.

Unknown to the brothers, their hastened and purposeful walking has not gone unobserved by some of the locals. Squatting at their doorsteps with hookahs, or shopping in the bazaar, or staring out of their workshops, they have scrutinised the fakirs, instantly realizing that they do not belong to any of the local shrines or dargahs. The visitors are, however, perfectly safe, for their parrot-green garb of holy men bestows upon them a degree of anonymity and protection. Their obvious lack of familiarity with the surroundings also serves them well.

Later that same afternoon, Hafeez Tarkhan, exhausted and sweaty after coitus, is sprawled half-asleep on a stringed cot, intermittently swatting at the flies buzzing over him. He has deserted his workshop to seek comfort in the shade of his home for the duration of the noon heat. The cool, darkened veranda lies in stark contrast to the harsh sunlit courtyard. Cords of wood and abandoned carpentry projects are piled high around him.

He is awakened from his drugged stupor by the agitated voice of his wife, Qulsoom, who is clutching at his shoulder. Mistaking her urgency for passion, he reaches for the hem of her kameez and is taken aback by her irritated rejection. It is only then that he notices the look of concern on her face. She speaks in a hushed voice,

"Hafeez, there are two men at the door asking for you. They are dressed like fakirs. I don't think they heard me, but I was able to get a really good look at one of them. I think they are Sikhs. I saw the glint of a kara on one of them. You know, Hafeez, how quick I am to pick up on these little clues, and how you are always telling me not to read too much into such things, but . . . "

Hafeez's benumbed mind is still trying to come to grips with his wife's torrent of words. Why would she ever think the visitors at their door were disguised, and what could be so urgent about two strangers at their door? They could just as well be customers inquiring about some job he is supposed to have completed. Each passing day brings more of them knocking on his door, each one expecting him to be at their beck and call at all hours . . .

Hafeez and his wife had been married hastily, by arrangement, in a mosque in Sialkot. He knows little of her personal history before they exchanged marital vows and knows as little of the causes of her personal anxieties. Over the years, he has found himself unable to cope with her need for constant reassurance, her frequent and prolonged bouts of paranoia. He has often wondered whether his wife had ever been fully sound of mind. There have been occasions when he has found her staring vacantly into space for what seemed like hours, or looking up at the outer door as if in anticipation of something, without the least indication of self-awareness. At such times, she has become a complete stranger; days pass without a single word exchanged between them. Yet, it is always his fondness for her that overcomes all his misgivings, and their relationship has continued to survive thus in a state of mutual forgiving and tolerance.

" . . . and for someone who is passing himself off as a Muslim holy man, he is counting the beads of his rosary with his left hand," she whispers hoarsely in his ear, breathless in her excitement, like a child who has uncovered some dark and juicy secret.

"And there are folds in his loose beard as if it has been rolled up or bound for a long time. The other one, who is younger, is hiding a short way down from our doorstep and appears to be standing on guard. Hafeez, if they are out begging for food, how is it that their bowls are empty, although our house is the furthest one on this street? And why is he asking for you by name: 'Is Hafeez Tarkhan at home?' he asked me when I answered the door. Hafeez, you have to be careful, they look kind of ferocious to me."

By now Hafeez has heard enough and decides to investigate the matter for himself. He quickly pulls on his kameez, straightens his dhoti, and, impatiently signaling her to be quiet, ambles over to the door. Peering from between two loose bricks in the outer wall, he notices that there are indeed two bearded men at his door, and they are dressed in fakirs' green garbs. He searches their faces and clothing for clues to their origins but can unearth nothing. The Sikh's kara that his Qulsoom claims to have seen is not in sight, and they both look genuinely devout. But fakirs out begging so early in the afternoon, when cooking in the houses hasn't even begun just yet? Is this why their begging bowls are empty?

Suddenly the awareness dawns on him: Of course, Qulsoom may just be right in all her babbling. How quickly he forgets what he has so reluctantly come to learn about her over the past seven years: her intuitive conclusions are always more reliable than his own. These men might well be Sikhs, and he may just know why they have come knocking on his house.

He has indeed been waiting for just such a day ever since he moved here with his wife.

It was about three years after the partition and his father's agonizing prolonged death, when Hafeez finally made up his mind to move back with his new bride from the adopted city of Sialkot to his hometown of Kotli. And it had been Qulsoom who had persuaded him to buy this particular house, putting forth several sound reasons for her choice. One of the previous owners of this house had apparently been a carpenter and some of the implements of his trade still littered the house. Strewn all over the rooms and verandas were discarded but useable planks and cords of wood. It also helped his decision that the property was selling cheaply. A previous owner had dug up all the floors in search of a rumoured treasure. The walls had also been subjected to a thorough search. The house had lain neglected, and cobras had made their nests there. A snake charmer had been hired to evict them.

The years following the partition were those of turmoil and hardship for many of Kotli's inhabitants, but for a few they were a time of great opportunity. There were those who were quick to lay claim to the more coveted dwellings of the wealthier Sikhs and Hindus. The moneylender Bunya Dinanath's sumptuous house was the first one to be "claimed." The house itself proved to be barren, anything of value having been already carted off in the first few days following its evacuation. However, a few deeds and promissory notes were discovered in the safe, and many of the villagers were now finally able to take legal claim of their own properties and have their debts written off. The flamboyant locals had been notorious for running up debts to finance lavish weddings, and this was close to uncovering a fortune for most of them.

Hafeez had shrewdly noted that several wealthy upper-caste Hindu and Sikh families had once lived on the same street as his new house. It was also rumoured that in the house next door, a cloth bundle had been discovered buried behind a wall. When untied, the cloth immediately disintegrated into powder revealing a large number of worm-eaten currency notes whose denomination could not be determined. In the middle of the heap of notes were some locks of hair and a tiny gold ring attached to a bit of red string. The ring must have been a ceremonial one for a coveted infant's finger; it was the only item of value yielded in a diligent search of the house.

For Hafeez, it now seems the time to collect on his investment is finally at hand. If the strangers outside his door are indeed Sikhs returning to their homes, than something of real value must have lured them all the way from across the border.

Meanwhile, outside Hafeez's doorstep, Balwinder is marveling once again at his brother's foresight in choosing this time of the day to approach the house, with the streets deserted. He stands close to the door while Sukhi is content to stay back under the wide awning. Waiting for a response from within the house after he has rattled the chain several times, Balwinder has enough time to notice how unchanged this street, his street, is.

The fist-sized open drain still runs down the middle of the street exactly as he remembered it. In even the lightest of downpours it had a tendency to overflow. You would expect the people who designed it to have figured out a solution to the problem and widened the drain, but then he recalls what a challenge it had been as a child to step across this hurdle as it stands. During the season of floods he would watch the muddy water progress each day ever higher and closer to their doorstep, until miraculously receding before it could do any damage. His father had correctly anticipated this seasonal threat, marking the highest point in the street the waters had been known to reach, and building the doorstep three steps higher. This foresight had allowed for a sizeable alcove inside the main door, lending privacy to the inner courtyard and veranda. Balwinder now runs his fingers fondly over the familiar grain of the four-paneled outer door of his house. The weathered veneer could do with some leveling; otherwise, the intricate woodworked scalloping is still grand almost fifteen years after he had hoisted it in place on its hinged flaps. The main beams of the frame firm to his touch.

In the harsh noon shadows, the haunts of his childhood and youth come alive before his eyes. To the left of this doorway lived his friend Puran. Next door was Balbir's house and further up that of Ranjit. A step down to the right was his cousin Manjit's home. Manjit, my Manjit. He sighs and clumsily clears his throat. Had it been the memory of this one doorstep that had drawn him all the way here? Or was it the voice of a child, suddenly left all alone, counting down Tilo in a game of hide and seek—"waray, one, two, three . . . "—before switching to Punjabi, the echoes still in these perennially open doorways and streets. The boys and girls on this street, some of them well into their teens or even twenties, would all gather at dusk to play here in an age of innocence and binding trust, long before the clumsy self-awareness of youth, before the realization of each other's sexuality, before flirtations, courtships and betrayals, before adulthood . . . Manjit had never been able to suppress her giggles when it was Balwinder's turn to go and seek. She was always the first to find him in all his favourite hide aways.

The sight of his brother clumsily adjusting his chuddar yet again interrupts his reverie.

There comes a slight scraping sound from behind the door. Hafeez, it seems, has finally decided that he has no other option but to confront his visitors. He clears his throat nervously by way of announcing his presence, as Balwinder steps closer to the door and repeats just loud enough for the words to carry across the door: "Are you Hafeez? Hafeez, son of Khaira Tarkhan? Your shop was closed and we were directed here. We have an urgent matter to discuss with you."

The inflection of the spoken Punjabi flows easily over Hafeez's ears but he realizes, for the first time, that he and his wife may be in danger. Surely they must know that his wife is also inside the house with him. Should he risk all and shout loudly for help? Perhaps his neighbour, Sarfraz, has already noticed the strangers loitering outside. Should he not run out into the street and seek help from any passerby he can find? What if he simply refused to open the door until the visitors walk away? And miss a golden opportunity to escape from eking out a bare living assembling doors, windows and the such for the houses of the wealthy?

If only there were some way to get Qulsoom out of the house . . . He stands in the dark alcove unsure of what to do.

"Yes, I . . . am Hafe-eez," he finally manages to stammer.

"We have come to talk to you about a certain job we want you to do for us. Can we come in and talk for a few minutes?"

Hafeez hesitates again, and then, asking them to wait for just a while longer, rushes over to the veranda where his wife has been listening to the exchange. Ignoring her protests, he manages to hustle her quietly into the tiny inner storage room, the kothri at the back of the house, latching the door from the outside.

He returns to peer outside once again to see if the visitors are still there, and when he finally opens the door, they hastily step into the inner courtyard as if grateful for its cool darkness. He notices how disheveled and weary they appear in their soiled clothes, and their empty begging bowls casually discarded near the entrance. With uncharacteristic directness, he asks if they have been traveling for long, but his query goes unanswered. He lowers two heavy manjis in the shade of the veranda and they sit facing each other in the reflected light. He offers them water, which they decline.

"If you really are Hafeez Tarkhan, then you can help us," offers the elder as a preamble. Hafeez notes that he seems to be in charge and of roughly the same age as him. His tangled beard is full and hangs loosely down the barrel of his chest. The dark irises in the wrinkled face bore into his, the mouth set solemnly, as if in full awareness of Hafeez's predicament. Hafeez also notices how they both follow his every move until their gaze wanders off to the interior of the house. Could it be that what they seek is inside the rooms, he conjectures, still fighting his lingering stupor and wishing he were more clear-headed. The younger one, who appears to be in his late teens, his beard not yet fully developed, is more relaxed, though intent on picking up cues from his elder companion and quietly following the elder's gaze. Whatever their relationship, Hafeez can detect no familial resemblance between them, though they both seem fully at ease with each other and not the least bit threatened by his presence.

"Now what is it you want me to make for you?" Hafeez finally manages to look the elder one full in the face and ask.

"Well, Hafeez Tarkhan, its not so much what you can make for us, but more of what you can allow us to do inside your house. We have a favour to ask of you. We believe you have something in this house that belongs to us. It is something that you may call an amanat, and we are now here to collect it from you. Believe us when we say that our intentions are entirely honourable. We need to be here only for a very short while, and once we are done, you will not see us again."

"And we will make it well worthwhile your time," the younger one interjects with a knowing smugness.

Hafeez, having always relied heavily on the practicality and common sense of his wife, now feels the urgent need to consult her. He knows she is within earshot of where they sit, but realizes that he cannot possibly leave these two alone in the house or give away her hiding place. He tries to contain his growing euphoria at having had his hunches proven correct, and realizes that he will somehow have to stumble along on his own through the haggling that is sure to follow now.

He turns his attention towards the visitors again and makes one tentative offer: "What if you tell me exactly what it is you want and then allow me some time to think it over? The house is in such a mess right now. Once I have it in order tomorrow, you two can return at the same time and we can then work out some kind of an agreement."

Qulsoom, from the safety of the kothri, can hear the arguments going back and forth. The visitors are adamant that the deed must be performed now or never, and they threaten to walk away, but Hafeez in his desperation counters each offer with an argument of his own. There is a prolonged silence at the end of which she is relieved to hear that some agreement has been reached finally. They ask him to get them tools for digging. They will need a pickaxe or a spade, but he claims he has none of these inside the house. Instead, he rummages through the clutter of discarded tools in one corner of the veranda and brings forth a wood planer.

"Maybe you can use the blade from this for digging. I have never been comfortable using it and my palm blisters every time I use it," he explains.

As Balwinder examines the implement held out to him, he immediately recognizes it as one of his very own. He lets out an involuntary sigh. Ah, the travails of a left-handed craftsman. The affectionately carved handle still slides snugly into the folds of his palm, awaiting the smooth and gentle forward movement from his left shoulder down to the wrist.

"Do you have any metal plates or glasses in the house?" he says finally managing to put the object aside and ask Hafeez.

As Hafeez goes off to look for them, Balwinder once again turns his attention to the condition of the house. Despite appearances, most of it has been skillfully repaired and very few signs still remain of the rumoured damage to the infrastructure. He is once again amazed to be able to instantly recognize each peculiar feature inside the house, uncovering the trivial but deeply personal history it holds for him. The stylized curlicues around the decorative half-domes on the front wall, the chipped circular leaf patterns inlaid into the floor of the middle veranda, even the protesting squawks of the rusty water hand pump under which Hafeez stops to soak his head, every detail stirs up deeply recessed memories and associations.

Observing his brother's apparent lassitude, Sukhinder, who had been jovial and relaxed outside, feels a bout of piqued petulance settling over him. Except for that one pale brick just outside the doorway that he has noticed has been leveled over time, nothing inside the house seems even remotely familiar to him. He vaguely remembers once tripping over that uneven brick outside, a long time ago, and then being laid prone in bed for several days by the injury. But no visible signs remain in the courtyard of his futile attempts to cultivate chopped branches from acacias and guava trees. No amount of diligent watering and patient coaxing could persuade the limp branches to take root and sprout. Then his father, after having watched him condescendingly for several days, had finally held his hand and led him to the kothri and revealed the miracle of seeds stored there in sealed clay bins. Sukhinder notes that there are also no signs of the circular tracks he had worn deep into the courtyard, racing his metal wheel over the strewn sawdust with its smell of turpentine. He now stands impatiently, waiting for a sign from his brother, willing him out of his stupor.

How Balwinder became a professional carpenter illustrated the guarded tolerance that the various religions and castes had come to accord to each other before the partition. Since the Muslims monopolized the main trade of metal craftsmanship, they were not eager to let a Sikh into it. Balwinder's father, a small farmer, had wanted more for his children, urging them to share in the prosperity all around them. The metal artisans had become prosperous during the war. When Balwinder was old enough to work, his father made the rounds of the metal workshops, asking if they could use a young apprentice. Most of the metal trade was family-run. It so happened that Khaira, the village's sole carpenter, was childless, bent with age and fast losing his eyesight. Khaira had reluctantly agreed to take Balwinder under his tutelage.

Balwinder recalls the humiliations suffered during the three years he had spent under Khaira Tarkhan. He had to keep the master's hookah freshly lit at all times from dawn to dusk. A door panel had to be planed and polished so finely that when it was placed flat on the ground, a pencil would roll smoothly across its length. There was the daily drudgery of drying out countless gunnysacks of soggy sawdust and selling them for a paisa each. All these tedious daily chores he carried out under a constant barrage of abuse.

As his eyesight had weakened, his old tutor had turned ever more bitter and frustrated, with little patience left over for an apprentice. To Khaira, who like most Muslims began all chores with his right hand, his apprentice's left-handedness was an endless source of ridicule and amusement; he would call down from his creator all manner of curses on all left-handed godless kafirs. Perhaps, Balwinder now thinks searching Hafeez's face for his father's features, in hindsight the boy had made the right choice in rejecting Khaira's tutelage and heading for better prospects nearby Sialkot.

Balwinder reminds himself that all that is now in the past and their task still remains uncompleted. Sensing Sukhi's impatience, Balwinder directs Hafeez to a spot in the middle of the sunlit courtyard and instructs him to begin digging there: "Whatever you find there is yours," he assures him with a patronizing pat on the shoulder, and Hafeez meekly heads for the courtyard with a brass plate in his hand.

The two brothers leave Hafeez to his work and enter deeper into the shadowed recess just inside of the main doorway. As Hafeez eagerly chooses a spot that appears to be exactly in the middle of the courtyard and begins to dig, going deeper and deeper through the layers of sawdust with ease, he can hear the two Sikhs getting busy, though he cannot see which spot they have actually chosen to work on. There is the sound of floor bricks being pried apart, wooden beams disassembled, packed earth ripped up. He tries to concentrate on the spot identified to him, and continues to hack away for over an hour, working through several layers of compacted sawdust and earth, before realizing that he has been duped. He drops the plate, and quietly hurries over to where the brothers are taking turns at their task. He notes that they have already uncovered several feet of the area adjacent to the main door and are now attempting to pry the wooden doorsill out of its seating without disturbing the door frame and panels. Once this is achieved, the three of them drag the heavy beam out into the brighter courtyard. The sunlight has by now receded to the rooftops and all three are breaking into a sweat from their exertions.

Balwinder gingerly inverts the doorsill, and loosens a thin rectangular panel, held in place by several short nails and running the entire length of the beam. This reveals a cavity in which are nestled three slim boxes, neatly wrapped in tarpaulin and marked in the Gurmukhi script. Balwinder gingerly lifts each box from its nesting place and places it beside him on the ground. A satisfied smirk begins to crinkle his eyes. He hands Sukhi the first of the packages to unwrap. Sukhinder uses his kirpan to undo the binding and unwrap the box. He is amazed at how both Hafeez and Balwinder are transfixed by the delicate filigreed work on the wooden boxes and the neat seating of each polished joint. Their hands brush the dirt away and tenderly explore the details of the carving.

"Your elders certainly mastered their craft well," remarks Hafeez, begrudging admiration writ large on his face.

"Actually, it was not my ancestors but your father who taught me all this," offers Balwinder, all smiles, his eyes shining with fierce pride.

"You mean Khaira Tarkhan taught you how to make boxes like these? You know, I was wondering how you were able to find out that Khaira was my father. He told everyone who would listen that he had no male offspring, that I was as good as dead for him."

When the first box is opened, a faded page of the *Granth Saab* falls out and Sukhinder retrieves it in haste, touches it to his forehead and then to his lips. Next to emerge is an untidy bundle of letters snared on a wire loop and a set of official deeds to some of the Minhas family properties in and around Kotli. Balwinder hands the latter to Hafeez. There comes a silver amulet bound by a red thread and cushioned between more loose pages of the holy *Granth*. Hafeez waits in silent expectation of what will eventually emerge into the dimming light.

With a swift and uncharacteristic flourish of his hand, Sukhi bring out a small bundle wrapped in silk. He peers inside it before handing it over to his brother with the remark: "It's all there, exactly as you had said it would be."

Balwinder reaches in and disentangles a ball of jewelry the size of his fist and, handing it over to Hafeez, remarks: "This is for our sister, paen-ji. Tell her we are sorry for all the mess we are leaving in her house. I am sure that you both will one day be able to restore this place to its original glory."

The mass of intertwined jewelry on closer examination turns out to be a gold necklace and six bangles that have been hastily hammered together. The delicate inlaid stonework is ruined beyond repair and, as Hafeez slides it into the side pocket of his kameez, they feel surprisingly light. His eyes meet momentarily those of the two visitors, and Hafeez once again debates mentally whether he should begin to trust them and reveal that his wife is hidden inside the house. The moment of indecision lasts only briefly and he decides to wait and see what else will follow. He watches wordlessly as the partially empty silk sash bundle is rebound and replaced inside the oblong box. The three boxes disappear into the folds of the loose clothing of the fakirs.

Balwinder now takes Hafeez aside and whispers in his ear a hoarse and urgent personal message of farewell: "Hafeez Tarkhan, I want you to remember that there is much more of this wealth inside your family home. All you have to do is figure out where to look. You must know full well that we cannot carry away all that we have hidden here. And whatever you do find is yours to keep. We are not coming back for more. Just be careful with what you find and spend it wisely. It is all hard earned."

His gaze lingers towards the exposed and darkening courtyard as he unlatches the outer door and steps out with his brother into the street. Malhaara, the streetlamp lighter, has already made his appointed rounds, and the corner oil lamp glows feebly in the lingering light of dusk. With one last look at the houses and their rooftops, the strangers adjust their clothing and head out towards the main street.

Hafeez watches patiently as the men finally turn the street corner and fade forever from his life. He rubs his eyes in disbelief.

Light from the single streetlamp finds its multiple reflections in the open drains. Hafeez stands quietly in his doorway for several minutes, trying to make sense of what has come to pass in the last few hours of his life, formulating the words to what he will finally tell his wife, imagining all her possible responses. The thoughts jolt his mind into the present, and remembering where Qulsoom is hiding, he rushes back indoors, his right hand reaching for the heft of the metal swinging freely inside his pocket. Carefully securing the door from the inside, sidestepping the heaped mounds of packed earth, wood and disinterred bricks, he hurries over to the inner kothri. Opening the door to the cool, dank room reeking of achar fumes, he finds his wife squatting on the floor directly in front of the door, fast asleep, a handle-less scythe gripped tight before her in both hands.

At dawn the next morning, Qulsoom Tarkhanan contracts Manni's tanga for the day, bundles her meager belongings into guthris and leaves Kotli and her husband forever. The tangawallah returns from the city earlier in the afternoon than usual, his tanga not yet fully occupied. Eager to pass on the juicy morsel of gossip that he has been unable to digest by himself: That saucy, secretive Qulsoom Tarkhanan has finally dumped her good-for-nothing, drug-addicted, charsi bhungi husband and run away to her ex in Sialkot. He is careful enough not to reveal that on her instructions he had to drop her off only half the way to the city with all her baggage. He left her inside the dark tunnel formed over the road by the interlocking vegetation of the ancient tahlis, as far from any dwelling as was possible. On his homeward journey from Sialkot, he was relieved to find no trace of either her or her bundles.

However, the scandal has preceded his arrival to deny him personal satisfaction, and he finds the village already abuzz with as many conflicting stories as there are idle tongues. And Hafeez is nowhere to be found.

After several days of wild speculation, although a few of the people actually saw Qulsoom leave the house, there is still no sign of Hafeez. His disgruntled customers have made repeated visits to his unattended shop, and then, cursing him loudly, have asked directions to his house. They have vented their frustrations by pounding on his padlocked door, but without the slightest response.

A week after Qulsoom Tarkhanan's departure by tanga, someone notices a key suspended from one of the panels of Hafeez's main outer door. As word of the discovery spreads, a crowd gathers before the door, noisily debating whether to unlock it, venture inside, and solve the mystery. Siddiq, the neighbour, even climbs up to the rooftop to peer inside but cannot see far enough into the yard.

It is finally left to Bhagga, who is owed money by Hafeez, to take the initiative to turn the key. The door swings inwards and seems to loosen from the frame. Bhagga's considerable body disappears in an undignified fall into the wide trench that runs the entire length of the inner courtyard floor. He hastily staggers up and, hearing sounds of scraping ahead, carefully makes his way into the blinding light in the courtyard.

Near one corner of the furthest wall, he notices someone scratching the ground with a metal plate. All around him are freshly piled mounds of soil, the newer ones dark with moisture and peppered with decayed sawdust. He watches Hafeez in a hushed, fascinated silence for several minutes, expecting some form of reaction to his presence, before calling out the other's name several times. Hafeez half turns in acknowledgement.

"What in Allah Karim's name are you doing here, Hafeez?" Bhagga asks, totally baffled by the other's behaviour.

"I am looking for the treasure that has been entrusted to me," comes the feeble reply, Hafeez not bothering to look up from his task.

"What treasure?"

"The one they said is buried here inside my home."

"Mere yaar, who said anything about there being some treasure buried here inside your home?"

"The Sikhs!"

"What Sikhs?"

"The ones who were in here just now."

Bhagga takes his time to digest this piece of information, before asking Hafeez how long he has been at his task.

"Since yesterday, when the Sikhs knocked on my door and Qulsoom, who had been spying on them, let them in and . . . "

Bhagga reaches out with his hands to gently persuade Hafeez to get up from the ground. He leads him by the arm to the coolness of the veranda and, seating him down at one of the two manjis already spread out before them, gets him water to drink. By then some of the other villagers have also ventured inside the house to satisfy their curiosity.

"You say that these Sikhs came into your house and asked you to dig for some treasure buried here?"

"Yes, and they dismantled the main doorsill and took something out of it. Come, let me show you."

He leads the gathered onlookers to the alcove. The doorsill, though exposed, sits firmly in its appointed niche and looks untampered. He runs his fingers unbelievingly over it, searching for the yard-long crevice he knows should be there. The wooden beam is solid to his touch. He taps it several times with his knuckles before looking up in bewilderment, for the first time becoming aware of the crowd gathered around him.

"Qulsoom! Qulsoom can tell you that she saw them here. Qulsoom . . . !" he calls out in desperation, and then goes off to the kothri to look for her. But she is nowhere to be found.

It is late in the afternoon. Hafeez and his wife are sprawled half-asleep on a stringed manji, intermittently swatting at the flies buzzing over them. The cool, darkened verandah is in stark contrast to the harsh sun-lit courtyard. He has deserted his workshop to seek comfort in the shade of his home for the duration of the noon heat.

As she drifts in and out of sleep, Qulsoom hears the sound of someone knocking on the outer door. She quietly walks over to the loosened bricks in the wall and peers out into the sun-bright street. She notices two worn-out fakirs standing just outside the doorway with their empty begging bowls. She looks closely at their faces to see if they are familiar and can be trusted before she can venture out to speak to them.

Hafeez is awakened from his stupor by the frantic voice of his wife. She sounds overcome by joy one moment and hysterical with grief the next. There are deeper, muffled male voices, apparently calming her. Sensing that something is amiss, he is instantly on his feet, rushing towards the door. "Qulsoom, Qulsoom, what is going on, what are you doing?" he begins to ask before even coming to a stop, and watches in shock as his wife first embraces a middle-aged fakir and then moves towards a younger one, all the while kissing their hands, their foreheads, and wailing hoarsely: "Sukhiya, Balwa, mera veer Balwa, mera veer Sukhiya." He notices that Balwa has suddenly disentangled himself from her grasp and is about to lunge in his direction. Hafeez freezes, but Qulsoom has been anticipating this confrontation ever since she has let her brothers into the house. She now holds them firmly back from her husband by announcing: "Balwa, Sukhiya, *this* is my husband. Let him go for now, he cannot harm us."

Balwinder seems reluctant to be held back, seeing Hafeez's ashen, puzzled face so close to where they are standing. He opens his mouth to inquire urgently: "Paenji, if he has ever harmed a single hair on your head, I swear by the Guru . . . "

Paenji, *paenji!?* Hafeez has to sit down on the floor to regain his strength and composure, and to think clearly, now the lingering cob-webs of sleep and drugs have begun to wear off.

The strangers move back to the relative darkness of the alcove by the doorway and are accompanied by their sister. There is the sound of floor bricks being pried apart, of wooden beams being disassembled, the muffled thud of the earth being broken. After an hour the doorsill is dragged out into the courtyard; the bottom dislodged, three exquisite wooden boxes are removed and inspected. Both the Sikhs keep a wary eye on Hafeez, while Qulsoom appears lost in a world in which he has already ceased to exist. He catches bits and pieces of their conversation as they exchange their family history of the past ten years: the events of the partition and how the attacking mob had separated Sardar form her brother Sukhinder at the temple of Gurudwara Nanaksar at Babay di Beri. There follows a prolonged silence during which she weeps. Hafeez wants to go up and comfort her, but finds himself unable to do so. He watches her elder brother put a hand on her head and awkwardly attempt to soothe her anguish.

". . . and afterwards, I was led with the other Hindu and Sikh girls who had met the same fate as me into a mosque in Sialkot and asked to recite verses from the Quran. I found that I was now a married Mussalman and had been given the name Qulsoom Bibi. I lived with him for three years, and when I did not bear him any children, he took me back to the Maulvi and thrice recited the words for divorce: Talaqti! That is when he stepped in and offered to marry me." She nods in the direction where Hafeez is. "He used to live on our street but was never fully aware of any of my recent personal history.

"We lived in the city for about a year, until I was safely able to persuade him to move back here to Kotli . . . How many times have I looked out of the door, listened for the sound of your footfall, and imagined how you would look . . . "

By then it is already dusk and she remembers all the chores that must be completed before dark. She continues to chatter incessantly, her voice now a hoarse whisper. She lights the oil lamps of the house and begins to prepare dinner. Smoke fills the veranda as she inattentively tries to get the hearth fire going in the kitchen.

Her monologue falters only once, when she realizes that there is a final act that still remains unfinished. She steps out to the courtyard and returns with Hafeez's prized fighting rooster tucked under one arm. The pampered bird, used to such rough handling only by other birds but not humans, launches into a series of screeches of frantic protest, lashing out with its cloth-bound, razor-sharp and painstakingly tapered talons. Sardar holds the noisy flapping bird steadily at arm's length, close enough to her husband's face, and looking him straight in the eye, she wrings the bird's neck with a single, sudden motion.

"Even though I have had to learn all the ways of Hafeez's people, I have lived in this mohallah like a prisoner, always fearing that someone would one day recognize me and uncover my past. Kotli has not been kind to him either, ostracizing him for what he did to his father. Throughout our marriage, he never really had the any idea of how many people here had known me before I left Kotli during the partition. He doesn't even know that this is my birthplace.

"Only once have I come close to really being discovered. Several years ago, a fakir came to our door, looking much as you do, and when I went outside to fill his bowl with flour, he blessed me with these words: 'Jiyo, tiye Sardarni, maula sab di kher kare!' I pretended to be offended.

"There are one or two others like me in this village but they have all come to accept their lot in this life. But I never gave up hope of seeing you all again and being reunited with our family. "

When the meal is ready, she heaps a plate full of meat, rice and achar and places it before Hafeez. She watches him intently to see if he will eat the non-halal meal. He continues to sit on the floor, rendered immobile, incredulous.

No one gets much sleep during the night, and by dawn, his wife and her two brothers finally gone, Hafeez remembers the digging and the instructions given to him.

He picks up the brass plate lying beside his manji with the half-finished meal and steps out onto the damp floor of his faintly lit courtyard. He begins scraping off layers of surface soil, his efforts eventually taking him deeper and deeper into the ground. He uncovers several desiccated tree branches and a partially corroded child's play wheel. In attempting to stretch his tired back he immediately loses interest in the spot.

Hafeez steps away from the courtyard and now moves closer to the alcove just inside the doorway. He begins exposing the years of packed soil under the doorsill, sweat pouring down his chin and onto the undisturbed ground.

Stalker in the Peacock House

Chakwa meṅ awaṅ? Na! Chakwi . . .
Chakwi meṅ awaṅ? Na! Chakwa . . .
—Verses from a Punjabi folksong

Having waited an entire year for their arrival at the Mela of Ronti, the slight nine-year-old boy known to all as Kittu is initially too timid to approach the colourful Pathan hustlers when they descend onto the fairgrounds, adjacent to the shrine. He has not joined his friends today in taunting the exotic northern visitors with cries of "Khoche, oy khoche, chhuriaṅ chaku tez karo ge?"

Though their arrival is in itself a much-anticipated phenomenon at the playground each year, this season promises more drama. Kittu surveys the Khan Chachas' pathetic lots from a safe distance, interest piqued by their dexterity at launching brief spurts of dun-coloured snuff out of the corners of their mouths.

He watches as they go about setting up their lean-to stalls a short distance from the rest of the improvised shops, and align their ten-yard firing ranges west to east, so that there is only the still water and bulrushes of the Nehr Mardan behind them. Their rectangular rubber sheets of recycled tires propped up for reclaiming used slugs, and their numbered balloons waving raggedly in the breeze and dust, the Pathans now stand haughtily by their garish stalls, each one dressed in the stereotypical bright waistcoat, baggy shalwar, and long black turban. Kittu watches as one of them casually scratches himself with his free hand, his crooked-barrel air gun haughtily slung over one shoulder, as he glares menacingly at each passerby, his open derision and fierce demeanour characteristic of the mountain-dweller caught in the vast open spaces and at the mercy of these somnolent, slack dwellers of the plains.

For reasons of their own, the Pathans have found, like virtually everything else around them, the name for the local canal of Nehr Mardan amusing. They get into countless arguments with the locals over its origins, accusing passersby in their heavily accented Urdu of crucifying genders, their turbans coming undone and slipping down their backs in the heat of argument. The knife-sharpener, the night-watchman pehredar, and a handful of others gather in a tight knot, to exchange notes on life back in their northern hometowns of Peshawar, Charsadda, Kohat and Mardan. To the locals these seem like names of remote and exotic cities in a foreign land.

Adding to the carnival's atmosphere is the spice of unsubstantiated rumours that these Khan chachas have been responsible in recent years for attempting to kidnap Kittu's friend, Asif, who was only rescued because Babaji Abdullah caught the assailant hurrying by in the street with a suspicious-looking sack on his back. What was worthy of note was that it had not been the squirming life inside the bag that had initially caught Babaji's attention but the fact that the Pathan had walked by without greeting him respectfully enough. Now here they were blatantly strutting their wares, haughtily anticipating the arrival of each dupe.

Kittu tries to approach one of the firing ranges to try his luck but he is shooed away by a fierce Pathan. Shahid, observing his friend's frustration, finally takes him aside and shows him how he can be taken more seriously by making the money in his hand more visible. "Hold it out like this and then watch them trip over each other to get to you," he whispers.

Shahid watches as Kittu misses the first three of his shots. The foresight of facing the firing ranges away from the crowds becomes obvious, as a dark smirk works its way across Khan Chacha's mustached upper lip when he deftly reloads the rifle for the fourth time. Equally amused, Shahid is also witness to Kittu's fourth shot striking only the upper right corner of the rectangular target. The next shot sneaks closer but is still off the target. The sixth one strikes dead on mark.

"Wah!" Shahid exclaims, his expression a mixture of relief and wonder; but by now the Khan is no longer amused, a crowd having begun to gather and cheer Kittu on with offers pouring in to pay for his remaining shots.

Smack, smack, smack! All three are on target, and Kittu goes on to claim all the major prizes lined up at the stall. He turns around eagerly to make his way to the next stall, tasting blood, only to discover that all the adjacent stalls have been hastily evacuated and their occupants are nowhere in sight.

His success at the firing range, however, has come as no surprise to everyone who knows Kittu well enough in the village.

"One thing you must know about me," he cockily tells anyone who will listen, "I am good with the slingshot, and the air gun, too. Very good! I once brought home three starlings and a dove in a single afternoon of hunting with my slingshot, and my mother couldn't believe I had shot them all by myself. At last year's Eid Mela, I shot four of the five balloons in one row and almost won the main prize. The reason I am this good is that I make my own clay pellets for my slingshot. So, when I am aiming at something, you can be sure that I will not miss."

Having witnessed Kittu's ability with the slingshot, and sensing a rare tenacity in someone so young, an elder maternal uncle, his mammu Anwar, has spent the past several months helping him perfect his aim. Proudly showing him his own impressive gun collection, his mammu has doggedly stressed on the one lesson that Kittu must learn above all others when dealing with the type of weapons owned by the Pathans. "Always remember the golden rule," he has stressed to his gifted nephew. "Whether it is a slingshot or a crooked rifle you are aiming with, finding the bias of the weapon in relation to your actual target should be your first priority. Once you have found the bias, the rest will come easily." Given the day's success, the lesson has apparently not been lost on the eager pupil with a penchant for showmanship.

With a crowd egging him on, Kittu has seldom been known to pass up an opportunity to display his numerous talents. Watch him closely as he winds up his spinning top in slow and measured moves, each fold a snug fit, until the twine is finally unfurled with the dramatic flourish of a whip. The walnut top is launched humming into the air to land wobbling like a drunk, close to the ground, before finding its center and steadying itself within the space of its shadow. Then, forming a noose out of his line, Kittu flips the twirling top onto his open palm. It continues to spin there steadily over a single crease, its spell not yet broken and its energy unspent even a minute later. As it begins to crawl up his wrist, he gently flips his hand with the palm now facing downwards, nudging the wobbling top back towards his knuckles. Finally, with one graceful swoop he launches the top before snaring it in midair. The audience breaks into applause. A few coins are tossed in the dust in front of the performer.

When it is not the season of carnivals, Kittu, who has yet to find consistency in his relationships with adults, gives all his attention to maintaining his equipment—his fishing lines, his hunting slingshot, his kites and their gear.

If you seek him out in the early springtime, you will probably encounter him in the deserted Eidgah. Long before the rains begin in earnest and the chill in the air has fully receded, the local countryside is swept by sudden gusts of wind that kick up dust and rattle doors and windows: Basant, the kite-flying season, arrives with a bluster and flourish all its own. Kittu's energies have until now been focused on preparing his kite-flying line, the near-holy ritual of dor sutna, and his strategies have all been mapped out.

Ever the perfectionist, he patiently works upon each step of the process with great care. The Pari Marka thread for the dhor has been bought well in advance when it was still affordable; a green glass soda bottle has been crushed and ground to such fine powder that it can now be sieved using his ammiji's finest muslin chunni, and the sheets of mud-coloured glue are ready and waiting for boiling in a tin can.

Each step of this procedure reflects the flyer's personal style and preference. The critical choice between the weighted thread for brute force and the light gossamer touch with the razor-sharp cutting edge has already been made. However, it is in the choice of dyes that Kittu has achieved an edge over similarly obsessed boys all over the Punjab in this heady season. Using a mixture of commonly used cloth-whitening aniline and a pinch of a blue cloth dye, he has arrived at a shade that is close enough to faithfully match the deep colour of an afternoon sky. It is this partial invisibility in broad daylight that will allow him to surprise his hapless victims, weighing down their lines with his rapidly baled blade of thread performing its magic in midair. Each victory will be celebrated with shouts of "Bo Kaata!" There will be the maddening, heart-thumping dash of the glass-laced spool, burning the base of the palm and the finger tips, the kite rapidly flowing way past the furthest rooftops, pigeon roosts, clearing even the bamboo hurdle of the radio fanatics, the brothers Shafiq and Rafiq's imposing antennae.

By the end of the Basant season, his rolls of killer thread almost consumed, Kittu will take to strategically rationing out the remaining portions, placing them further down the line to extract maximum effect. By then, even the therapeutic Aloe Vera near the rooftop stairs will have been reduced to tatters, having been pressed into repeated service as instant glue for patching the ravages of wind on his kite collection.

On such laid-back days, Kittu might spend an entire afternoon harassing the giant ants scampering across the cracked mud of the courtyard in his home. He uses his right thumb to crush the warrior ants as soon as they emerge from the hole in the ground, oblivious to the growing soreness until one of the creatures finds the tender softness between calluses and sinks its pincers. He winces in pain, leaping up and shaking his hand, snatching at the pain under his skin, snapping the thorax of the ant to leave the head with its vicelike grip still clinging to his flesh. He is finally able to pick out the pea-sized head with the forefinger and thumb of his other hand.

As I struggle up these stairs, I am amazed at how far and removed my life is today from that of the more agitated and younger Kittu at nine and ten, willfully terrorizing his hapless opponents, reaping unexpected rewards in the process. Where I once used to eagerly dash up the stairs daily at dusk to light the oil lamp inside the tower, I can now swear that jinns have been busy adding extra steps for me to climb. I am grateful that the oil lamp has been replaced with an electric bulb, thus making my life so much easier. The only obvious and sane reason I can now really put forth for climbing up here is to clean the stained-glass windows of the tower.

The glass and brick square structure before me is barely tall enough for a small child to stand upright in, yet when lit up from the inside at night it is visible for miles around. Crouched inside it, I can see all the way in the direction of the Qibla to where the new canal is being dug up parallel to the river Chenab. Further beyond Kotli, I can even discern smoke rising up from the chimneys at Rana Saab's brick kiln. If I now turn towards the south and look over the rooftops, I can distinguish some of the many fields and orchards that comprise his vast estate. I cannot see a single human being from up here.

I realize now that like everything else here this panorama before me does not really represent reality in its true colours. What I see is viewed through filters of coloured glass that range in hues from deep-water blue to the brightest parrot green of freshly sprouted rice. Rana Saab has more than once proudly pointed out to me that each of the intricate components of these stained-glass windows facing the four directions has been painstakingly selected to closely match the glory of the peacock's plumage; and just like those precious birds that roam the grounds freely here, each piece is now irreplaceable.

Each time I come up here, I am also reminded of a now discontinued family tradition of this house that was established a long time ago by Rana Saab and his friends when they were still children. I have been told that there was a time when they used to descend into the gardens of this house in the fading light of the lingering monsoon dusks, armed with muslin traps to gather fireflies. At the end of the hunt, when it was totally dark, the insects would be transported and released inside the tower. Once the lamp had been snuffed out, these trapped creatures would continue to scurry about behind the glass late into the night, the glass stains magically transforming their diaphanous, faintly flickering green lights, as I am sure that it must have been an impressive sight. I am also sure that as the night wore on, each pinprick of light would have been snuffed out. Today, the powdered traces of those nocturnal diversions still litter the floor of the tower.

Fortunately, for young Kittu's sake, no one else ventures up here anymore but I. If you were to look closely today, you would discover that a tiny portion of the glass of the east window has been shattered inwards. This window is only visible from outside the house. The damage appears to have occurred a long time ago, and on the floor before me lies the culprit: a sparkling green marble the size of my thumbnail. This peculiar, oversized marble with its night sky of brightly suspended bubbles, resting here amidst the shards of turquoise glass, can only have been recovered from the neck of a glass soda bottle. I know of only one person who could have deposited it here from the outside, and I am always surprised to find it here still waiting for me after all these years. Perhaps it is this secret knowledge of its source that has made me deliberately leave the evidence untampered, as if I would be tempting fate to implicate someone in the successful sabotage of Rana Saab's most elaborate edifice.

Having revealed this much about these premises, I must now approach a more difficult subject, that of our Rana Saab, the current owner of this sprawling mansion, and my reluctant benefactor. He insists on vainly calling it his Peacock House. And I, having lived here since being orphaned at ten, have kept painstakingly busy peeling off the onionskin layers of ostentation, pretense and myth.

Every inhabited house has an inner spirit, the hum of its heartbeat regulated by those who dwell in it and call it home. Sometimes these rhythms may radiate outward into the dark and attract others to come inside and seek shelter. However, in all my diligent searching for this, I have come away empty-handed. What I have uncovered instead is a clutter of human voices trapped within these walls.

If you listen attentively, you too can tune in and listen to these embittered and discordant rhymes, tell apart the incidents that have brought them here. Look carefully and you will see that the lament of these chants does not end here. Their reverberations branch outward, like ripples from a stone casually tossed into a still pond, and reach deep into the interiors of the neighbouring Kotli houses.

41

It is here, in one of the verandas protected from the early afternoon sun and opening into an inner garden, that our Ranaji, clad in an immaculate white cotton kurta and a hand-woven shalwar and chuddar, now sits resplendent in court. After a brief but bitter tangle this morning with his disgruntled spouse, he spent an hour grooming himself, and his confidence and composure have gradually been replenished. A handful of close friends and a steady stream of visitors attend to him. Out from sight, but well within earshot, is a wooden bench in the shade of a towering outer wall. Five men are seated here, while an equal number squat on the bare ground before it, patiently awaiting the fate of their petitions to this impromptu court.

Though Ranaji has not been a local resident for long and holds no official status, he wields an inordinate amount of influence over the lives of these waiting men. Having married locally long before the batwaara, Ranaji's father had purchased vast tracts of local agricultural lands, and abandoning his barren hometown of Sargodha, decided to settle in the lush environment of Kotli. After his father's death, Ranaji's inherited wealth and vast holdings have gradually allowed him such luxuries as these, so that on a mere impulse or notion he can adversely or advantageously influence the welfare and livelihoods of each of these men.

As the host and the guests sweat out the early afternoon in the shade of the veranda, their attention is partially diverted by the of a weighted silk fan suspended from the ceiling. A feeble old man wrapped in a threadbare chuddar is seated on a low stool in a corner of the room, rocking back and forth from his waist and tugging on a silk rope attached to the fan. His movements appear to be those of a man immersed in pious recitation. Gossip swirls idly like a moth circling the room; it barely falters in falling on the ears of the mute and servile presence in the room.

Barely a few feet away is a secluded room in which a heavy-set, middle-aged woman called Ranima by one and all sits sullenly at the edge of her bed. Although the curtains in the room are drawn and the warm afternoon sunlight fills the muggy room, she has smothered herself in a pale heavy woolen shawl. Like Ranaji, her husband of twelve years, she too is ruminating on the brief encounter of that morning. The confrontation would ordinarily have been nothing to rue over at this hour, yet its aftertaste lingers, sharp and astringent as a fresh paan. She should have been savouring her triumph, the flash of her outburst searing through all the constructs her partner had carefully laid out in his defense. But she realizes that there has been no relief from her anguish.

She rises from her bed to seek out the slim, gawky nine-year-old boy engaged in a solo game of carom in the adjoining room. She taps his shoulder lightly; the boy abandons his game and follows her obediently to her darkened room. Settling herself down on one side of the bed, she carefully arranges his body across her lap, curling his frail and lanky frame into a fetal position. Now, with her eyes half-closed, she begins to gently rock back and forth to the easy cadences of a mother crooning a baby to sleep, her words half-formed under her warm breath. The boy, who knows this ritual well, waits for the eventual warm rain to drench his face. And far from falling asleep, he stares wide-eyed at the fleshy round moon of the face hovering so close above him. The tears begin to flow freely, etching shiny paths into the folds of her flesh, amidst the heady mixture of body warmth, sweat and the flavour of paan. The storm continues unabated for what seems an eternity until her breathing gradually returns to normal. The boy is then able mutely to disentangle himself from her and tiptoe out of the room.

On his way back to his interrupted game, he manages to peek into the kitchen where his mother squats before a hamam of hot water. She is still busy washing the dishes from last night's dinner and this morning's breakfast.

This is Sughra, who, in her mid-twenties, sometimes has the appearance of one who has lived twice as long. Her chunni is modestly tied around her hair, and the hem of her mismatched kameez and the frayed cuffs of the shalwar have been tucked neatly under her. Her apparent serenity at her task is in contrast to the turmoil of her tangled thoughts. ". . . Here scrubbing these bowls and washing these bone china dishes, caressing with ash these shiny cold utensils and cutlery, and tossing dishwater down the drains, I have wasted my youth. In these households of the pampered and the privileged have I sacrificed all my personal ambitions and desires, I have watched in bitter solitude the squandering of their ill-gotten gains, thus it has been by birthright for us and for them . . .

"Hai Karim, see the mess your callousness has gotten us into. How will I ever possibly be able to extricate myself and my little son from this mess? . . . "

Meanwhile the attention of the men in the veranda is focused on political intrigues, in which Amreeka and the political upheavals of the novice nations of Pakistan and Hindustan figure prominently, the crops, the progress of court proceedings and land claims, the coming harvest and the following planting season, the wrestling matches and horse races at the winter Mela at the Urs of Pir Sabz.

When the performance of the new muezzin, Hashim, comes up for review, Kittu, overhearing the name of his personal nemesis mentioned for the first time in the conversation, leaves the drawing room and settles down on the cool cement of the floor next to Ranaji's chair. After a familiar preamble into local politics, the conversation flows inexorably towards Ranaji's favourite topic: his temperamental peacocks.

The waiting petitioners, realizing that the topic will probably keep Ranaji preoccupied for at least another hour of the afternoon, let out an audible collective groan, shuffling in their restlessness, noisily clearing their throats and spitting into the dust.

"So, Rana Saab," the nambardar asks in an ingratiating preamble, all oily charm and obsequious concern, "do the birds keep you awake at night with their noisy calls? Sometimes, when the wind is just right, I can hear them all the way on my property."

Ranaji, who has never been known to be in a condescending frame of mind, swiftly retorts: "Of course they do. If you can hear them all the way out there, do you think we here would be able to sleep through the racket?"

There follows an awkward silence, before the host softens his tone and disarmingly offers: "But then what would our Peacock House ever be without its peacocks? You have to learn to take their nakhras in stride like so many squabbling wives in a harem . . ."

The attentive audience snicker as they observe Ranaji immerse himself further into his familiar element, his words implying that the mere fact of ownership has rubbed off the house's charm upon the owner. A short-lived breeze enlivens the stifling humidity of the veranda.

"These are royal birds and as such they deserve royal treatment, and our greatest challenge in raising them has always been their diet. When it comes to eating, they are fussy as toddlers and feeding them is a meticulous art. Luckily, our Sheedu has mastered this art. Provide them an unbalanced diet and their feathers will lose their colour, and the eggshells will not harden enough to withstand the weight of the roosting peahen."

"Now, having told you this . . . ,"Ranaji pauses in the dramatic build -up to his revelation, his right hand involuntarily coming to rest on top of Kittu's head, "I will also have to let you all in on a little family secret. When Abbaji Marhoom built this house and introduced the first batch of peacocks here, he did not have much success initially in breeding them. The birds kept shedding their feathers until the flock looked as sorry and drab as plucked chickens. This state of affairs continued until one day, upon seeing his pathetic birds eagerly feeding on a heap of insects piled beneath a glass windowpane, Abbaji Marhoom came to the sudden realization of what needed to be done."

At this point in the lecture, Kittu, distracted by some commotion behind the bushes close by, rises and disappears into the garden.

When he is out of view of the men, he looks around and discovers a disheveled blue feather resting at the base of a motia bush. Carefully folding and pocketing the feather, he descends further into the seclusion of the garden, isolated now from the outside world by a high brick wall draped in thorn-laden vines. This towering structure, running a great distance northward along the unpaved road and a seasonal stream, has been the cause for grief in Kittu's life on more than one occasion. How many of his kites has he watched helplessly borne here by south winds and deposited behind these very same imposing walls?

He wanders through the garden, dazed and satiated by the profusion of such bounty in a time of drought. Here jacarandas and gulmohar bloom, shedding delicate petals fine as ivory; scarlet trumpets of lilies droop on fragile stems, fiery begonias drape brick walls and clouds of wild. In his exhilaration, he begins to call aloud the names of the blossoms around him: "Motia, motia, suraj mukhi, ghulab, gul-e-lala," the act calming that part of him that needs the reassurance of his own voice, "amrud, amrud, anar, anar, jamnu, jamnu, amb!" His act of naming eases his fear of the unfamiliar. "Amrud, amrud, amrooood!" His call startles a koel out of the branches of a jamnu tree, launching it into the air with a rising cry *Koo koo koo-OOOH!* More than the resonant vibrations of this call, it is the feeble tickle in his nostrils of the static charged, moisture-laden air that jolts his senses. He turns around to retrace his steps back through the inner garden, before noticing the gardener quietly at work amid the pansy flowerbeds, his hoe in hand, his pupil-less eyes raised to the sky.

Working concentrically, the blind gardener has been running his fingers lightly over the fresh blades of budding grass. This is Sain Chacha, and Ranaji values his skill at being able to distinguish, by touch alone, the persistent weeds from the overgrown blades of grass. If he occasionally snips a young flower bud instead of a weed, it is a rare sacrifice and gladly tolerated. As Kittu instinctively follows the gardener's vacant upward gaze, he notices through the dense foliage of overhanging branches of tahlis that the crisp blue of the late afternoon sky is now being edged out by dirty, ragged clouds.

By the time he has reached the massive outer gate of the mansion, more clouds darken the sky, and an east wind is beginning to churn the foliage into a dizzying froth. Swinging out of the shadow of the metal arches, he leapfrogs from one side of the narrow paved street to the next, lost in the lilt of his personal limerick about a pair of songbirds alternately inviting and rejecting each other: *Chakwe meñ awañ? Na! Chakwi* . . . And then hopping over to the other side of the path without a missed beat: *Chakwi meñ awañ? Na! Chakwa . . . Chakwe meñ awañ? Na! Chakwi . . .*

For the time being there is no real need to hurry home, as the clouds have been threatening a storm for days without delivering. If he is lucky enough, he can even catch the halvai stirring the day's stock of milk into cream to make his wondrous sweetmeats of mithai.

Early one sweltering Friday afternoon, the announcements over the village tandora are about two important forthcoming events. Sakhiya, the drummer, unable to read the message nailed to his drum, recites it by rote as he makes the rounds of the deserted Kotli streets. He stops frequently, quiets his drum, and lets his booming voice carry his message deep within the cool shade of the houses:

"Sunno, hear this! On the day of 12th Muharram, being Tuesday and a school holiday, a vilayati team from Amreeka will be showing a film and holding competitions for the healthiest children aged three to six. There will also be races for seven to ten-year-olds. The scheduled programme will begin at the Dara-tul-Aman grounds after the Asr prayers. One and all are invited to attend!"

He concludes the message with the announcement that fresh beef will now be available every Sunday morning at Chacha Rasheed's butcher shop.

On the appointed day, Kittu and his friends, Shahid, Zahid and Abid, spend the better part of their morning diligently tracking the progress of the gadget-laden truck that has arrived on the outskirts of Kotli. It has bumped along and clawed the arduous seven miles of potholes, mud slicks, and makeshift bicycle paths that make up the road from Sialkot to their village. Approaching from the east, the sturdy vehicle prepares to confront another challenge. It must now maneuver through the narrow streets of Kotli to get to the Dara-tul-Aman grounds at the western end. Some of the curves and bends here are so sharp and narrow that the truck has barely an inch of clearance. Observers, including women in purdah leaning from rooftop banisters, offer helpful but conflicting advice to the driver to swerve a palm's length this way or that.

Later in the afternoon, when it is time for Kittu to leave for the fair, his mother is delayed by extra work at Ranima's house. When she finally rushes back home, there is an impatient and skittish Kittu ready for the races. Ever since the tandora announcement two days ago, he has had his heart set on the races. He fidgets restively, unable to stand still or keep his hands in his pockets, impatient, as his mother continues to fuss over him. His hair is now a slick mass of water and oil that she weaves around his head in shiny curls and puffs, as he agonizes over each passing minute, dreading that he will not only miss all the races but the rest of the day's activities as well.

The clothes he is wearing are all hand-me-downs wheedled from Ranima, her employer and benefactor. In spite of his mother's repairs, his shorts are too long for his legs. The stitches show through the fabric, because the thread does not match. The bright silk bush-shirt is polished from wear but the rich herringbone weave is impressive.

"Please let me go, Ammiji," he pleads. "I will be late. All the other boys will already be there. Let me go before Saeed claims all the prizes for himself."

Still his mother continues to linger on the details, deliberating the exact place to pin the rosebud, humming to herself.

Finally, satisfied that she has done all she can to make him look adorable and presentable, she continues to hold him at arm's length, gulping in sudden intakes of air. On an impulse, she reaches out with a crooked small finger, and skimming some of the surma out of one of his eyes, places a tikka between his eyebrows. Her eyes are already brimming over when, with one final kiss carefully planted on each cheek, he is launched into the world. He dashes out of the house and through the streets, as passersby hurriedly step aside and stare after him. He follows the freshly cleaned and lime-lined drains, clearing the distance between the Hindu temple and the narrow street to the village well with a few long strides, and arrives breathlessly at the crowded clearing of the Dara-tul-Aman.

In the commotion that greets him at the playground, he is quick to notice two things: the rosebud pinned to his shirt pocket has slipped and fallen somewhere; and all the races scheduled for the day have been run. Several of his classmates are catching their breath, slumped against a wall. He has barely had time to grasp the situation before his nemesis, Saeed, ambles over, a wide grin plastered across his face.

"O-y K-i-t-t-u! Look what I have won at the races while you were hiding under the bed at home and missing out on the competition for the skinniest boy," he teases, showing off his newly won prize of a red-

and-gold writing pen nestled neatly inside a shiny black plastic box.

"What races? Oh, this is not fair . . . " Kittu fights the warmth beginning to well up in his eyes, his breath now coming in short gasps, aware
that if he begins to cry the surma will smudge his face.

"They should not be handing out fountain pens like this as prizes for
merely running fast," he finally manages to stammer. "These prizes
should be reserved for the best penmanship or something else equally
worthy . . . "

"And you, Kittu de bache, do you think you would have won for
your brand of penmanship?" Saeed sneers.

"I might have . . . I would have won! If only my ammiji had not been
delayed at work, I would have shown you how fast I can really run. You
want to race me now, just you and me and we will see who really is the
fastest. We can settle this for ever right here."

One of the uniformed organizers overhears Kittu's agitated voice
and, after gently maneuvering him aside, asks him his name and age.

"Kittu Karim Allah Bashk, ten years old," he lies, stumbling once
again over his surname.

"No, no. What I want is your real name."

"KITTU! Kittu KARIM Bushk," comes back the unwavering
answer, threatening a tantrum if challenged any further. Once his name
and age have been noted down and a number assigned to him, Kittu is
promptly handed a transparent plastic package that contains a tube of
toothpaste and a brightly coloured toothbrush. The rustling package
contains a leaflet on which is printed a picture of two hands locked in a
handshake. He notices that the image is printed above a band of stars
and stripes.

He turns to the matronly attendant who has handed him the package and inquires about the remaining races for his age group.

"Oh, the races . . ." She glances at the clipboard in her hand. "Karim
Bushk, you have just missed the last one of them. You are, however, just
in time for our film."

With this piece of information, she guides him to a spot in front of
a whitewashed wall where all the other children are seated on the ground
inside squares drawn of fresh lime powder. Some of the children have

turned up with both their parents.

A hush descends over the audience as the first flicker of light projects in a bright cone from the back of the covered truck. The screen comes to life, with images of children moving on and off the screen. Men and women in starched white uniforms distribute packages to outstretched hands while the flag with the stars and stripes waves from the trucks.

Some of the children in the audience stretch out their hands too, to grasp the handouts. Others make silhouettes on the screen with their hands. The uniformed attendants admonish them. Shhhh, they whisper, index fingers held vertically across their lips.

"America has generously come to the aid of its friends all over the globe," says the soundtrack.

An hour later, when the show ends and the smattering of applause kicks up even more dust, the crowd rises noisily to its feet. The men linger briefly to admire the wondrous gadgetry that has made the film possible, appreciating the sturdiness of the converted military truck, and the starchy, dry authority of the uniformed workers. However, there is only so much that can hold their attention so late in the day, and they begin to disperse gradually into the streets to head for home. The film equipment is hastily repacked under the tarp, and the truck is once again guided through the narrow streets. This time it is followed by a much smaller crowd of children and fewer adults.

One of the last to leave the grounds is Kittu, who reluctantly heads for home, this time taking the longer route, the shiny package held tight in one clammy hand. He kicks a pebble skillfully across the polished street, then comforts himself with his favourite rhyme, hopping from one side of the street to the other: *Chakwa meñ awañ? Na! Chakwi . . . Chakwi meñ awañ? Na! Chakwa . . .*

He almost misses the entrance to his own street.

He notices that all of his neighbours are now gathered with his mother outside their house. She is the first to rise to greet him, her look of pride turning into one of alarm on seeing his tear-streaked face, as he rushes past her into the house without a word.

She notices that his panting is punctuated by sobs once he is safe inside the home.

"Ammi, I told you to let me go sooner but you would not listen," he finally blurts out, turning towards her, trying even harder now to fight back his own disappointment and the heat of his tears.

". . . and when I got there, Saeed had already won all the prizes and all the races were over, and then we saw a film about poor people and they gave me this to take home with me."

He proudly holds up the package to her, bravely covering his mounting sobs. She pulls him onto her lap, showering his face with kisses, her own hot tears now beginning to flow freely.

"My Kittu, mera chunn! What a clever, brave boy you are. I am so proud of you. Why do you let that spoilt child Saeed ruin all your fun and bother you so much? You know you are way too clever for him and others of his type. Come here, now tell me more about the film . . . "

As he chatters on, she fondly recalls how as an infant he would follow her everywhere, an unobtrusive shadow by her side, an uninquisitive child who would passively remain seated where he was placed. An onlooker might have concluded that the child lacked curiosity or imagination. Yet, here he was now, vibrant as sunlight, his eyes sparkling with exhilaration. At such moments, how like his father he seems to her. She finds a clean hem of her kameez and uses it to wipe the tears, first from his and then her own eyes.

"One day your abbaji will return to us . . . and he will be so surprised to see how you have grown up, and how fast you can run, and how good you are with the slingshot . . . one day . . . "

At the mention of his missing father, Kittu's well of tears dries up and he struggles to unravel himself from his mother's embrace. He knows what is sure to follow as she begins recounting of their litany of tragedies, how his father abandoned them when Kittu was only a year old and has not been heard of since; how she must suffer the further humiliation of doing odd jobs and washing dishes in three different households in order to keep them both alive.

"In my heart I know that Karim will one day come back for us," she repeats in between her sobs, "and we will again be a family like the rest of the people. And I will no longer have to work in three different houses, perhaps only one, when he goes out to work, and you will have new clothes and lots to eat and . . . and . . . "

But by then Kittu has long since slipped out of her reach, is already on the rooftop struggling to get his kite aloft in the feeble evening breeze. Shahid and Zahid, upon seeing him across the rooftops, call out to him to come down to the street to play. Before heading out of the house, he stops to splash some water onto his face, noticing that his mother has dragged out her suitcase from under their common bed and is rummaging in it.

He knows what she is searching for.

For a long period, this object has resided in the forbidden domain of Jinn Baba. When he was younger, Kittu's mother had described to him the world beyond theirs as the domain of demons and monsters. As a child this admonition had kept him out of mischief and harm's way, but as he grows bolder with age, those forbidden places had begun to seem more enticing with promises of adventure. Sometimes his curiosity about the world of the adults would overpower his ingrained fear of jinn, pari, and booth, who wandered the world chanting adam bo! adam bo! at the scent of man.

In his early years of childhood, left alone at home when his mother went to work her long hours, any sudden lapse of self-confidence in him would often hurl Kittu into the hostile domain of Jinn Baba lurking just outside his sanctum of safety. The walls of the house would begin to move in on him, closer and closer, threatening to crush him in their midst and swallow him whole. When and if his mother ever returned, he thought, she would surely find the house empty and the walls back where they were supposed to be, and her precious son would be nowhere to be found. There were other times during this period when the house moaned and creaked under the weight of shifting spirits, and he would go outside to sit atop the stairwell and wait for his mother's return. More than once she found him curled up there, whimpering with fear. She would gather him up in her arms and carry him inside, his eyes urgently scanning the courtyard and the veranda.

"Ki ay mere chunn? What are you staring at? What is it? Tell me!" She would question him and he would be too scared to articulate his fear. She would curse her kismet and her vulnerability in this hostile world. However, Kittu's recent meticulous exploration of every inch of their house had finally banished Jinn Baba and others forever to the dark of the night.

It was a long time ago when he stumbled upon the object his mother is now seeking for comfort with such urgency. The image resides inside the cloth pocket of the cardboard suitcase she has always kept under their bed; since its discovery, it has become a shrine he visits frequently. He has evolved a personal ritual, one in which he will prop up the image next to his mother's palm-sized mirror, and staring back and forth from his reflected image to that in the photograph, he will wait for the two faces to merge. He has scanned the familiar profile endlessly from every possible angle, hoping to catch the person trapped beneath the veneer in an involuntary twitch or sneeze, and thus give a sign of being alive. He has searched all over the house, but he has failed to uncover any other clues to his father's existence. Could this be the only residue he has left behind on their lives, from a chapter blossomed briefly and then evaporated into half-fabricated memories? Had his father been so real to them that Ammiji to this day cannot speak his name without turning her face away? Where is he now that they need him so much? Why does he not want to be with them as much as they want to be with him? These are the questions that rage through his young mind.

He notices that a part of the oblong paper has snapped off from frequent handling. The young man in the photograph sits on an elaborately carved chair next to a round wooden table. He sits stiffly, his face tilted upwards at an unnatural angle, leaning on an elbow, his chin propped in the palm of his open hand. Next to him is a large bowl of cloth or paper flowers, behind is a painted backdrop of highly stylized mountains, several willowy trees, and a lush waterfall. Three shadows of the same human head overlap across this painting. The seated character, dressed in a dark three-piece suit, appears uncomfortable and overly self-conscious of the bright lights, and his eyes bore intently at a spot above the camera.

Kittu's father has become this sepia-coloured photograph with a spider-web of cracks across its glossy surface. Even though his mother keeps reminding him that he resembles his father, he has so far been unable to tell the similarity. The image holds no clues to his queries. In place of answers there remain the vague emotionally charged memories labeled as his father, Abbaji, planted in him by his mother from a very early age, until he sees a familial resemblance in every middle-aged male moving through his or his mother's life.

Searching for clues to his personal origins, even his name has become a puzzle to him. "Why did you have to give me such an unusual name as Kittu?" he asked his mother once, unable to bear any longer the daily taunts of his classmates.

"And why not Kittu, mere chunn? It is a great name. It is the first name your father knew you by. 'Mera Kittu Mittu!' he would proclaim, proudly holding you up in the light so that your dadi amma could see you better. Your father wanted it this way and you should be proud of your special name. No one in this whole wide world has it. Only you. Mera Kittu Mittu," she repeats, enjoying the roll of the name over her tongue and fondly ruffling his hair. From that day on Kittu has this very special badge to wear and defend. He will get into fights to defend it. No "Tichoo" or "Achoo" will do. From now on, it has to be "Kittu" and nothing else.

During one of those early days, while on his way to school, he had happened to step into his nanni's house. She had taken one look at his miserable face and made him sit next to her for the next three hours while she cleared the breakfast dishes, began the laundry, kneaded the dough, washed the rice for supper, and then sent him out with two paisas to buy treats for himself. He returned some time later with two peppermint pillows melting deliciously under his tongue. He helped Nannaji in the workshop by operating the wheel of his bellows. He had ended up spending the rest of the morning with his slingshot in target practice on the unfortunate house sparrows nesting under the veranda ceiling.

At noon, he had lunch with Nanni and Nannaji, before returning to the rooftop to play some more, and Nannaji returned to his workshop. Much later in the afternoon, when he had been all worn out by the day's activities, he was finally ready to head for home. At home, he once again enjoyed a meal lovingly prepared for him by his proud mother and by the next morning was back at Nanni's house.

This state of affairs would have continued endlessly had not his mother paid a visit to her parents. From that day on, she made sure each morning that he had entered the school compound and that the class monitor or Masterji had taken him into their care.

Now in grade three, he has already mastered the instinctive art of rote and recitation, while freeing a major part of his mind to wander the countryside outside the school. He flees the confines of the open class-room like a caged bird set free, hovering over the neighbouring streams and ponds, gliding into deep-shaded trees and over freshly planted fields, searching out doves and starlings unaware of the intruder in their midst. When he tires of the game, he switches to plotting out deadlier strategies for kite flying. The teacher drones on and on with the recita-tion of the five times table as the rest of the class echoes the refrain: Punjo chokay vee, punjo chokay . . .

His wooden tablet takhti is diligently coated daily with freshly dried paste so that he can hone his writing skills. Yet, no matter how skillful-ly he maintains the prescribed angle of the precise cut of his reed pen, fine penmanship eludes all his determined efforts. He remains chal-lenged by his inability to contain his exuberance within the confines of the dictated flow of graceful curlicues and sweeps of the Urdu script.

"I can already see that Kittu da bacha here will never be a profession-al calligrapher," Masterji needlessly points out to the class, seizing Kittu's slender earlobe in a vicelike grip of forefinger and thumb. As this has become a routine exchange between him and the class teacher, wily Kittu has learned to counter each one of these encounters. "But Masterji," he winces, "I do not want to be a calligrapher when I grow up. I want to be a good masterji like you." The ploy never fails to induce in masterji a sheepish and self-satisfied simper before he moves on to the next victim's handiwork.

At the end of the afternoon, when classes finally do come to an end to the accompanying shouts of chhutti, he races home, the wooden takhti held high horizontally at arm's length like an extended wing of the occasional airplanes he sees flying overhead. Once at home, he hastily gobbles down the food his mother has left for him, pours himself a bowl of water, slurping it all the way down his kameez collar, and is off to meet his friends for a brief game of gulli dhandha. Then too soon it is time for the Maghrib prayers and sapara reading at the masjid. Here, there is more learning by rote; the Quranic verses repeated in a singsong nasal semblance of Arabic, first by Hashim, the new muezzin, and then by the assembled class of twenty boys.

When his mother, hurries home from her work, she brings with her day-old portions of leftovers of yesterday's dinners and lunches and the morning's breakfasts, gathered from her employers' homes. This rice dish has become the story of their life: a mishmash of leftovers from the feast that is the lives of the fortunate; each mouthful a burst of new flavors, a poor man's multi-textured biryani. "Khitchri!" Kittu shouts gleefully, proudly eyeing the rich hodgepodge being offered up to him.

Sometimes, while pensively observing the extravagant lifestyles of her employers, Sughra is unable to comprehend either the scale of their benevolence towards her or their frivolous wastefulness; watching with a choking frustration as so much good food being wasted right before her eyes. She has seen Ranima toss out a whole bowl of day-old kneaded dough just because it had begun to ferment. The same fate awaits day-old rice that no one has touched the previous night, and the meat that is no longer tender and is unceremoniously dumped into the garbage.

On the rare occasions when she does cook at home, she offers Kittu all the tasty morsels she can spare from the clay cooking pot, skewering pieces of steaming meat or tubers onto chipped firewood that is oozing with resin. Sometimes, knowing his favourite treats, she will toss a potato or yam into the cooking fire, and then fish them out for dessert after their dinner, when the lone kerosene lamp is lit and raised on top of the gauze-lined freestanding almari used to store all their food.

This has been the established routine of his life with his mother for as long as he can remember. However, there has now been a recent disruption to it by the increasingly frequent visits of Ranaji to their house. Kittu's thrill of each new day and the unexpected gifts it brings is suddenly becoming tempered with the bitter knowledge that the reliable world around him is beginning to fall apart. Every time Ranaji has come to visit them, and it is often in the evenings when Kittu is away at the mosque for sapara lessons and his mother is back from work, he finds the outer door to the house locked from the inside, and he has had to wait outside patiently before they will let him in.

He has also been quick to figure out that if he returns home too early from the masjid and Ranaji is visiting them, he will be hastily sent away with some money to buy a treat for himself. The earlier he returns, the higher will be his reward. However, the real trick is evading Hashim's vigilant eye, and in spite of all his resourceful ingenuity, this is a task he is unable to pull off often enough. There have been several occasions when he has been forced to stand facing the masjid wall, clutching his earlobes, and chanting meri tauba, meri tauba, in penitence under his breath.

As Ranaji steps into their courtyard, his arrival is announced by the protesting squeal of the stiff leather of his new khussa that has not yet been fully broken in, the right foot still indistinguishable from the left. Today, he is wearing a sumptuously flowing kurta of boski silk with gold cufflinks, the front buttons left partially undone. In greeting him at such close quarters for the first time, Sughra notices that the thick dark head of hair and the curling mustache are both flecked with henna and stand out in sharp contrast to the pepper gray of the bushy eyebrows. The visible hair on his chest is white. She realizes that this multi-hued man, with the tight shiny skin and the easy swagger of a much younger person, is completely in his element. She has to remind herself yet again to be subservient and meek in his presence at all times; after all, it is a great honour for them that he has blessed them with another personal visit.

She drags into the open courtyard the larger of the two stringed manjis that are standing upright in the veranda, hastily covering it with her cleanest duree, and keeping her head lowered inside the overhang of her bright, flimsy chunni, demurely keeping her eyes averted at all times. She is glad she had saved this fine muslin stretch of cloth for only such a special occasion. As she pours water from the clay matka into a bowl and holds it unsteadily out for him to drink, her glass bangles chiming, he glances briefly at her face in trying to get her to meet his gaze. He notices that beneath the wear and tear that life has written across her face there is a youthfulness in her shy smile and lowered eyes, a vitality of which he had not been aware of until now. And in this shaded part of the house, as he looks at her in an entirely different light, he realizes how closely she appears to resemble Ranima from an age when he was still wooing her. Moreover, when she had risen to fetch the manji from the veranda, he had had the inexplicable urge to lie down at her feet and unburden himself of all that ailed and possessed him when he was away from her. There had been the briefest of moments as their nervous glances had collided, releasing in him a sudden flood of unforeseen emotions, a quickening of his pulse that he had forgotten still existed within him.

Though not a word has been exchanged between them just yet, he begins to unbutton his kurta before happening to look up at the surrounding walls of the overlooking rooftops. He rises quickly and drags the manji back under the cover of the veranda, newly aware of the grace in her light step as she crosses the courtyard to latch the outer door from the inside.

These weekly visits, ostensibly for a body massage, have become an awkward ritual over the past two months. The first of these visits had caught her completely offguard, and she was surprised at her pleasure in his visit. After all, she had been working at his house for over three years now and they were just beginning to become less formal with each other. That day they had sat uneasily at a considerable distance from each other, he out in the courtyard while she next to the hearth, not knowing what they expected of each other. In her exhilaration of the moment, she even lost her awareness of her drab, wrinkled clothing and uncombed hair. Their conversation was restricted to the usual formalities as they waited for Kittu to return with the soda bottle she had sent him out to purchase. For his next visit, Rana Saabji brought a box of syrupy jalebis that he knew Kittu loved so much, still piping hot from the halvai. For her, he had brought an ornate metal surmadani, the first of many such gifts. That first time, her insecurities had got the better of her, as she nervously wondered about the true purpose of his visit and his presents, and when he half-jokingly suggested that he was here for a massage, she did not know what to say in response. Gradually, she got over that, and they had moved with clumsy formality, from small talk to his actually removing his kameez and lying prone on his stomach while she administered the massage.

At the present stage of their courtship, they are both fully conscious of the fact that it has not been an easy relationship to maintain. He has had to show a vulnerable side under his impetuous formality, and she has had to overcome her awe and intimidation at his considerable physical presence.

As she now steps into the inner room to fetch the oil, a shadow falls across the doorway, and she does not turn, aware that the bulk of his half-naked body is blocking the doorway. Sensing his presence in the room more than actually seeing it, she does not dare to seek out his eyes, to ask or to understand, aware only of the sudden arousal within her own body, and the abrupt lifting of the weight and tension of her years of self-denial. As she stumbles in her confusion, his steady arms have lifted her and are carrying her away.

Much later, she will recall the incident in concluding that it has been nothing short of miraculous that their relationship has survived so long up to this stage. During Ranaji's first few visits, Kittu had a hard time tearing his eyes away from the man's face, so disconcerted was he at having discovered some dark secret that he could not fully comprehend. Ranaji, for his part, had become increasingly irked by the child's unwavering gaze, until one day, for no apparent reason, he launched into a tirade against the boy.

"Mammu, mammu, MAMMU! When will you stop calling me mammu? Call me Rana Saab or Chachaji, or even Tayaji if you have to. How many times have I told you, I am not your mammu? Go ask your ammi and she will set you straight."

He had managed to splutter his indignation through a mouthful of betel juice, his gums and teeth heavily flecked with paan.

Sughra correctly anticipated that this would be their first confrontation with each other. She raised her own voice to proclaim sardonically that Ranaji was indeed like a maternal uncle, a mammu, to Kittu. "After all, what else can you be to him if not a mammu? My mother was closely related by marriage to your father. Ranaji, how else can you expect my little son to recognize his own relatives."

The mention of this elaborately intertwined network of bloodlines rankled her suitor, and she sensed from the blood rushing to his face that she had touched a sore spot.

"What relatives of mine?" he screams in red-faced indignation, yet unable to tear his eyes from her mouth that was set in a half mocking sneer, her eyes darting sideways as she avoided his gaze. He had never wanted her more than he did at this moment. However, there was face-saving to be done, and the child was now intently watching them.

"Why do you keep insisting that you are related to us? Your husband broke that bond when he refused to come and work for me when I so desperately needed him at the kiln. How dare you still claim to be of the same family as mine? After all I have done for you, all the favours I have granted you, all the money you make working in my household, all the gifts I have showered on you and your ingrate son. Have you any idea how many girls would be eager to work for me in my house . . . and without any monetary compensation at that?"

He pauses, for a moment, at a loss for fresh accusations.

"What am I running here—a charitable gharib-khanna?" He finally splutters, comical to her in his inability to contain his exasperation. He continues to seethe until finally, unable to peacefully resolve their argument, he rips the motia garlands wrapped around his wrist and hurls them at her in frustration.

Kittu meekly watches as the heated debate ends in his mother finally breaking down in tears, with Ranaji continuing to mutter to himself about all the ingrates he has had to feed in his lifetime. Paan juice dribbles down his chin, staining his silk kameez like bloodstains, and it is several minutes before he is able to regain his composure sufficiently to quietly exit the house.

Kittu has also noticed that Ranaji in his nervousness and haste has taken away the unopened box of fresh jalebis he had brought for them.

The memory and unpleasantness of that encounter had been hastily tucked away by both of them by the time of Ranaji's return the next week. And as a mute uncomprehending witness to the confusing affair unfolding before him, Kittu has observed his mother go about her daily chores as if dazed and half-asleep, her mind occupied by an inner dialogue, a smattering of her conversation finding its way to her lips. Sometimes she will lie idly in bed complaining of being too tired to work, her head tightly bound with a dupatta, and send him out to inform the various households that she will not be coming in for work that day.

The air-cooled almari with all its perishable food sits on four stubby legs that are nestled in the summer inside clay pots filled with water to keep out the ants. Nowadays she sometimes forgets to top up the water in these pots and then the ants have to be fished out before Kittu can have his milk. The flat open courtyard of the house, the top layer of mud acquiring a weekly coat, is now left unattended, and is beginning to crack up, forcing him to take his game of clay pellets and marbles outside.

There are other times when he will walk into the house and she will continue to be preoccupied with some chore, and there will be no acknowledgment of his presence. This, he is coming to realize despondently, is a very different person than the one he has known, whose undivided attention he has always commanded.

It is now only in the presence of Ranaji that she comes alive, hurriedly tidying up the visible parts of the house, hiding the broken and the unsightly behind the almari or under the bed, rebuking Kittu for messing up his clothes or not washing his hands properly after eating. During the visits, often he is asked to go outside to play. The tiny alcove in the wall housing the handheld mirror is now cluttered with the numerous gifts Ranaji has brought for her: a bottle of scented coconut oil, carved wooden combs, bottles of exotic attars and elaborate surma-danis each with a tapered applier welded to the cap. It is a rare event when Ranaji will bring him a box of flavoured green burfi, cut into diamond shapes and brushed with silver and gold leaf, its creamy texture tampered with drops of gum arabic.

To an outsider this affair would appear to be a lopsided and abusive one, but Sughra has awakened very early to the fact that she must now swiftly make the transition from a mere servant in the residence of a powerful man to a discreet mistress. In the process, she has acquired an enhanced self-worth, mastered the art and nuance of the implied apathy, the intermittent and unpredictable outburst of tears that will further solidify her hold over her attentive lover.

At the Peacock House, with Kittu out exploring the garden and rain clouds beginning to edge out the sun, Ranaji is still rambling on about his pets:

"Abbaji Marhoom finally figured out that since the peacocks will not eat any meat, the missing ingredient from the birds' diet must be the juicy insects that they so greedily consume . . . "

Ranaji points to the stained glass structure towering over the estate.

"Can you all see that tower up there in the sky? That structure was actually designed to gather insects during the night to feed our peacocks. The light inside not only serves as a beacon in the dark and is visible all the way from the other end of Kotli, it also attracts swarms of insects. If you come here in the early morning, you will find the grounds around it littered with moths and such. Sharifu collects these daily and feeds them to the birds. Ever since the time the tower was put in place, the call of the peacocks has continued to echo through our grounds."

"As you can see, there is more to the stained glass then mere decoration. Moreover, speaking of decoration, if you look closely you can see a dark turquoise glass in the middle of each side of the tower. My abbaji acquired this very rare shade of stained glass from a supplier in Delhi."

"Wah! Ranaji," the nambardar interjects in open admiration. "I would never have guessed that in a thousand years."

"And that is why you will always be a nambardar and we the owners of the Peacock House," Ranaji chortles, relentlessly bettering the thick-skinned official before him.

"But enough talk about my beloved pets. All this discussion must surely have made you all hungry. Sharifu, go and see if the dhahi baras that Ranima has been preparing for us since morning are ready."

As Sharifu disappears into the interior of the house, the gathering turns quiet. The underlying blend of irritation and pathos in Ranaji's voice has not been lost on the assembled men. There is only one obvious area of Ranaji's personal failing: even though the peacocks on the estate have continued to breed and thrive, he has no offspring of his own to pass on his vast wealth; he knows that with him, an only son, will die out his lineage and family name.

The contemplative mood of the gathering is suddenly interrupted as Barkat, Kotli's jovial head street-cleaning jamadar, drops in.

"Ranaji," he inquires, breathless from his jaunt, his pleasure genuinely writ across his face. "I was on my way home from the sabzi mandi and thought I would come in and say salaam to you all. I pray that all is well with you."

He proceeds to squat down at the foot of the stairs after removing his shoulder scarf and placing it on the bare earth beneath his uncovered legs.

Dainty china bowls, heaped with sweet and sour dumplings in yogurt and topped with tamarind sauce, are brought out. After passing the bowls around to all the seated guests, Sharifu turns his attention on Barkat. He attends to the jamadar by first scooping out a fist-sized hole in the soft soil directly in front of where he is squatting. Into this depression he presses a freshly plucked banana leaf, pouring the snack directly into this makeshift bowl.

After the snack has been consumed in silence and eagerly complimented, a freshly loaded hookah is brought out and handed to the host. He passes it over to the most venerable of his guests, Babaji Abdullah, to take the first puff. No one notices that after the hookah has completed its first round and finally returned to Ranaji, he inconspicuously fishes out a mouthpiece from his kurta pocket and slides it onto the shared hookah tip. The mouthpiece disappears unobtrusively back into the pocket when the hookah is passed around again.

The lecture on the mating habits of peacocks resumes, Ranaji taking immense pleasure in describing the elaborate courtship rituals of the peacocks, and their manners of love that he gleefully terms as Ishq.

"At the first signs of rain, the peacock begins his advances by spreading his tail feathers. He shuffles them into a fan so that they are adequately arranged. Then, shaking them like a tree at the nearest female, he will put on a grand display. However, you have to also remember that when he is courting, the male will perform the same dance every time something bright comes into his vicinity or between him and the female. One particular male has actually attacked our horse-drawn buggy twice as it was being pulled out of storage for a visit to the city. And more than once the same bird has been at risk of being run over by Babaji Abdullah's gleaming Mercedes when he has come calling here. Even our own Sughi has been given the same treatment. This happened one day when she came in here straight from a wedding wearing a tinsel-lined chunni."

At the mention of Sughra, Barkat tactfully clears his throat and rises "Well, Ranaji, it is getting late and I must be heading for home. I have a busy day ahead of me. You should see the mess the merchants have left behind for us to cleanup in the morning at the sabzi mandi. Rab rakha!"

His departure is a cue for the other guests, who tactfully rise and depart. Ranaji now turns his attention to the men waiting patiently on the bench for his attention.

Later that same afternoon, when Sughra is finishing up washing the dishes and Kittu is busy playing Ludo with one of the servants, Ranima sends her personal attendant to fetch her. Kittu watches his mother nervously dry her hands on the edge of her kameez and adjust her chunni over her head before wiping her feet and stepping timidly onto the lush carpet of Ranima's bedroom.

She has been in this room only thrice before, each time to rub Ranima's shoulders or massage her legs. The room feels claustrophobic to her, cluttered with decorative and functional objects. She quickly notices that Ranaji is seated in a sofa at the far corner, busy reading a newspaper. Ranima, sitting at the edge of the double bed, rises stiffly on seeing Sughra and steps up to open a large cupboard next to the bed, barely containing her restiveness. Eyeing Ranima's heavily embroidered shawl, Sughra is suddenly insecure and more conscious than ever of her own threadbare kameez and the tattered rims of her chunni that she has repeatedly sewn back in place.

"Come in, Sughi. Come on in. Come over here and see what I have to show you."

Ranima struggles with a drawer before prying it half-open and carefully lifting a large bundle. As she unwraps the creased, rustling brown paper, Sughra catches glimpses of a deep crimson-coloured suit that appears to be heavily embroidered with a gold trim lining. Ranima spreads the heavy suit out carefully across the bed, her pudgy hands caressing out the wrinkles and gently brushing the fine metal-wire handiwork. In the bright light of the room's interior the silken dress seems to flow like a dark stain against the woolen bedspread, offering up shades of deep burgundy and highlights of gold. It is the most amazing dress Sughra has seen in her life.

"Do you know what this is, Sughi?" Ranima asks, running her fingers once again across it to smooth out the creases.

"No, Ranima. It looks to me like a wedding, jora?"

"Haañ," she exhales, murmuring to herself. "The very dress I wore on my wedding night. It has been so long since that day, I think Rana Saab has forgotten what I looked like wearing it."

She glances up to see what effect her teasing has had on her husband. He puts his newspaper aside to stand next to her and squint at the dress, a bemused and flustered look on his face.

"Well, Sughi, it is of no use to me anymore. For all anyone cares, it could just as well never have existed. Do you know what I am going to do with it, Sughi?"

Sughra opens her mouth to speak, but seeing the severe expression on her benefactor's face she is unable to utter her protest; she senses that this confrontation has everything to do with herself and nothing whatsoever to do with the dress.

"Since I can no longer fit into this jora and you look a lot like I did when my palanquin first came to this house, I have decided to give it to you. I believe it will look equally lovely on you, Sughi."

Ranima motions her to come closer, adjusting her heavy chuddar with the other hand.

"Come here, come closer and let me see if it will fit you. I can always have it altered if needed."

"But this is your original bridal dress, Ranima," Sughra blurts out, backing away nervously from the bed. "How can you possibly think of giving it away just like that? And why would you give it to me? It is just too sumptuous for someone like me."

In her desperation, she tries unsuccessfully to establish eye contact with Ranaji for support and extricate herself from the situation.

"Where would I ever wear it, anyway?" she finally counters, limply this time for she is already imagining herself in the dress. "You know my husband may never come back and no one else will want to marry me at this age."

At the mention of her husband's name, the warmth of tears relieves her heightened apprehension. She tries getting away, edging towards the doorway, and notices that Ranima has cut off her means of retreat. In her desperation, Sughra has stumbled over a side table and brought a covered spittoon crashing to the floor. Ranima is quick to help her to her feet, and drawing her closer to the bed.

"It is all right, Sughi. Don't be nervous, just sit here with me for a moment and think it over. Take the dress; it is my reward to you for all the years of service you have bestowed upon us. I am sure Rana Saab approves and would also like you to have it."

She looks to her husband for support, quickly wrapping up the suit with a silk sash. Sughra has been slow to realize that all this time, not once has she heard Ranima address her husband directly. She wonders if the rumours about their morning squabble have anything to do with her present ordeal.

"Go on, take it, Sughra," Ranaji finally intervenes, unable to bear any longer Sughra's growing discomfort. "Ranima is giving it you as a reward for all your efforts. Go on, take it. It will make her happy."

He lifts the bundle up and holds it out to her. "Do us both a favour and take it. You know Ranima can no longer wear it and you can surely find some social occasion that calls for such a dress."

Kittu rises from his game upon seeing his mother emerge from the bedroom, her eyes bleary and her cheeks marked with tears, the bundle clutched close to her body. But, before they are able to leave the house, Ranima offers to pack for them some of the chicken biryani left over from the day's lunch.

She appears startled on noticing Kittu standing next to his mother.

"Oh Kittu. Look how tall you have grown since I last saw you," she murmurs, bringing his face close to hers and staring myopically into his eyes. She kisses his closed eyelids, then each of his eyebrow, his hands, his forehead, a deep susurration rising in her breath.

When she is finally able to look up at Sughra, she sighs loudly and wipes her eyes with the open palms of her hands: "If only Allah Kareem would bless us, too. He alone knows how Ranaji and I have visited every hakeem, every pir we have ever heard of, tried every taveez thaga and wird; it has all been to no avail. Unfortunately, for me, it seems the lines of my kismet were drawn on someone else's palms."

She scolds Sughra in a shaken voice: "Look how the buttons on his kameez have come loose. Sughi, why can't you take better care of this child? Look, how skinny he is getting to be. Don't you feed him enough?"

She fishes for the tiny cloth purse tucked next to her bosom.

"Here, take this and get him some new clothes," she says, handing Sughra the money, and holds out the cloth-wrapped dish to Kittu. Once again she is unable to resist running a hand affectionately through his hair, smoothing down the waves and puffs, and tilting his face up to hers to lay a parting, lingering kiss on the forehead.

"You look so handsome each day that I wish I had a daughter I could marry off to you," she teases unsmilingly in handing him the package.

Mother and son leave the grounds of the mansion silently, huddling close together, mutely letting their feet guide them home over the familiar path.

Once they are safely inside the home, her trembling hands struggle to untie the wrapped food until Kittu reaches out and undoes the knots with his teeth. Spiced aroma floods the room as the two reach in with their fingers, she pushing the tender pieces of meat towards Kittu's side of the plate, without looking up. He has never seen her look so downcast before, and as soon as they have had their fill, he rushes out to the street, leaving her alone to recover from the shock of the afternoon's events.

Much later the same day, when it is nearly dusk and he has returned from the sapara class with a crisp new yellow kite with blue circles for eyes that he has clasped under one arm, he tries discreetly to head for the rooftop. Ranaji and his mother are no longer sitting in the veranda and have moved to the single inner room. This in itself is not unusual, but the sounds emanating from the inner room deserve his closer scrutiny. Since he knows the door will probably be locked from the inside, he gingerly places one ear against it and listens intently.

He has heard these animal grunts and muffled sighs before, and upon inquiring from his mother, has been told that this was what a vigorous body massage sometimes entailed. This time, however, he is unable to attach ownership to the muffled urgency of voices, and is about to move away when he hears something unexpected: there is the sudden harsh sound of human flesh being slapped. This is followed by Ranaji's deep resonating voice:

"Ranima, Ranima, one way or another I will show you who the master is in this house. I have had it with you . . . "

In the silence that follows Kittu can hear his heart pound in his chest loud enough for them to overhear.

" . . . a day will come when I will divorce you and send you back to your parents' house and take on another bride, one who will bear me an heir, a golden child who will care for me in my old age and . . . "

Further silence, and then:

" . . . you will have to be taught a lesson and your place in this house. You will have to learn to respect your majazi khuda, the one that you should be idolizing in your home, won't you?"

The question hangs in the air for a few moments before it is followed once again by the sound of a slap. Once again, there is a long muffled sob and a prolonged silence. Kittu cringes inwardly and continues to listen, unable to move away, yet careful not to lean too close to the door or breathe too loudly. He wonders if they would also beat him if he were caught listening at the door.

The hushed interval stretches out of the room and gradually seeps into the entire house, silencing even the chirping of crickets and the sparrows in the veranda. Kittu notices that a gecko has boldly crawled across the wall to within inches of his face, refusing to flinch in his presence and dart away. The slit eyes blink independently before the creature disappears into a wall crevice.

He is now left with two unanswered questions racing concurrently through his mind: What is Ranima doing in their house at this late hour of the day and why is Ranaji beating her?

Unable to resolve either of these issues, he summons up enough courage to edge away from the door. On his way to the stairs, he notices the faint glint from a tinsel-lined scarlet dupatta draped over the veranda manji. He knows it does not belong to his mother and concludes that Ranima must have left it there.

In the gathering dusk, he struggles to keep his kite aloft even though the wind has died down and the sun has dropped beyond the trees in the distant horizon.

Straggly lines of crows are beginning to wind their erratic way westwards, when he finally descends the stairs and discovers that Ranaji has left the house and his mother, dressed in Ranima's gift of her scarlet wedding jora, is sitting by herself, idly running a comb through her hair. Normally, she would ask him to perform this chore for her, but she seems too self-absorbed today to notice his light step on the stairs as he slips out. She is humming lightly to herself, and does not acknowledge his presence. Impulsively, he walks over to her and puts his arms around her neck, and is shocked to discover that one of her cheeks is swollen and the left eye is partially shut.

She hastily pushes him away, turning her face into the shadows, continuing to hum to herself.

Dusk creeps in early as the rooftops crowd each other to shut out the sky, light visible only in the punched-out squares of the windows seen through the banisters. Swallows emerge from the awnings to dart after mosquitoes. Smoke from hearth fires lingers low and the aroma of dinners being cooked sets the mongrels to restlessness as they move out of Kittu's path. He encounters Manni Tangawallah's tired horse, as it plods homewards, half-asleep after the day-long return journey to the city, and has to climb up a raised stairway to make room for it to pass. He dodges past Malhaara out on his daily routine of lighting the street lamps. He also encounters his neighbour, the machinist Azam Karighar, struggling on his bike to make a U-turn in the narrow street. He edges past the halvai's shop, keeping his eyes averted from the neat stacks of fresh mathai, and the apprentice frothing the milk to fill yogurt bowls for setting during the night.

He approaches the tandoor nervously, as it is crowded at this time with housewives laden with kneaded dough and the day's ferment of gossip, lest they recognize him or ask where he is headed so late in the evening. He moves to the unlit side of the street, manages to remain unnoticed.

On his way he does not dare look up at the wooden lion gargoyles underneath the awning of Dr. Aziz's house. He hurries past the vacant Dara-tul-Aman where only a few days ago he had sat to watch a film, and where the races were held and he had arrived too late and Saeed had already hogged all the prizes leaving nothing for him but a toothbrush he had no use for. He hurries past the tea stall and the barber's khokha, making his way past the open mill still functioning at this late hour, an industrious Sain still at work, loading the last of the day's bins with fresh wheat to be ground to flour, the *tukk, tukk, tukk* of the mill's engine a ubiquitous heartbeat punctuating all the villagers' waking hours.

The Malhaara's shaggy dog has been furtively following him, and without missing a stride he manages to pick up a piece of gravel from the roadside, load his slingshot and let go. There is a sharp whimpered yelp before the creature retreats back into the dark.

He heads past the Malik graveyard, careful to keep his eyes averted from the graves this late in the dusk, past Matha Rani's square compound with its neatly laid offerings of the day, and past the long unused Hindu crematoriums choked and overgrown with weeds. Bats have suddenly begun to unravel themselves from the jamnu trees at the Kalri graveyard and race on eastwards ahead of him, but he is no longer afraid of these or other terrors that come alive in the dark.

Once the Kotli houses have receded into the background, he must wade through ghostly carpets of mustard, trample underfoot their bright staining blossoms, this ochre glowing in the dark. The rising damp of the evening dew also stains his sandals. He only comes to rest when he is next to a massive outer wall that fills his sight with its flaking white-wash and patched stain of mildew.

There is barely enough light in the gathering gloom to reflect off the crystal of green marble, as it arcs across the dense humming air between the ground and the brightly lit stained-glass window. The momentum carries it just far enough to lightly tap a peacock hued diamond of glass, shattering it inwards into a hundred pieces. The marble rolls down to lie among the layers of powdered bodies of fireflies, their miracle lights long since stunned out of them.

With my energy and frustration all spent, I headed for home in the total darkness. By the time I arrived, weary and dispirited, I discovered that Ammiji had not yet returned from work. I waited for her until I grew hungry, and then ate the fresh daal roti waiting for me in the almari. Some of the remaining biryani from the noon meal had also been left there for me. It suddenly struck me as odd that when I walked out of the house it had still been fairly bright inside, yet the lamp on top of the almari had already been lit for the evening.

After the meal, I set out to look for her in earnest. Since I already knew from my games of hide and seek that there were not many places to hide inside the house, I began by scanning the rooftop. I searched the tiny inner kotri, and then even looked under the bed in the main room. When I found that she was not at any of the neighbours either, I concluded that Ranima must have called her to work. I set out for Rana Saab's house.

She was not there. Both Ranima and Rana Saab were genuinely concerned, and he even accompanied me back home to wait for her. We sat and waited until the first light of dawn, while I proudly showed him the rolls of kite dhor remaining from last Basant. Finally, as the day broke, Rana Saab brought me to his home and decided that I would stay with him until my mother returned.

In searching for her, the usual places were scrutinized: the depths of all the local wells were dragged, the three bridges over Nehr Mardan were examined more closely. It seemed impossible that someone could disappear so easily and completely from the face of the earth.

Soon, everyone else returned to their routines, and since I was already living in Ranaji's house, I was given a separate room of my own. I have lived here ever since.

Wiry and raw-boned Kittu at nine, now here I am, at nineteen, chubby and well rounded, with rolls of healthy fat, ever unable to resist indulging my sweet tooth and unable to leave any meal without exceeding the point of satiation.

The much-anticipated downpours never materialized that season of monsoon, though the clouds continued to crowd the skies. Shortly after my mother's disappearance, as I adjusted to life in a new place, Rana Saab returned from an extended trip to his ancestral home of Sargodha, with the sensational news that he had married again to someone from his own family. He would now be dividing his time equally between his two homes.

If Ranima was affected in any way by this development, she showed no sign. When Rana Saab was at home, they continued to live their lives much as they had before his second marriage. I never heard either of them express the wish to have the second wife come and visit them in Kotli.

A few months into autumn, Rana Saab received the joyous news that he was the proud father of a son. There were joyous celebrations at both the houses, and the boy was named Afzal in honour of Rana Saab's father. Thus, in the end, Rana Saab finally redeemed himself and made up for his single failing in an otherwise fulfilled life.

Afzal is now almost ten and visits us regularly. Everyone keeps remarking how closely he resembles Rana Saab as a boy. They seem to say this only in his presence. But they may just be expressing a genuine sentiment.

Over the past few years, Afzal and I have become very good friends. Whenever he visits Kotli, and this is beginning to happen more often, we spend hours together exploring the house and the surrounding countryside. I remember once trying to teach him a song I used to sing at his age, and finding that he already knew the lyrics.

Chakwa meñ awañ? Na! Chakwi . . . Chakwi meñ awañ? Na! He had teased.

Yesterday, when we snuck up to see the damaged side of the tower, he extracted the marble from the rubble and asked me if he could keep it. Then at lunch this afternoon, when we were both alone, he offered me something in exchange.

Holding the marble in his hand and peering at the food, he whispered conspiratorially: "Do you know that out of all the foods I like to eat, the one I love most is Khitchri?"

I know, I know, a part of me wants to say; I have had enough time to figure it all out myself.

Shafiq, the Sacrificial Circuit

". . . One day, on seeing for the first time a sandstorm approaching from the direction of Iraq and turning the noonday sun to blood, my roommate Abrar rushed out into the street with his arms raised to the sky in joyous rapture, wailing: 'Karbala, Karbala, this is the blood of Karbala, of Hassan and Hussein and all our shaheeds.'" —*from Shafiq's letters home.*

"To the imagination of we landlocked Punjabis, the sea is merely a deep and vast river in flood whose opposite shores are never both visible at the same time. As such, Shafiq, you should find it inherently no different from the floodwaters you have been swimming in all your life."

Babaji combs his fingers leisurely through his long white beard, pausing to let his words sink in, the restrained tone and warmth of his words hanging like mist in the chilly air.

"Moreover, even though the sea may initially appear to be much deeper than the familiar churning waters of the Chenab at Maralla, where you have so often fought the undertow, to a strong swimmer like yourself, the depth of waters should be insignificant. Does a tightrope walker look down to see how high the rope is over the ground?"

Babaji places a hand gently on Shafiq's shoulder. "Have faith in your own ability to overcome all such obstacles that are placed in your path. Who knows, Allah Kareem may have placed them there merely to test your resolve."

Once again, the words hang suspended in the air, as if awaiting a response. Having never before traveled over an ocean, my elder brother Shafiq has been apprehensive about his upcoming voyage to Kuwait, but he appears to be somewhat mollified by Babaji's words.

This night is unseasonably cold. Even though we are all swaddled in thick woolen chaddurs and huddled around the three angithis in the middle of the room, we can't help shivering. Together the flickering light from the kerosene lanterns casts angular shadows onto the whitewashed ceiling. We are here because our parents consider Babaji their spiritual mentor, and this gathering at his house has become a Friday night ritual. These days, the only time our entire family is gathered in one place is when we are in the comforting presence of Babaji.

As Shafiq's departure for Kuwait approaches, we decide to pay one last farewell visit with our cousin Jamil to his boarding school at Abbottabad. We have correctly anticipated that he will welcome any opportunity to escape from the drudgery of his hostel life.

During one memorable weekend, the three of us travel all the way by bus to the apricot and plum orchards of Mansehra. We even manage to squeeze in a brief afternoon of fishing with bare hands for river trout near Dhudhial. Jamil manages to document our trip with his camera. With his shirtsleeves rolled up to his elbows and his gray woolen trousers hitched to his knees, he splashes around like a puppy, scaring the trout from their refuge under the giant rocks; pausing only briefly to take in the breathtaking scenery and quote Tennyson: "In the afternoon they came to a place where it seemed afternoon forever . . . "

Eventually we wind our way into the hill stations of Murree, Gorhagali and Nathiagali, ending our trip in feeding the albino fish at Lhasi Masjid, close to Jamil's school. As we toss slivers of roti into the pool and the fish swarm over to us, we take one final photograph. Perhaps it is because of the proximity of the masjid, or the spiritual nature of its healing fountain, bubbling up miraculously from beneath an underground spring to feed the lake, that I shall forever remember Shafiq's assertion that in his opinion all fish are holy, or ought to be, and should always be treated as such.

"Then how could we ever possibly justify eating them?" I point out the obvious in ignoring Shafiq's own fondness for fish. His laughter is of pure joy in the moment. Sadly, that luminous moment passes before it can ever be documented.

"Maybe we should exempt the edible ones as unholy," he concedes. I notice that Jamil is already depressed at the thought of seeing us leave and the outing ending so soon. This is also the last time he will be seeing his friend before Shafiq sets sail for Kuwait.

Those glossy, square, black-and-white images of the trip now lie before me as I write this. Jamil has been complaining once again about being in so few of them; as I flip through them, I find that most of the photos are indeed of Shafiq and me. We are invariably posed in the foreground of some stunning natural scenery or solemnly pointing out various salient features around us. Here is Shafiq's face in half-profile close-up. A lock of his hair, which unlike mine was always wavy, falls across his wide forehead and completely shades his eyes, endowing him with the glamourous looks of our film heroes. And the more I examine this one sunlit image, the more I am amazed that even at this moment in his life, he remains as illusive a human being as he will ever be.

"The voyage lasted nine nights and ten days," Shafiq writes to Jamil in his first letter from Kuwait. The aerogram bearing the British postage with the bold imprint "KUWAIT" stamped across the Queen's profile arrives two weeks after being posted. The voyage was hampered by engine trouble and foul weather at Karachi and later near Gwadar, but all this failed to dampen my brother's infectious sense of wonder about the world around him.

He writes: "Almost daily we touched the shores of a different city: Karachi, Muscat, Dubai, Qatar, Bahrain and finally Kuwait. In my mind each one of the names of these cities now has a harbour; its waters have individual hues. We were accompanied for most of our journey by dozens of very persistent dolphins that kept abreast of the prow; squads of flying fish darted outward from the ship's wake and seagulls landed on deck to steal stray scraps of food.

"One night, when the sea was unruffled and smooth as oil, the surface came alive with a soft inner glow. Thousands of saucer-sized jellyfish floated up from the depths, each beacon like a miniature radio tracking light, a turquoise iris flickering alive in the quiet ripples. I began to wonder if I was observing some form of electrical manifestation at work. Such sights I have seen that I wonder if anyone in Kotli will ever believe me.

"Another night, I fell asleep just after crossing the Strait of Hormuz, — the stony slopes of Muscat were visible through the portholes of our deck— I awoke the next day to find that the shore had disappeared from sight. I distinctly remember that the engines of the ship had not been engaged during the entire night. It was only when I went above deck to have my breakfast that I found out that our ship, the SS *Adrissa*, had swung around on its moorings during the night and remained at anchor at the same spot. Without any steady landmarks to guide you, it is easy to lose your bearings at sea.

"The harassed and demented crew of the ship scrubbed the exposed upper decks with the precision and single-mindedness of military men; it is as if the ship would not be permitted to enter another harbour unless each and every one of its decks were spotlessly clean. Mr Mansoor Cheemaji, my Electronics teacher back at the Polytechnic Institutes would have remarked on such efficiency.

"Every time we dropped anchor a horde of local merchants and entrepreneurs would invade our ship. Yemenis bearing ritual facial scars would clamber aboard to sell us anything and everything imaginable, from sealed tin bottles of Aab-e-Zamzam, the holy water from Makkah, and stone rosaries and silk prayer mats, rolls of silks, shaneel and boski, to elaborate handicrafts made from seashells and coconut husks. Adding further to this carnival atmosphere, half-naked deep-sea divers would appear in boats and beg the passengers to toss coins into the water. No sooner would a coin hit the surface than someone would already be diving after it. I noticed an efficiency of a different sort at work here. If you tossed in a Pakistani paisa or anna into the water, no one would bother retrieving it.

"The bedbugs of Karachi had already receded in our memories, as we stretched out on our bunks and makeshift beds in the deck halls for unberthed passengers. Our entire luggage was piled in the middle or around our fort-like perimeter. I found myself keeping company with some other bachelors from Pakistan. A short distance from us, where each family strung up bedsheets and chuddars to claim their private space, a small community, divided along cultural lines, had sprung up between the bulkheads and the exposed piping of the metal ceilings. It took me all of two days and nights to get used to the constant rocking motion of the ship, but once I was over this, I effortlessly fell into the laid-back daily routines.

"Everywhere I found innovative solutions to old technical problems. I particularly admired the design of the trays in which all our meals are served. These were divided into five compartments of unequal size: one to hold curry, one for rice, one for achaar, one for the fruit piece or sweet dish and one for roti, dossa or idli. As the ship rolled hopelessly from side to side, the contents of each of these compartments sloshed within its confines and did not spill over. There it is again, such efficiency!

"One crisp afternoon, the ship rammed into a sleeping dugong that had been afloat on the water surface, and we came to a complete stop, as the carcass was wedged high onto the prow. The crew tried out various implements to untangle it. I was told that this has never been known to happen on this route before, as the dugongs do not travel so far southeast from the mouth of the rivers Tigris and Euphrates. Perhaps our Babaji's fanciful stories of mermaids with eyes like saucers were actually more about dugong sightings than real-life mermaids.

"Later in the journey, I passed my evening hours tracking the ship's wake from the twin propellers as it receded into the distance like parallel train tracks mingling in the far horizon. At such times, the curious sensation of the ship being at a standstill while the water rushed by it only made the distance traveled from home seem all the more tangible. However, eventually I came to feel completely at peace with myself and the twinge of homesickness completely evaporated.

"Our first sighting of Kuwait City on the tenth day of the voyage was of minarets and domes gleaming on a distant shore, dotted with scrub and palm trees, while white-sailed dhows floated on a silken ocean. Flocks of seagulls rode out the wind to greet us and dive-bombed the decks.

"The ship anchored a mile offshore, and we had to descend into launch boats with all our luggage in order to reach the shore. This proved quite a challenge, as the ship heaved or fell away from the launch with each swell.

"There to greet us at the port were Chachaji Suleman and some of his friends. After we disembarked and headed for the bachelor quarters at Dogha, the ship sailed on its last leg of the journey to Basra."

Long before his departure for Kuwait, ostensibly to seek work, my restless brother Shafiq and I had led a very unremarkable but rambunctious life in Kotli, and though we may have been a handful for our parents, our lives were not marked by any extraordinary events.

Early in his youth Shafiq had become intrigued by all sorts of complex mechanical appliances that he found lying around our house. He must have been about five or six when Abbaji remembers catching him trying to pry open the cardboard grille of our battery-operated family radio so that he could peer inside. From that day on, fearing that Shafiq would hurt himself, Abbaji hid all the screwdrivers in our house. A few years later, Shafiq was caught trying to open Babaji's malfunctioning phonograph with the sharp end of a knife. And though I was three years his junior, and he later denied any memory of it, I distinctly remember him showing me how the hand-powered mechanism inside it worked.

We were kept busy in our chosen strenuous exercise of stringing up a series of radio antennas from bamboo poles. These poles had originally been installed over our rooftop as pigeon roosts. One of our greatest challenges and frustrations in those days was keeping the wires free of roosting crows and flying pigeons, while achieving sufficient height to track the faint radio signals Shafiq was becoming so enamoured with. We also had to be careful not to raise any insurmountable barrier to the kite-flyers in our neighborhood. I can still remember the endless hours of dragging those exposed wires in different directions in varying alignments, while Shafiq fiddled with the dials and the jumbled innards of his radio kits, searching for stronger signals.

Whenever he got lucky, and this was not very often the case, he would leap up excitedly and yell up to me, "Bas, bas! This is it. Don't move around anymore. I think I am getting a good hum." And, this would invariably be followed by "No, no; I'm losing it now . . . can you move a little more to the east? . . . No, no . . . more to the north? Rafiq, what in Allah Kareem's name are you doing up there? I am beginning to lose it."

This exchange could sometimes last the whole afternoon and, yet, who could say no to someone who could coax the sounds from the other end of the world out of a lifeless tangle of tubes, knobs and wiring. Our obsessions would surely have seemed demented to any outside observer, but the tedium was relieved by the fact that opposite our house lived Jamila and her younger sister Bushra. We would often see the sisters take turns in keeping an eye on all our antics; occasionally looking up from their daily chores, and once in a while waving back to us. At such times, the heat of the noonday sun and the burning floor beneath us would be soothed away, as if a cloud had suddenly cooled the face of the sun, and we would redouble our rooftop clowning.

Looking back, I realize it was the first arrival of electricity in Kotli that set in motion the events that had such profound and tragic consequences for our family.

In the winter of 1954, the Kotli Loharan Town Committee received a letter from the national "Department of Electrecty" announcing that one of their crews would soon be arriving at the village to set up power lines. The project was to be completed by the end of the third quarter of the following year. The Town Committee was to facilitate the crew and allot a plot of land for them to set up their base camp.

For years the inhabitants of Kotli had returned from their infrequent visits to the nearest city of Sialkot, marveling at the miracles that electricity, or bijli as it was known, was providing to improve the quality of life of its citizens; and wishing that the power lines could somehow also be extended all the way to their village. On clear nights, they could see from their rooftops the glow of the city lights in the southwestern horizon. And now the powers that be had decided that this wish was finally to be granted.

The news was broadcast through out the village by Sakhiya and his drum in the form of a traditional tandora. I was with Shafiq when he first received heard it. He was particularly excited, as he had recently applied to the Polytechnic Institute in Sialkot to study electronics. So, when Sakhiya ventured into our street with the letter nailed to his drum, I watched Shafiq take him aside and ask him if he was aware of the full import of the message he was delivering.

"What message?" the unsuspecting simple-minded soul had asked.

"The one you are spreading around Kotli today."

"The tandora?"

"Haan, mere yaar Sakhiya, yes, the tandora! It has already become a thing of the past." My brother asserts his opinion by punching his agitated right fist into the palm of his left hand. He put a patronizing arm around the drummer's neck to guide him back from our street.

"Welcome to the Kotli of the future. You, mere yaar, are also to be replaced by the miracle called bijli. Who needs a man with a drum around his neck, walking around the entire village and shouting out the message at every street corner, when with one flick of a switch everyone can immediately hear the news, whether they are inside their houses or out in the fields? This news of bijli that you bring is eventually going to put you out of business, Sakhiya. Better start looking for something else to do. By the way, what else can you do besides beating that poor drum?"

For Hashim, the newly hired muezzin at the mosque, Shafiq also had the same message. With barely a year at his new job in Kotli after his graduation from his madrissa, Hashim was already learning to get by with a minimum of effort, and his students were beginning to fear his stern unprovoked rebukes. He was also beginning to wonder how Maulvi Saab ever expected him to work with students with such a low potential for ritualistic piety. He had spent months with his current group of fidgety and voluble boys, trying to get them to keep their right feet in a vertical position while squatting as prescribed in the final stages of namaz. Yet he still had to make the daily rounds himself and physically position several of the stray feet. "They snicker and fart during namaz, and chatter incessantly during sapara lessons," I had overheard him complain to Maulvi Saab, his employer. "And I cannot leave them alone for a single moment. I have not seen such insolence and irreverence in so many young boys gathered inside a single holy place!"

Shafiq told him that once the electricity arrived in Kotli, Hashim would be out of his coveted job just like Sakhiya.

"And how is that going to happen?" Hashim had inquired.

"Well, you have heard the Egyptian recordings I played for you of the adhan and the Quranic recitation of Surra Al-Falaq on Babaji's phonograph. Do you think your Arabic will ever sound half as good as Qari Baasat's, or that you will be able to carry a single note with such eloquence or piety as he does? With the arrival of bijli, all anyone will ever need to do is turn on a switch inside the masjid and the adhan will be read out loud and clear from the record player to mosque speaker to the furthest rooftops. How can you ever hope to compete with that?"

And seeing his carefully constructed vision of his own comfortable future about to be toppled over, Hashim had sought reassurance from his employer. "Maulvi Saab, can it be true what Shafiq has to say about the phonograph eventually replacing me when the supply of bijli reaches the masjid?"

"La hul wala quwat, illa billa hul azeem," Maulvi Saab had spluttered as they were performing the ablutions of the wudhu for the Isha prayers, his obvious irritation alarming all the other namazis. "How many times have I told you not to listen to that lunatic Shafiq? What will he dream up next, machines reciting Fajr prayers while the Umma grabs a few more minutes of sleep in their beds?"

But Hashim's insecurities had already got the better of him and were coming home to roost. Maulvi Saab had called Shafiq a lunatic, and Hashim knew in his heart that he was anything but that. He had been a disbelieving witness to Shafiq's coaxing of a mess of wires and glowing tubes of finicky ancient radios and other such devices into flickering life; had seen him pull in from the filaments of the antennae on his rooftop the cacophony of myriad voices of the outside world. And though the eloquence of the recorded Quran recitations on the shiny phonograph had always left him in tears, the threat of what Shafiq's message signifies had not allowed him to put the matter to rest. He had reasoned with himself that if he were to merely sit back and not confront the threat more aggressively now, only Allah Kareem knew where he would be headed in looking for his next job.

It had become furthermore difficult for Hashim to stand idly by, when Shafiq had managed to convince Maulvi Saab to allow him to play the recitation of the Quran to the assembled congregation before Friday's Jumma prayers. Those who heard the recording agreed that, Mashallah! they had never heard the Quran recited with such passion, such perfect elocution and such sustained pitch. No one took note of how Hashim had reacted to this praise directed at what he had considered a merely gaudy and overrated piece of shiny machinery.

A month later, when the Friday broadcast of the recordings threatened to become a routine at the Jumma prayers, he covertly substituted the Arabic record with one from Shafiq's collection of popular film songs. The next time the phonograph was wheeled out before the congregation in the masjid, the rapt and pious listeners were treated to the strains of a popular film song: *Hawa meiñ urtha jaye, mera lal dupatta malmal ka, Ho ji! Ho ji!*

The damage to Shafiq's personal reputation was complete. He and his phonograph were promptly banished forever from the masjid. No one had seen how Hashim gloated in private and then returned to the challenge of his duties with a renewed dedication.

In the following months, as he went about his studies, Shafiq eagerly kept himself abreast of the progress of Kotli 's march towards electrification and modernity.

Once the surveyors had completed their job, the next three weeks saw donkey carts delivering the requisite sixty-six wooden poles to the outskirts of Kotli. By then the crew from the electricity department had already ensconced themselves comfortably in their new quarters. Fully conscious of their elevated status in the village hierarchy, they were convinced that nothing short of such luxury would adequately reflect their growing influence. They had rented enterprising Bhagga's recently completed sumptuous eight-room haveli at the northern end of Kotli. Then they set about hiring labourers to cheaply carry out the work of laying down the wooden poles along the marked route. This was one of the tasks originally assigned to them by their headquarters, but the crew were shrewd enough in their assessment to conclude that the only way to maintain their newfound authority locally was to be never seen doing manual labour themselves. Within a few days they managed to farm out their own workload to the eager, underemployed local men.

The lead hand of this electrical crew was a pot-bellied Lahori named Sharif Ullah. Upon his arrival in Kotli, this ponderous, insecure and squat little man reminded everyone of Dinanath, the pre-partition bunya who had held nearly half of Kotli in bondage. He was also the type of person who once at rest you imagined would have a hard time getting back in motion. Surmising from similar appointments elsewhere that he held an extremely coveted position in a potentially lucrative profession, he began his assignment by making some shrewd changes in how others would interact with him. One of the first of these was to limit his speech to a deliberately affected drawl of Hyderabadi Urdu, and refusing to exchange even a single word of the humble Punjabi. He would communicate his pretensions through a mouthful of ubiquitous paan tucked inside each cheek, so that his slurred speech always sounded as if he were speaking through a mouth half full of water.

In Rana Saab, Sharif Ullah found a soulmate. They took to spending hours exchanging esoteric nuances of chewing Lucknauvi-style paans, and the correct choice of katha paste, betel leaves and zarda. A multi-compartmented paandaan could always be found at these meetings, placed equidistant from the two. They were further united in their mutual passion for the breeding of peacocks and fierce fighting roosters. But it was their utter disdain for the work of honest, dim-witted workers that brought out the worst in both. Whenever curious onlookers stopped by to chat with the overbearing Sharif Ullah, he would be overheard scolding his subordinates: "Abay, kya kar rahe ho,kambakhto…"

As work on the electrification project began, it became increasingly obvious that the route of the power line went nowhere near Rana Saab's remote Peacock House. It did not take much guile for Rana Saab to convince Sharif Ullah to make diversions from the sanctioned route. Now the straight and sanctioned path of the power line was going to set off obliquely on a northern mile-long detour, before swinging back to its original destination. And when all was said and done, the electricity department was left sixteen electric poles short for the Kotli project.

There the matter would have rested had Shafiq not chanced to glance at the original drawings of the outlined route. He brought the matter to the notice of everyone who would listen to him, and he was puzzled to find out that no one else shared his enthusiasm in confronting Rana Saab or Sharif Ullah on this issue. Had Shafiq left the matter there, I doubt if it would have later been blown so out of proportion.

Once the sixty-six available poles were in place, new warning signs were affixed to each pole: "Danger 220 Volt Dept. of Electrecty." Our cousin Jamil, who happened to be home from boarding school on his summer vacation, saw these signs. He pointed out to Sharif Ullah that there were at least three spelling mistakes in the sign and that only a handful of people in Kotli could read English.

Sharif Ullah dismissed all of his concerns by scornfully spitting a glob of betel juice onto the ground before him: "Aray Jamil babu, jao tum apna kaam karo . . . angrez to chale gaye, tumhare haath apni zubaan chhor gaye . . . just leave us alone to do our business. Just because you attend an angrezi school doesn't mean that you can tell us professionals what to do. The Department of Electrik-city has been posting this very same sign all over Punjab from the day the Angrez left our country, and no one has ever objected to it before."

Sharif Ullah had finally found an outlet to vent his mounting frustrations over the project by berating our friend: "Anyway, it would be impossible now to alter the master stencil from which these signs were printed. I would advise you and your friend Shafiq to leave all such matters in official hands . . . especially, Shafiq, if you both know what is good for you both. You know very well that the power line to your streets has not yet been installed."

However, the temptation to set things right was too great to resist for long, street power lines or no power lines. One sweaty moonless night, Shafiq and Jamil decided on their own to rectify the spelling mistakes.

mistakes. They set out late one night with a can of white paint and brushed in the hundred and thirty-two missing "i"s. By the time they were done, the wet paint was still not fully dry and had begun to streak down the metal boards and splash onto the streets below. Of course, by morning everyone in Kotli also knew who the perpetrators were, and amidst the rounds of accusations that followed, Kotli must have seemed a very unwelcome hometown to both my brother and our self-righteous cousin.

Shafiq's next letter home from Kuwait brought us some joyous news: "I already have a job working as an apprentice electrician/pipefitter at the Ministry of Electricity and Water's meter shop in Shuwaikh.

"Not that I had much of a choice in careers. It was either work as a steam plant operator or a pipe fitter at the newly constructed salt and chlorine plant next door. Luckily, there was a shortage of electricians at the meter workshop of the distillation plant here in Shuwaikh.

"My five roommates at the bachelor quarters, locally known as the 'dhera' in Dogha, are also Punjabis. Suhail and Anwar are pipe fitters from Sialkot, while Iqbal Cheema and Khalid Mansoor are plant operators from the neighbouring towns of Dhaska and Sambrial. And let's not forget the most pious and colourful one of them all, Abrar Ali Zaigham, my colleague from Gujranwala.

"It has taken me some time to get used to living within the environmental limitations of Kuwait. While onboard the ship that brought me here, all the water we drank had come from Bombay and tasted unfamiliar but sweet. Yet, now that we are on land, the water still tastes slightly off. I had come to Kuwait thinking I was being banished to a Kala Paani, the land beyond the last ocean where culprits are banished forever. However, what I have found is the land of Khara Paani, the kasela mineral-tasting local blend of brackish and distilled water that we all drink. The only other potable water available here is shipped from Basra and Abhadan by special dhows. This is then delivered to the households in small tankers drawn by donkey carts, the Iranian maashkis delivering it two canisters at a time to the water tank in the middle of our courtyard. I had never before thought of water as having any monetary value and here I am relearning its true value. Chachaji Suleman tells me that when he arrived here in 1953, he had to survive living in a tent at the bedu camp on just two pails of water a day for bathing, cooking and drinking. Our current life in the dhera seems luxurious in comparison.

"How I miss the taste of our own sweet water from the village well.

"When I left Kotli, Maulvi Saab told me that I was going to the land of 'true believers,' and as such I should always be vigilant yet open-minded about what I could learn from culture of our Prophet. What I have found instead is a travesty of all the personal beliefs I have been raised in. The irreverent manner in which everyone treats the Quran is shocking. I have seen it tossed casually onto the floor. Moreover, the Egyptians have gone so far as to transform the holy Friday of Jumma into Gumma, and the pilgrimage of Hajj is known to them as Hagg. Figure that one out!

"One thing I do like about the locals is that they address all non-Arab foreigners as Rafiq or 'friend.' You my brother, Rafiq, will be welcome here since everyone already knows your name.

"Only four months in this place and I am already beginning to categorize everyone I meet by his country of origin. A large number of my colleagues at the distillation plant are from the southern Indian state of Kerala. Nambiar, or 'nambardar' as I call him, is my direct Supervisor.

"The plant is located on the shores of the Shuwaikh mudflats, and in my spare time I am like to watch the antics of the mudskippers that thrive in its tidal wetlands. At low tide, thousands of them wriggle out of their nests and slither or hop about from one mud pile to another, deftly dodging the beaks of swooping seagulls. I never imagined that there were fish like these mudskippers that actually choose to live out most of their lives on land.

"On summer nights, when all the scheduled tasks are complete, I sometimes go to sleep curled up on the floor beside the door of the rectifier room. This locked room is kept air-conditioned at all times, and during summer, the air escaping from under the door makes it the coolest place in the entire plant to sleep or sit and read. One night while napping at this spot, I woke up with a start to see that I had a visitor: a tiny kangaroo-like rat about four inches high. It was watching me intently, its whiskers twitching with nervousness while the rest of its body rested on its long tail. As soon as I made an effort to rise, it bounded out of sight. The next night the same thing happened, and over time I learned that if I did not make any sudden moves, the creature would continue to sit there quietly while I slept or sat and read. I later learned that my inquisitive visitor was a desert jerboa, and though it is rare to encounter them indoors, it never occurred to me to bring along my camera.

"This affair went on all summer, but by early winter my friend was gone. Throughout the winter I went about the daily routine of meter readings and line repairs and I often wondered what had become of my desert visitor. Abu Jassim, one of the bedu operators at the plant told me that jerboas do not drink any water during their entire life, getting all the moisture they need from their diet of seeds and nuts. He also informed me that the flesh of the jerboa is a rare delicacy. Maybe that would explain the sudden disappearance, and I wondered if Abu Jassim was being selective in imparting this knowledge to me. Meanwhile, I read up all I could find at the local British Council library on the habits of jerboa rats and stumbled onto their habit of aestivating or hibernating to pass the summer. However, this was the middle of winter and I remained puzzled by the disappearance of my new friend. I know, you will think I am reading too much into this, but one picks one's friends where one finds them.

"One day, a water basin at the meter shop was plugged, so I poured some hot water down the drain to flush out the blockage. When this did not work, I tried pouring some caustic lye into the drain and followed this with some more hot water. I let the mixture sit overnight. The next morning the drain remained plugged. In desperation I poured some acid down the drain in a last-ditch effort to dislodge the obstruction. A day later, when the blockage still remained, I gave up on the problem and went back to looking for something equally useful to do.

"Upon returning the next morning, I found the drain unclogged, and in the bowl of the basin were scraps of skin and fur: the remains of my pet jerboa. It had probably holed up in the unused drain to hibernate. Or, was it to aestivate? The library book I consulted also informed me that these solitary, nocturnal creatures have a low tolerance for heat, and are often known to plug the entrances to their individual burrows. You can imagine how distraught this made me feel at my actions. For several days following this debacle, I actually thought of trapping another jerboa from the desert and letting it wander inside the plant. Perhaps it would take to watching over me as I slept. Thankfully, nothing came of my desperate fantasizing.

"The dhera I share with my roommates is located opposite one of the last remaining sections of the ancient wall that once surrounded the entire city of old Kuwait. Adjacent to one of the south gates through this wall is the central police station. Every time I pass by this place, I notice the scaffolding in the courtyard, the suspended rope noose clearly visible through the open gates. I have yet to see the noose in use, but I did once see a man being caned by three police officers, while their superior sat close by smoking a cigar. The prisoner's punishment was to last until the entire cigar had been consumed. This type of deterrent seems harsh, but criminal activity is extremely rare here. I have seen the local shopkeepers leave all their wares fully exposed and unattended, whenever they have to leave for prayers.

"Rafiq, you know how I have always been drawn to intriguing natural phenomenon. Well, last week I learned from the local paper that a whale had followed a ship into the harbour at high tide, and then after was trapped by the ebbing tide, and had become beached on the southern shore of Fahaheel. On first hearing about it, I could not wait to see the whale for myself. In order to get to Fahaheel, you first have to travel to Ahmadi by a strange contraption called the 'dhumbra,' a cross between a large bus and a sixteen-wheeler truck, and the hour-long journey is an adventure in itself.

"On reaching Fahaheel, I immediately headed for the beach, alongside hordes of other excited families who appeared to have come fully prepared for a picnic. However, long before we reached the carcass, the stench hit us, and we had to turn back. We could see the whale splayed out like a deflated balloon. Someone was already retching onto the sand. The death seemed to have been such a waste and in my disappointment, I wished I had got there sooner. What bothered me more was the carnival-like atmosphere all around me, with hawkers selling water, fresh fish and heaps of pearl oysters.

"I journeyed back was by taxicab, and as the Maghrib adhan sounded over the car radio, the driver pulled over to the roadside in the middle of the desert. There were six of us in the cab and we alighted to perform our symbolic ablutions of the wudhu using only sand to wash, as no water was available. Then facing towards the fast waning light of the western horizon, we formed a straight line to pray. It was as deeply moving and exhilarating an experience as it was unexpected, offering prayers out in the desert like this in the company of complete strangers whose language I did not yet fully understand, and facing Makkah, so close over the horizon and yet so far away.

"How far away Makkah really was came home to me when Babaji, Bebeji and Tayiji Fatima arrived from Kotli to stay with us before traveling on to perform the Hajj. They had arrived by the same route I had taken, and Tayiji Fatima looked so gaunt and drained by the journey that at first I had trouble recognizing her. It was as if we were greeting an entirely different person than the industrious and tranquil one we had known all our lives. I had always known her to possess immense personal strength, and to see her in this state was a great shock. When Chachaji Suleman asked her about the voyage, she grew even more remote and withdrawn. Babaji and Bebeji, however, looked healthy, though they too had suffered from seasickness through out the voyage. I was thrilled to talk to Babaji again and felt comforted by his presence, however short, in our midst. Babaji even managed to tease me about my initial trepidation on traveling over the ocean.

"All three of them seemed so frail and vulnerable that a part of me wanted to go along with them, as Makkah and Medina were closer now then they had been all my life. Ahead of them was a physically grueling month-long journey. But the emotion in their eyes when they spoke of the streets of Makkah, the emerald dome, the sabz gumbad at Medina, was palpable. They had grown up peering into the top end of their tasbihs, in which a tiny image of the black square in Makkah is embedded. And I could now see a lifetime of devout obsession reaching its culmination.

"I have said I was tempted to join them for the Hajj, but then I decided to wait until the following year, when I would be more financially secure. They set out for the Hajj from Wafra one Friday dawn; the arduous journey would test their resilience and faith all over again as much as the voyage had. After seeing them off, we returned to our homes and strung up a white flag on the rooftop, to signify that someone from our household had also set out for Hajj. Similar flags could be seen waving in the breeze on several other rooftops, once the Hajjis returned, we would follow the local custom and replace these with green ones."

From this date on my brother's letters take on a darker, more contemplative tone and to this day I remain mystified by the personal confusions and allusions he was trying so desperately to convey to us.

"Nowadays, I spend a great deal of my spare time at the beach and always come away amazed at the abundance of wildlife around me. From the mudskippers, the raucous seagulls, the industrious plovers and sandpipers and the rested winter migratory birds, to the gesticulating crabs, how each creature goes about its business of daily survival in opportunistic niches of what seems like a giant chaos.

"If, one day, I were given a choice to live out a lifetime as another creature on this earth, I would surely choose to be a mudskipper, willfully squandering my life inside a wet and slimy world that exists between the corrosive salinity of the seawater and the abrasive rasp of the desert sands.

"When it has not rained for months on end, I begin each morning eagerly scanning the sky. Sometimes I am rewarded with the sight of swaths of congealed humidity that look like curdled milk. However, I have learned that these are fake clouds, just like the nighttime flares in the desert that appear to be noonday suns.

"Observing these phenomena closely, I have been rewarded with a revelation that I want to share it with you all. The desert must surely be Allah Kareem's last unfinished landscape. It now seems to me that while he was at work on it, our maker became distracted and wandered off, perhaps to return at a much later to elaborate on its solitudes.

"Located close to the Shuwaikh plant where I work is a shimmering palace that emerges out of the sand like a mirage. It belongs to one of the several royal pretenders to the Kuwaiti throne. As the sheikh who owns this palace needs a pipe fitter to carry out some renovation work inside his premises, he was able to persuade the powers that run our distillation plant to relieve one of their workers for the job. As I am the newest employee at the plant, I was volunteered for this job.

"Since I was offered a room to stay at the palace and did not relish the prospect of commuting to it from the dhera in Dogha on a daily basis, I decided to pack my bags and take up the offer for the duration of the project. I am now for all practical purposes living inside this palace. And one of the first things I noticed on moving here is that there is a giant storage shed adjacent to my room. This shed is kept locked at all times, except for when I have to fetch some of my supplies for the project. It is guarded by a fierce-looking Yemeni attendant who lets me borrow the keys for the short time it takes me to gather whatever I need from the room.

"One sweltering afternoon, while I was fetching some steel piping from the shed, I happened to peek behind the tarpaulin partition. There I saw a large, cluttered backroom, lit by a single bulb, and a thick layer of dust coated everything. Heaped close to the entrance were several massive faded silk carpets, rolled up and bound with rope. These were probably recent additions to the treasure trove. They were propped up against an ornate desk the size of a large dining table. To one side were a dozen fancy upholstered chairs with their stuffing falling out. Several ancient clocks in various stages of disrepair lay by the floor, and I was tempted to take each one apart and repair it. Closer to the back wall was an early Islamic ceramic tile collection half packed into wooden boxes. Further back, where the dust and cobwebs were even thicker, I could distinguish volumes of leather-bound books in glass-paneled shelves, chipped statuettes of angels missing wings or arms or even heads, a life-sized clay winged lion, an Egyptian alabaster cat, several eagles of various sizes. And further back from these were more bits and pieces of unrecognizable furniture, statuary, masonry, and other artworks.

"I discovered that not only had I stumbled upon a hidden treasure trove, but that buried underneath the clutter was a unique and unexpected gem waiting for the right technician's touch. Tucked beneath a dirty oilcloth, in the midst of all this detritus of a vanished lifestyle and lavished glory, was a massive floor-model radio that seemed to have been abandoned. What I had uncovered was not just any old radio but a massive electric prewar German BLAUPUNKT–LU 760 U, in possible working or repairable condition. I felt as excited at the discovery as I would have been had I stumbled upon an ancient tomb. I knew even then that I would not be able to keep my hands off it for long. Given a few afternoons to work on it, I was absolutely certain I could bring it back to life.

"Rafiq, you know how I love these old radios, especially the prewar ones, and this one was a classic beauty. I innocently inquired from the palace attendant if I could be allowed to repair this radio, but I was not prepared for the reaction I got from him. He bluntly told me that not only would I have to stay away from that portion of the room in future, but also that if I so much as breathed a word about the contents of the shed, I would have to immediately pack up and leave the palace.

"The image of all that vast wealth, stockpiled and tucked away in the inconspicuous storage shed, swam for days in my head as I went about my work. When I asked the palace cook and the driver, the brothers Abraham and Mathai Verghese, about it, they both found my revelation hard to believe.

"Mathai, the younger of the two, asked me if I had ever noticed the elaborate inlaid tile work on the walls and floors of the two rooms to the rear of the palace. I answered yes.

'Well,' Mathai continued, warming to his favourite subject, 'what can these people possibly know of fine living when they can continue to use these two rooms merely to pen their goats? If you ask me, all I can see in their past is slave trading and caravan robbing.'

"I realized that Mathai was venting his personal frustrations, and that he always got carried away whenever he talked about the peculiar habits and attitudes of his employers. I never heard him say anything good about them the entire term of my stay at the palace. Yet I was amazed at the depth of his bitterness, and began to wonder how he could eat his employer's salt and be so ungrateful to them at the same time.

"However, Mathai was not willing to let the matter rest at that. I had apparently struck a raw nerve somewhere in him. He tugged at my elbow and asked: 'Mr Shafiq, do you know that most of the local attendants in this palace are actually modern-day slaves? Ask them if any of them has a surname or citizenship of any sort. Just ask them directly and see if you still do not believe me.'

"I was to later find out that the sheikh had indeed acquired one of these attendants only a few months before I had arrived. This attendant claimed that he had been smuggled here inside the bowels of an Iranian dhow that was delivering fresh water to Kuwait City.

"I sometimes accompany Abraham on his Friday-morning shopping trips to the Kuwaiti souk. Most of the merchants in the souk seem to know him very well, and it is fascinating to watch him become a vicarious sheikh himself, with nothing but the best brought forth for him to select: the freshest meats and vegetables, the fattest of the spotted grouper hamour, and the plumpest tiger prawns. Surprisingly, there is none of the usual haggling that is involved in all such traditional transactions here.

"During one of these visits, he even managed to find a cooked mudskipper for me to taste and satisfy my curiosity. It tasted terrible and I could not imagine anyone actually eating it, much less risking his life for it. He has also taken me locust tasting, an experience I have yet to recover from.

"Much later in the morning, we ended up sitting on the dock, watching a group of dhows sail into the quiet harbour. The boats must have been away for an extended period as several of the crews' family members gathered to receive them. And as soon as the seamen landed, arguments broke out amongst their relatives, the crew and the pearl traders. They were still haggling when we left them an hour later.

"As we drove home, I noticed a man wading knee deep into the seawater at ebb tide, his arms raised to the sky, his singsong offering traveling across the breeze. There was nothing even remotely Islamic about his gestures or his prayer, and I was intrigued. Abraham told me that the man was probably a fisherman or a pearl diver who was performing some ancient pagan worship of the sea. I guess that even though the locals are all fully converted to Islam, old habits die hard.

"As soon as I had finished laying down the piping inside the palace compound, the sheikh put me to work repairing the engines on one of his motor launches. Later on, other tasks followed this one and I began to wonder how long my so-called sabbatical from the plant was going to last. If I had not become obsessed with that damn radio rotting under the oilcloth, I would probably still be toiling away somewhere inside the palace.

"While I went about my routine jobs, my mind was preoccupied with hatching a plot to get back at the radio. I realized that the only way I would ever be able to get back into the shed would be by acquiring a key of my own. My resourceful friend Abraham was able to locate a duplicate key that he allowed me to 'borrow' for a day. Once I had the magic key, I could secretly slip into the shed during afternoon siesta and unhook the ventilator flap at its back. By climbing an adjacent wall, I could then crawl into the shed whenever I wished to. I also knew that during noon hour, the area behind the shed was always deserted, and as long as no one saw me enter or leave, no one would be the wiser of my presence inside. It was a perfect plan, and as I ran it back and forth in my mind, I could detect no obvious flaws in its execution.

"I chose to put my master plan to work immediately following the mid-afternoon Zuhr adhan on a Friday afternoon, when all the men would be away at the masjid. I unlocked the door and slipped into the shed unnoticed. While I was unlocking the ventilator flap, I could not help taking a peek at the radio. And that is how I discovered the model number printed on a paper label glued to the cabinet. I discovered the circuit diagram flaking off the inside wall and also the missing schematic to the radio. I detached and then climbed out of the tiny ventilator flap to the rear, locking the door from the outside.

"On my next visit, I had to resist the desperate urge to plug the radio in and see if it worked. My earlier experiences had taught me that providing power to an unused radio without pretesting it could severely damage its components. I knew that a dry shed was often the harshest storage environment and that rodent infestations were among the radio's worst enemy. I also knew that in spite of all my efforts, the radio was never going to sound like it did when it was new, or begin receiving stations in the correct locations on the dial. I would have to test the voltage, rebuild capacitors, and replace tubes, buffers, electrolytics, capacitors and resistors. I would have to lubricate and clean all the contacts, the pots and the tuning capacitor.

"I began the task by first stripping the radio down to its essentials, in order to test each of the components for its integrity. As it turned out, the cabinet was totally infested with spiders. At least none of the vital tubes was missing.

"Working patiently and discreetly for almost a month, I did manage to finally get it as close to a working order as I could. When I finally plugged it in and turned the dial, I immediately heard a faint scratchy sound emanate from the labyrinth of wires and radio parts. I had not been expecting a miracle; all I had wanted to do was to bring the long-dormant radio to life again even if for only a moment. And I accomplished just that. I saw the tubes glow dully. One moment there was a faint glow as of an ember spreading through the tubes . . . and then I saw a spark leap out of the circuit coil and onto the surrounding mess on the dusty carpet. Before I could react, the glow became a low flame that spread and began to acquire a life all its own. In a moment the entire area around me was ablaze. I tried to smother the flames with the oilcloth, but to no avail. Panicked, I crawled out through the ventilator flap and raced along the wall towards my room, half-expecting the shed to explode into a giant fireball behind me.

"In fact, after the initial spurt of flame and smoke, the fire took almost half an hour to reach the ventilator flap. By then everyone else had also noticed the smoke.

"So the fire continued unabated, and the shed was still smouldering the next day. I was amazed that no one inside the palace lifted a finger to put out the fire, or called what passes for the local fire brigade.

"My newfound popularity among the attendants wore out after the sheikh's return from his overseas sojourn, so I figured someone must have pointed a finger in my direction. Though I was never openly accused of causing the fire, I found myself relocated back to the plant. My hiatus, or 'sabbatical' as I had been calling it, was supposed to have been a short one, lasting a week or two at the most. Little did I know at the time that over a year later I would still be at work at the palace. As I write this letter, I am now back at the daily grind at the meter shop."

Once again, he quotes the poet Ghalib in writing an apology: Bahut be abroo ho ke tere kooche se hum nikle!

"Having lived here now for over four years, it is becoming increasingly obvious to me that we outsiders are not the only ones smitten by that desert Pied Piper, oil. The locals, too, are watching their lives, which had remained virtually unchanged from the last century now begin to unravel.

"Last week I went to open an account in one of the newly established banks, so that I could transfer money home in a safer manner than the cash transfers of Hundi. While I was there, a fierce-looking bedhu dressed in heavily soiled clothes walked into the bank with bundles of currency notes. The first thing he did upon entering was to ask the attending farash if there were any 'real Kuwaitis' working at the bank. He wanted someone local whom he could trust with his cash. The farash promptly came back with the explanation that he was the only Kuwaiti working at this bank and was only an attendant and not permitted to handle cash. The rest of the employees were all non-Kuwaitis, either Rafiqs or Farangis. As I watched, the old man shook his head in disbelief, his eyes full of contempt for the men gathered around him, and immediately walked out of the bank with all his fortune still piled high in his ghatra.

"This place continues to amaze me. Only yesterday, I was involved in a similar incident that took place right in our own street. Since it had been raining for two straight days, a lot of water had collected into a shallow pool in the middle of the street, and the mud and sand had turned into a slippery slush. A Bedhu was driving through this mush when the wheels of his car got stuck in it. All of us in the dhera could hear the engine reving and the wheels churning the muck and, curious, we ventured out onto the street. We discovered that the car was a 1955 model Chevrolet, its lovingly polished scarlet paint and gleaming chrome grille were splattered with mud.

"Seeing all of us gathered around his car, the driver eventually emerged and asked us to push. We heaved and pushed for almost an hour, yet no matter how hard we tried the bulky car would not budge.

"As we were pushing, I happened to glance into the interior of the car. Seated next to the driver was a white goat that completely occupied the front passenger seat. Two burqa-clad women sat silently and immobile in the back.

"It was at about this time that our Iraqi neighbour, Abu Ali, finally emerged from his house to see for himself what the commotion was all about. Within minutes of his arrival he had negotiated a deal with the driver. We watched in amazement as the women and the goat were ushered inside his house. Abu Ali returned with a spanner and a set of pliers, and proceeded to unbolt the front door of his house from its frame and hinges. Once he had it loose, he slid it into the puddle and under the rear wheels of the car, and signaled to the driver. The wheels squealed once more, and found purchase on the door, and the car swung out onto solid ground. The two men embraced, cash exchanged hands, the women and the goat were summoned back, and the driver got into his car and drove off. We trudged sheepishly back to our rooms.

"Another day at the plant, my colleague Adil Matar abu Jassem saw me reading a *National Geographic* magazine article on the expansion of oil exploration in the Arabian Peninsula. This was a special edition on Kuwait's imminent independence from Britain in February 1961. Seeing me studying the attached world map, he asked if I could point out Kuwait for him. When I did this, he looked incredulously at me.

'You mean to tell me that is how small Kuwait really is?'

"I knew I had to let him down easy, but I could not help letting slip 'Actually, that is how large the rest of the world is!'

"Score one for the non-locals, the Rafiqs."

The first sign that something was going horribly wrong in the life of my dear brother arrived in the next letter:

"I have just now stumbled on the discovery that the local's name of 'Rafiq' for all non-western foreigners is actually used in a derogatory manner. And, here I was, already putting out the welcome mat for you to join me in Kuwait.

"I have further revelations to make in this letter: I am suddenly becoming very conscious of the fragile state of mind of some of the people I see around me. These people have definitely been damaged in some way; it comes through in their peculiar mannerisms and obsessions.

"Let me tell you about an amazing onion eater at my plant. Abu Daud from Egypt is about fifty years old and looks all of seventy. He is a welder at the plant workshop. I get to see him almost daily in the lunchroom. His daily meal invariably consists of a slice of goat cheese, a khubos, and a slice of pickle. However, before he can get to this main course, he insists on consuming a raw onion that he slices and chews one sliver at a time, over a period of nearly fifteen minutes. Fortunately for us, he is aware of our aversion to his compulsion and consumes the appetizer while sitting a short distance from our tables. Though onions are not one of my favourite raw relishes, I am always puzzled in observing this man's obvious joy in his solitary passion. His stubby fingers tear impatiently into the the inedible paper skin of the outer layers, which he tucks into his coat pocket; the snaps off the moist, fine-veined and semi-transparent interior layers, the shade of burnished copper and gunmetal; and then he masticates the translucent succulence within the pungent heart as a dull glaze descends over his eyes. The room is small so there is no way to avoid witnessing this procedure. My eyes water and I have to suppress the urge to gag. Only when the entire onion is consumed does he return to one of the tables to resume his meal. He claims he has been doing this for the past forty odd years of his life.

"Then there is my good friend Abraham Verghese, the palace cook, who, on recalling a famine in Kerala, tells me how often he had to chew the soaked bark of trees when there was nothing else to offer to eat. Even now, he is still unable to tear his eyes away from the heaps of fresh food piled before him in the market, or in his kitchen fridge. He tells me, 'You know, Shafiq Bhai, everytime I take the car out for a drive, all I can think of is my battered bike. It was among the many personal items that I had to surrender in order to obtain my visa to Kuwait.'

"To this list of brittle and fragile people, let me also add our very own Chachaji Suleman, who is living out his bachelor life in the austerity of dheras and pining for his family still back in Kotli. He lives out his emotional life elsewhere, a life that is anywhere but in this barren land. He obsesses about the fruit trees he has growing back home in his garden, loving them as much as the fruit he fondly remembers they once bore, enumerating the names of the fruits as if that alone could provide sustenance and inspiration in this arid land.

"Every place he has lived for the sake of his profession, whether it is Sialkot, Abhadan or Kuwait, he has attempted to recreate that lost orchard in Kotli. Gardens spring up around him. He shows a wrinkled photo of his namesake mosque, the Iranian Masjid Suleman, and tunes into radio broadcasts from Teheran. He weeps to the music of Khorasan, lecturing me on the nuances of the Persian radif and maqam. His flood of nostalgia for that abandoned and idyllic life in Abhadan before the oil industry was nationalized and he relocated to Kuwait, while other colleagues ventured off to Arabia, Bahrain and Qatar, is as palpable as his longing for his family. In their absence, he relives the infancy of his own offspring through the local children playing around him. He has painstakingly collected just the right gifts to take with him the next time he returns home: a wind-up bear and an airplane equipped with four spinning propellers for his two sons; silk dresses, golden-haired dolls with blinking eyes and lovingly selected boxes of chocolates for his three daughters."

Much later, Shafiq writes that he is delighted to hear the news that he has been betrothed to his childhood sweetheart, Jamila, the one who used to signal to him across the rooftops. However, the letters that follow these are equally cryptic, yet ominous and disturbing. Abbaji and I decide to keep them from Ammiji. Shafiq's disillusionment with Kuwait and the people around him, the sand and the oil, is now becoming more obvious. He writes: "I am beginning to be sickened by the people around me and by their demands on me, and this place saps my energy and my will for tomorrow."

However, on reading this, Abbaji and I try to comfort ourselves with the realization that this is also the Shafiq we know so well: the dark and melancholic, joyless creature, fearing the light for days on end. I became aware of this dark side of my brother's personality long before the advent of electricity to our town and the ensuing events. On these occasions, a dark cloud would seem to descend unheralded upon him, and he would rudely shoo his friends out of his room, locking himself away during the long bouts of depression that were always sure to follow. My parents would continue to joke about the jinn they had locked away in their dungeon, until he would finally emerge from his hermetic bouts to take long walks through the fields, sometimes walking all the way to the town of Kharota or heading off eastwards to the newly dug irrigation barrage. I always knew that after wrestling with his personal demons, my brother would safely emerge renewed and be all the better for it.

He also writes that he finds himself increasingly turning away from the world of humans in favour of the natural world, finding solace in remote and secluded places. There is a small beach next to the plant where he particularly feels at home, returning to it often for solitude and reflection.

In an intriguing and lengthy scrawl of a letter that follows, he writes to me of having finally mastered the art of roaring with the lions: "When the weight of this world becomes too much to bear, I sometimes lock myself in the compressor room late at night. I then proceed to add the roar of my own anguished screams to that of the massive motors that hum nonstop day and night. I think I have managed to isolate an underlying note at which all such machinery hums, and have learned to match it exactly in pitch and tone, if not in volume. After these sessions, I feel strangely centered within myself, even though I am unable to speak for hours afterwards. It feels a lot like Iftari, the dusk breaking of the fast, all appetites sated, the gnawing 'feed me, feed me' quietened for a short while longer.

"Mere bhai, where have I banished myself? To this lifetime of voluntary labour, so far away from all my loved ones? What is it in me that drives me to punish myself thus? What has driven me to the ends of my known world when all I really craved for was right before my eyes? Why did I abandon all of you merely to satisfy my own vanity? Our family could just as well have survived with a little less income.

"One day, on seeing for the first time a sandstorm approaching from the direction of Iraq and turning the noonday sun to blood, my roommate Abrar rushed out into the street with his arms raised to the sky in joyous rapture, wailing: 'Karbala, Karbala, this is the blood of Karbala, of Hassan and Hussein and all our shaheeds.'

"Rafiq, get me out of here, for unlike the temperamental Abrar, when I am tempted to rush out into the street, you will all have a harder time dragging me back indoors. This phenomenon of the annual ochre march of fine sand from the north is known to cause short circuits in the power grid; it also causes nausea in humans, and will infrequently drive a fragile mind over the edge. This dust is so fine that I feel its grittiness in my mouth even when I am inside a hermetically sealed room at the plant.

"Where the desert was Allah Kareem's last unfinished landscape, its solitude is now something I dread to contemplate. Moreover, there is even less relief at the seashore where I used to spend so many hours in contemplation. The strip of beach is now littered with garbage and has been overrun by a raucous flock of seagulls. Even its familiar denizens are now alien to me, the amorous crabs rattling over the pebbles in gesticulating to their mates, and the mudskippers still undecided over the choice of environment to live out their allotted tides. It sometimes feels to me as if I have come into this world in the body of a mudskipper that is condemned to a tenuous hold over a patch of slimy mud between the water and the sand, desperately guarding the thin film of moisture against all the elements, a film that is as diaphanous as the condensation over a clay canister, a sherba full of water.

"Where I used to find solace, I find only desolation. My jerboa, my trusting messenger from the desert, is gone. Perhaps it came to me as one last opportunity for redemption, and I failed it, miserably.

"I now wake on some mornings when the desert has oil on its breath and am reminded once again that this is a land of mirages; I will find nothing here to anchor my sanity. A leaden weight is pressing down on my chest and my mouth is dry and bruised, as if I had bit into sand during the night of roving on the beach. As I arise from the bed, I put on this mask, adjust this expression to greet the day, and am startled by the gaunt stranger who stares back at me from the mirror. It is as if overnight I have acquired a second skin, a dun-coloured patina of fine sand that will not wash away.

"Who am I and what am I doing out here? I have finally decided to pack up and leave.

"I must get back once again to the land of green moistness and rivers, and massed thunderclouds that pour forth for weeks on end without exhaustion. I want to revisit those lost monsoon seasons where nubile girls once set up rope swings under the jamnu and mango trees, and the koels would call out from orchard to orchard. I miss the sickly sweet aroma of overripe guava, the sharp bouquet of raw, green, wind-tossed mangoes, the cloying scent of motia blossoms.

"But I know you well enough, Rafiq, to realize that you will write back to me with your usual cynicism: Shafiq, my dear brother Shafiq, the young girls you knew as nubile have all been married off, and the only songs they now sing are lullabies to their children; the koels have all been hunted down and eaten, and it hasn't rained for the last six months. However, I write this knowing full well that you will not have the heart to tamper with my idyllic vision of the life I want to come back to.

"All I now know is that I want to be anywhere but here. In writing this, I acknowledge that I, too, have become one of those brittle and fragile men who live out their shriveled lives of denial, and whom I once so despised and wanted to shun.

"Once I am married, I will live each day amidst the warm embrace of my extended family members and never again venture so far away from home. I shall even refuse to travel as far as the city. I shall treasure each moment of my life with my Jamila. No marriage by proxy for me like my roommates, who live out their entire lives in isolation from their parents, wives and children. They might as well have sent the substitute bridegroom, the sarbala, for their wedding ceremonies.

"Maybe when I return home, I too will grow a beard and spend the rest of my life pacing between my workplace, the masjid and my home. On the other hand, I may even be tempted to join the growing army of the disciples of Shakeel Al Mabrouk, a name I have coined for my Kotli friend, the miracle workers who, as you have written, has discovered the secret of early retirement while still in his teens. And, just maybe, this time I can share in the bounty of Allah's blessings. I could well use a miracle myself.

"Every time I step out into the tandoor of the noonday heat, I recall an image of the street singer Malhaara stopping opposite our house, his nasal chant traversing the space to our balcony. I see the frozen look on Ammiji's face as she looks up from some domestic chore, and hears the words of his improvised chant of Kotli's banished youth: Hai ni maye, tere ladle kithe gaye? Somehow I always imagine him saying Hai ni maye, tera ladla Shafiq kithe gaya? (O mother, where is your beloved Shafiq now?)

"One of the first things I am going to do at home is set up a radio repair shop. How I would love to continue doing what I love the most: teaching villagers to ferment their dough over the heated body of a radio cabinet. I know that by now there must surely be a niche in the local market for such obscure skills.

"My roommates no longer bother to disguise their scorn at my decision to return and settle down back home. They are also equally dismissive of my inability to adjust to this life of voluntary labour in Kuwait. A year back home, they say, and you will be begging your uncle to call you back here! Be grateful you have it made here. Thus have they all chided me at one time or another.

"And I have received the same treatment at the plant as the final days of my departure approach closer.

'Shafiq, do you have anything else planned? Is there a plan B, a contingency, just in case things do not go your way?' So my Canadian manager, Mr Fred Meaden, has been inquiring of me upon learning of my decision to resign. 'Shafiq, it seems to me you have forgotten why you came here in the first place. Wasn't it just to get away from that place you call Ko-ta-ly?'

"Rafiq, you should hear him stumble over the word Kotli.

"And when it is the nambardar's turn, he, too, is equally flippant about my future plans: 'Mr Shafiq, you have been a very good worker,' he says, 'and we would hate to lose you. But if you have already made up your mind then there is no argument any of us can offer to make you stay. There is a shortage of skilled electricians like you here in Kuwait, and I can probably have a replacement for you from Kerala within this quarter.'

"I wish I could gather all these cynics in one place and tell them for the last time that what they are looking at is the original 'sacrificial circuit,' a circuit that is built as a redundant component into every complex electronic configuration. A vital and integral part of any system, it is specifically designed to fail under conditions of extreme stress, system overloads and malfunctions. The collapse of this one unit ultimately saves the rest of the system. I was meant to fail under these circumstances. And I know that there is a multitude of others to replace me.

"Not in vain did Tarek bin Ziad burn all his boats.

"Tell Jamila her mudskipper will very soon be coming home for good. I wish I could write to her directly and pour my heart out, but for a while longer you will have to be my messenger. And be sure to tell our sly muezzin Hashim and Maulvi Saab that they will have no trouble from me this time around. I have already been mellowed by enough mischief to last a lifetime. And tell Babaji that I have learned my lesson and I am sorry for not having taken better care of myself, or heeded your advice earlier.

"For the past month I have been trying unsuccessfully to reserve a seat for myself on one of the newly introduced BOAC Comet jets for the flight to Karachi, but due to the approaching Eid season the scheduled flights been fully booked for the next two months. I have now reluctantly registered myself for the 15 April sailing of the SS *Dara*,

D-A-R-A as in our very own common grounds of Dara-tul-Aman in Kotli."

A week later an urgent letter follows to proclaim: "You will be glad to hear that I finally have a reserved berth waiting for me for the sailing date as someone has fallen sick and canceled their reservation. As this is going to be my second time aboard ship, I should probably feel right at home the moment I step aboard. I hope that I will still be home in time for the month of Ramzan and Eid. Moreover, my roommates are now beginning to disguise their taunts in playful teasing: You know very well that this will not really be a final goodbye. We are so sure you will be back soon enough that we even have a betting pool going. Where else on earth will you find food as fine as what our mess serves?

"Fimanallah!"

"Once safely aboard, I learned from the tags on the door of the cramped cubicle I had been assigned that my cabin mate was someone named Shafiq Ahmed Malik. An hour later he peered into the cabin and introduced himself. I felt glad to be sharing the cabin with another Punjabi headed for Lahore via Karachi. He appeared to be much older than I was, though I was to later discover that he was exactly my age. When he told me by way of introduction that he was from the village of Kotli Loharan near Sialkot, I was then able to mentally plot out the route we both would probably be sharing once we reached Pakistan.

"We dragged as much of our heavier luggage as we could and stacked it in the middle of the tiny cabin, sending the rest below to the hold for more secure storage. Later we stood peering out from the deck, our clothes flapping noisily in the wind, as the ship weighed anchor and headed eastwards for open seas. Shafiq pointed out that the sea was choppier than on the day he had first arrived in Kuwait, and though we searched the horizon for them, we could not spot any dhow sails on the water. The Kuwaiti shore rapidly receded, and it being a blustery day with low visibility, within a few minutes had disappeared completely from our view.

"When we returned below deck to our cabin for dinner, I got to know your brother a little better. I found out that he was leaving the Gulf and returning home for good. I was amazed to learn that he had been in Kuwait for only four years before deciding that he had had enough of it. I recall that more than once he mentioned that he was unable to get out of his mind the parting words of his uncle, Chachaji Suleman, imploring him to stay.

"We sat and chatted late into the night, exchanging snippets of our personal histories. He showed me some faded and creased photographs of his family that he claimed he had carried in his wallet throughout his stay in Kuwait. He told me these had been taken just before he left Pakistan. I think I remember that there was a photo of you, Rafiq, pointing at something in the water as you stood next to a masjid. And when I asked him why he had ventured overseas in the first place since he was quitting so soon, he offered me a long and technical explanation about how young men of limited means from Kotli have always been setting out from their homes for overseas, and how they were the sacrificial ... I forget the word, machines? I think that is what he called them. He even had a theory to back up his explanation, and where he fitted in the scheme of such things.

"You see, I was already beginning to appreciate, even then so early in the voyage, what an extraordinary person your brother was.

"Our homemade supply of rasam finally gave out when we pulled away from Bahrain. Shafiq told me that his Malayalam friends, knowing of his fondness for the south Indian soup, had managed to pack a tightly sealed metal container for him. It was supposed to have lasted him further into the voyage. But his friends hadn't counted on my being there to share it.

"At the time of our arrival at Bahrain, it was raining heavily and the sea was beginning to turn a threatening gray, reflecting the sky. An unseasonably cold rain accompanied by hail began as we stood anchored off Dubai and those on the exposed decks, though protected by tarpaulins, began to search for vacant areas in the lower covered decks. No one had ever seen such inclement weather this late in the year. I also noticed that the wind-driven rain and choppy swells made it nearly impossible for the passengers to embark or disembark the ship by the heaving launch boats that waited below before returning to the shore.

"An hour later, when Shafiq and I were back inside our cabin, we heard a sudden loud scraping sound from the bulkheads, and a shuddering motion rocked the ship. A crewman informed us at that a cement cargo ship had raked the starboard side of our ship, but that there was apparently no serious damage to either of the two ships. The captain then decided to move the ship to deeper waters to wait out the storm. The forecast was for even worse weather.

"In the evening, with there appearing to be no change in the pace and fury of the storm, we headed for deeper water. In heading further north from the shore, several of the hawkers, cargo handlers, port officials and the relatives and friends of passengers who had come aboard to bid farewell were caught unawares onboard when the storm hit, and were unable to disembark.

"As far as I remember, we spent the remainder of that evening inside our cabin, while the storm continued to roar outside. Seeing that we were unable to remain focused on our card game any longer, Shafiq suggested we venture above deck again for some fresh air. The ship was by then lying at anchor several miles from the Dubai coast, and though the rain had temporarily let up, it was still cold and windy. He showed me the narrow curved area of the deck directly above the propellers, where he said he had spent a considerable part of his first voyage in tracking the ship's wake, imagining the ship to be stationary as the water sped by it.

"By now, with the sea a roiling mass, we watched from the farthest point of the stern as ever-higher waves slammed into the ship. Each of these waves was now capped by a crest of froth. Our ship was straining against its anchor and threatening to tear loose and launch us further from the shore into even deeper waters. As we scanned the horizon, we became aware that we were anchored close to a busy international shipping lane. We watched the dim shapes of giant oil tankers loom out of the gathering dark of the evening, or their pilot lights blink in the distant horizon, before being swallowed up completely. A freight carrier even passed so close by us that the froth from its stern washed over to our ship.

"An hour later, we were still debating whether to go below deck and get some sleep. Karachi was already beginning to seem so much closer now. We both knew our relatives would already be waiting there, holed up in the bedbug-infested Kashmir Hotel and visiting the port daily to hear of the eastward progress of SS *Dara*. Once we landed we would begin the two-and-a-half day journey by express train from Karachi to the junction of Wazirabad, and then transfer from there for Sialkot. I remember thinking that I was now closer to Pakistan then to Kuwait, and that if only this storm would blow over we could once again get back to the business of sailing for home.

"When a sudden squall of rain brought in a shower of hail, catching us by surprise with its ferocity, we decided to move back below deck. We resumed our card game at about midnight, and about an hour later, when we could sense the ship was swinging back in motion and could hear the engines hum back to life, we retired to our bunks.

"Three hours later—it seemed only a few moments since I rested my head upon the pillow— I was awaken by an explosion. After the ringing in my ears subsided, there was a moment's silence, and then, without warning, complete pandemonium broke out. The night air was rent by the sound of screams, fire alarms, and footsteps ringing on the metal floor. The explosion had ripped through the deck somewhere below our cabin, and our door had cleaved inwards, tossing some of the piled luggage onto our bunks.

"There was sufficient light inside the cabin for me to notice that Shafiq had also arisen from his bunk and was struggling to stand upright from beneath the luggage. I also made a mental note at the time that the reassuring hum of the engines underfoot had also been stilled, and that even though the ventilation system was dead, the air was filled with the faint smell of cordite. The deck's rhythmic heaving and sinking with the waves informed us that storm had still not yet died down fully.

"As we both stumbled out into the narrow alleyway outside our cabin, I found out that here, too, the carefully stacked pieces of luggage had come loose and spilled onto unwary sleepers. The only lights to guide us through this labyrinth and the mass of passengers were the overhead emergency lights and the faint glow from the doorways opening on the stairs to the upper deck. We were also surrounded by the sound of distant screams as the passengers were now beginning to stir fully and mass around the stairwells. In the process, they were also trying to dodge the debris dislodged from the ceiling. I also noticed that some of these people were as yet unaware of what had actually happened and were trying to sort out their strewn personal luggage.

"I headed for the crowded stairs to the upper deck, intent on getting out onto the open deck. A faint white haze was escaping up the stairwell closest to us. As we pushed our way through the crowd of panicked passengers, the fire bells suddenly began to ring shrilly and we could now clearly smell the smoke as well as see it.

"At this moment, I noticed that I had run out of my cabin barefoot and recalled that my sandals were tucked neatly under my bunk. As I was debating venturing back below deck after them, I saw that Shafiq had collapsed to the floor and was clutching his left arm. His left forearm was covered in blood. A pea-sized gash on his biceps had already begun to clot over. Using my handkerchief I hastily made a tourniquet for him and instructed him to try and keep his arm raised. I was relieved to find that we had both survived the ordeal alive. But as I turned to peer back at the mouth of the stairwell, an explosion within the bowels of the ship knocked us onto the floor. I knew that it would now be all but impossible for either one of us to venture back to our cabin until it was safe and the fires had been brought under control.

"By now we were surrounded by an incoherent bunch of men, all of whom were shouting as they hoisted their families into the lifeboats that were suspended by massive davits and pulleys. A ship's officer, who had obviously been caught off guard as he was out of uniform at the time of the explosion, tried to impose some order on the chaos.

"Shafiq and I attempted to assist in repairing the malfunctioning lowering mechanisms for one crowded lifeboat. Someone else was shouting to the occupants of the overloaded lifeboat to get off as the earlier collision with the cargo ship had damaged the davits beyond repair. So we both turned out attention away from the boat to take stock of our situation.

"As soon as we stepped back from the lifeboat onto the deck again, someone managed to untangle the pulleys of another lifeboat and get it level with the deck. It seemed only a few moments before this boat was also swamped by the frantic women and children. But as we stood aside, watching the overcrowded lifeboat being lowered to the water with over fifty women and children aboard, we could see that not only was it not seaworthy, but it would be difficult to lower it safely down through the almost thirty feet to the water level.

"Once the boat had cleared the deck, we watched in helpless horror as the lifeboat, freed from the side of the ship, swung outward and slowly overturned in midair, tossing all its occupants into the water. Within a few minutes, most of the human forms that we could discern in the water had gone under, disappearing into the murky waves.

"As we moved away from the railing and the sight of the forlorn, overturned boat in shocked silence, a number of men shouted out the names of their loved ones and leaped into the water after them. Since this had been the only lifeboat that could safely be reached from our deck, the awareness finally began to dawn on us that getting off the burning ship was now not going to be as easy a task as we had thought.

"Surveying the open deck, we could see areas where the fires had crept up and found combustible material to feed on. There now began a desperate rush to clear the upper bridge deck of all such materials in order to contain the fire. Wooden benches, bedrolls, tarps, wooden trunks, bundled clothes, carpets—all were tossed overboard in a frenzy of activity. Suddenly, all these possessions that we had been so reluctant to part with began to seem trivial.

"In the ensuing flurry of activity and confusion, I noticed that some of the wooden benches we had pushed overboard were now being used as rafts by the few survivors who had either fallen off the ill-fated lifeboat or had leapt overboard. We could only shudder at the prospect of having to jump in amongst them to escape if the entire deck caught fire. Several of the passengers who were milling about around us still appeared to be in a daze, but were quieter now and had gotten over the initial shock.

"I remember seeing a group of about a dozen men standing in two straight rows in the middle of bridge deck, seemingly oblivious to the chaos and the fires raging around them, offering their final namaz. But neither Shafiq nor I was willing just yet to give up. By then the ship was heaving and falling violently with each crest and trough of the waves. And over all this commotion was the steadily rising crackle of fire that was fast becoming a roar, the smoke turning dark and backlit by the flames.

"Exhausted by our efforts in clearing the deck, we sat down with our backs to a stack of rope that had been spared as a safety precaution. Noticing how drained Shafiq appeared to be, I offered him a cigarette. He protested that he didn't smoke and returned the cigarette to me. I lit my cigarette off a smouldering piece of wooden banister, the dull irony of the moment escaping neither of us.

"This moment of repose was interrupted by two major explosions that rocked our deck, leaving me flat on my back. These explosions seemed to be located deep inside the bowels of the ship, the crackling of breaking glass and the roaring of the flames now drowning out all other sounds.

"There was now sufficient reflected light to see the havoc that had been wrought around us in the space of just an hour. Watching the column of billowing smoke rise out of the tilted chimney into the gray sky, we were hoping that other ships in the area would now see our distress and soon come to our rescue. But by then the deck beneath our feet was already beginning to heat up and burn my bare soles, and we could see the paint on the hull plates blister as if it were being boiled off in patches. At the rate the ship was deteriorating, I knew that there would soon not be any haven above or below the decks.

"In a brief moment of reflection, I began examining the formerly crisp sharp features of the neatly maintained decks. Every outline I lay my eyes on was blackened by the fire, smoke and soot. It seemed as if the vessel was ageing right before my eyes, as if all the surrounding structures had been stressed through a corrosive shower of acid, so that it had reworked all the exposed surfaces, deteriorating them instantly. Where there had been solidity and firmness, there was now a honeycomb of pitted craters. I looked at my hands and feet, half expecting them to be blistered, too. I could now feel the heat with my bare feet, and in my heightened imagination the metal plates appeared to be uneven, as if they were on the verge of buckling.

"The waiting surface of the water below us had by now acquired a thick oily film that swirled over the restless waves, and the sky looked as gray as the water. In the early dawn light, the cloud cover appeared somehow to be more distant than it had been at first light. The amorphous column of smoke still continued to billow upwards even as the wind ripped it away from the funnel as soon as it left it. There were also several points in the middle of the ship that were smoking and had huge gaping holes in them. I was sure that these columns of smoke would be visible for miles, and that other ships in the busy shipping lane we were in would have surely marked our location by now. I voiced these desperate observations to Shafiq in the hope that they would calm our nerves. As I did so I thought I noticed the steel floor beneath us already beginning to list starboard.

"In an effort to stave off panic I rose up from the pile of ropes and asked Shafiq what we were going to do now. Shafiq merely shook his head, whether in reply or to clear his head, I don't know.

"At thar moment, our attention was drawn to the crew members and passengers gathered a few feet above us. They appeared to be shouting and gesticulating in our direction. We looked up to where they were pointing and saw the remaining tatters of the tarpaulin above our heads burst into flame. A babel of urgent voices called out to us in English, Gujarati, Punjabi, Malayalam and Urdu to jump. We knew that we were running out of options. Since the fire would not let us escape the deck, the only way out would be over the railing. My eyes kept wandering to the flotsam bobbing in the water, some of which was recognizable as humans clinging precariously onto whatever was available. The thought of going into that chilly water made me shiver in anticipation.

"However, there was a brief reprieve from our plight when our spirits were lifted by the sight of another ship heading towards us, followed by others. It was tortuous to watch their painfully slow progress against the onslaught of the waves. But the sight of the approaching ships and their lifeboats created another round of desperation and panic in those who were already in the water. We watched as the first boat to approach us was nearly swamped by those strong enough to swim to it and climb aboard. Others managed to cling desperately onto it from all sides, and the boat headed back to its ship.

"However, from our relatively elevated perspective we could also see other boats heading our way at some distance. Now that rescue seemed so tantalizingly close at hand, there were widespread shouts of joy at the thought that we were all now soon to be safe.

"Shafiq and I were still leaning over the railing, and tossing out rope lines to the people in the water and shouting out instructions. I noticed an old woman in the water was desperately trying to hold on to a floating bench. She soon lost her grip and began to slide back under the waves. I turned to Shafiq. He was no longer by my side.

"I am not sure exactly what happened. Did I really notice Shafiq leap into the water out of the corner of my eye, or did I imagine it? I searched for him in the water, but to no avail. In the meantime, the old woman had managed to climb back onto the bench.

"Almost an hour later I was plucked from the deck by the third wave of boats to arrive. But by then, none of the remaining bodies left floating in the water was alive."

I feel the icy chill of the water as it rises to receive my brother. Clutching desperately to the tarpaulin of the inverted lifeboat, he feels the waxy fabric slip through his numbed fingers, and he is back again in the water. The turbulence of the seawater appears sluggish under its fine slick of oil. It is now at eye level, reflecting the fire and the brightening sky of dawn. He looks up at the column of smoke towering over the ship as it disappears into the congealed mass of clouds. A human form leaps from somewhere above him and disappears into the water a few feet away. The lifeboat heaves partially out of the water onto its side and begins to sink.

As far back as I can recall, I remember our mother would gather us at dusk every Thursday, to head for the local shrine of Mira Saab to offer fateha prayers. After covering our heads reverently with handkerchiefs, we would race through the verses of our mumbled prayers, drop a few coins into the collection box, and top up the mustard oil in the clay lamps that would be lit each night at the head of the nine-foot grave. Before leaving the shrine, carefully walking backwards the way we had entered so as not to show any form of disrespect to the departed, Ammiji would take some soot off the wall above the alcove lamp and place a tikka on our foreheads to ward off the evil eye. Protected and blessed in this manner, we would make our way home over the rickety wooden bridge that at the time spanned the canal of Nehr Mardan.

At the age of about three or four, Shafiq discovered on these weekly trips that if he tossed the few remaining drops of oil still clinging to the empty bowl in his hand into the path of the flowing water, and then immediately rushed to the opposite side of the bridge, he would be greeted by a swirling slick of translucent colours that would form and reform into a magical, constantly evolving kaleidoscope.

That distant memory now surfaces in the dull morning light and is swallowed by the water.

"Babaji, Babaji!" Ammiji pleads between sobs that rack her frail body as she struggles up the steeply winding staircase.

Abbaji and I carry her across the veranda.

Her voice is a hoarse whisper now: "Babaji, what can you see? What can you see now? How is my son? Is he well? What does he have to say to me? Is he well enough to return to us now? How much longer will we suffer like this in his absence? Tell him that I have had enough of this mischief from him and that he should return home immediately, and I cannot bear his separation any more."

The torrent of questions races out of her mouth as Abbaji and I support her and stumble towards Babaji's prayer mat. She finally settles down with bowed head close to his ear with her right hand coming to rest on his shoulder, her breathing still lost in a strenuous fit of wailing.

Ammiji's desperate pleading for details of her son's fate has become another painful ritual for our family, as the spring of that fateful year yields to summer, and no news has yet emerged of my brother's ultimate fate. Abbaji and I do our best to hold her firmly back from stretching out and completely prostrating herself on the prayer mat.

Babaji, who is by now fully aware of our distress in the midst of his prayers, curtails his meditation and turns with a heavy heart towards us. He does not look at either one of us directly, only turning slightly towards Ammiji and comforting her.

"Sabr, paen meri, sabr," he whispers soothingly to her, his hand resting on top of her covered head. "I know that I told you I have seen Shafiq jump into the water. But there is much more that I have also seen."

He looks away at the distant wall as if the images are being projected on it. Ammiji continues to tremble like a leaf shaken by a sudden autumn chill.

"However, in falling into the water, I also see him begin a new life. He has lost his memory. I can tell you that he has survived and he is eventually going to be all right. He is going to learn to lead a new life again and in the process he will forget all those he left behind, and finally be at peace. We all know how he has suffered in this life with us. Let him be, paen meri. Set him free from this world. May Allah Kareem grant us all solace. Ameen, soom Ameen."

Even before we had met or spoken to any of the survivors and talked to Lateef Bhai, who, given the confusion at the time, may or may not have seen Shafiq jump from the burning ship, Babaji had correctly recounted the events.

Upon reevaluating all my personal efforts on his behalf in recording his remarkable life on these pages, and piecing together his story from his letters and the words of those who knew him or witnessed his last voyage, I realize that the facts and images that I have so faithfully and lovingly compiled do not do justice to his memory, or capture even a fraction of his indomitable spirit. Instead, what I have put down has been tinted by our grief, which continues to permeate every brittle moment of our conscious lives. We have succumbed so willingly to its unyielding hold, as if in gingerly exploring the familiar jagged edges of a cavity, our tongues every now and then stumble upon a raw nerve.

All we ever had of him was this oblique glimpse in a splintered mirror, with the essence of the whole always eluding us. Perhaps we had been called upon to bear witness for the briefest of moments, the flash of energy that was one human's triumph over his personal demons. As we attempt to recover from the shock and once again pick up the individual threads of our lives, we have become like ships passing in the night, sailing on to other seas and other horizons. Yet, our lives remain weighed down by this insurmountable loss; we are endlessly peering back over our shoulders in the anticipation that one day he will catch up with us, and then we will be able to move forward with one body and one heart.

In the years to come, Babaji will continue to comfort us thus, assuaging our grief with several new revelations, gradually evolving each episode of these visions, so that Shafiq moves further and further away from the corporeal life he had shared with us. And we, in our own desperation for closure or redemption, will continue to seek and find consolation in them.

We will continue to mark each anniversary of the accident with offered prayers and a family feast of Shafiq's favourite foods, remembering always to accompany these offerings with a glass of fresh water from the village well.

His radio and record collection lay alongside Babaji's forsaken gramophone, unattended amidst the paraphernalia of his many obsessions; silenced, it seems, forever. I have tried to take an interest and revive them, but the memories associated with each item is so poignant that it seems too early to approach them just yet.

I sometimes mark the anniversary in my own personal way by pouring a few drops of mustard oil into the waters flowing under the bridge on Nehr Mardan. My brother, who carried with him throughout his brief life this boundless fascination with the physical world, taught me a long time ago the immutable laws governing the immiscibility of oil and water. I know that if he were here today, he would still continue to be enthralled at bearing witness to the phenomenon of the refracted, swirling colours, and the eventual triumph of the resolutely flowing water over the sullen resistance of sluggish oil.

Mitti da Baawa

Mitti da baawa meiñ banaaniyaañ,
jhagga paaniyaan, ve ute deni a khesi.
Na ro mitti deya baaweya, tera pyo pardesi
— *Punjabi folksong*

Even before he has had time to pull his bike up the ramp to his
doorstep, Azam Karigar detects the burnt smell of the dinner
awaiting him inside the house. Hungry and tired from his day's
work in the city and the hour-long bike ride back home, he is already in
a churlish, unforgiving mood. With his kameez sweat-plastered to his
back and his calf muscles clenching, he flings the door open, and, stooping to ease his tall, lanky frame into the doorway, hurriedly leans the
bike against a courtyard wall.

Heading for the kitchen, he can hear the muffled sound of desperate feet scampering in the background. He finds the kitchen floor littered with unwashed dishes and an assortment of cooking pots. A clay
pot of burnt lentils has recently been spilled into the smoking hearth
fire, and the evidence then partially covered over with ash. Faint embers
of resinous firewood glow still amongst the charred food. Her favourite
rag doll rests among the litter on the floor. And she is nowhere to be
found.

Having already discovered all her hiding places inside the house, it
takes him only a moment to locate her. She is trying desperately to
squeeze into the narrow space between the two rooftop chimneys. Azam

grabs his young wife by her arms and drags her downstairs behind him without saying a word.

"How many times must I . . . ?" he begins, the words whispered hoarsely through clenched teeth, before running completely out of self-control, conscious now only of his light-headedness and the upwelling of bitterness inside him.

He turns around to face her, raises his right arm in reflex and strikes her flatly across her exposed left cheek with his open palm. In an instant, he has adjusted his stance and is aiming for the top of her head, ignoring her deep throaty moaning. Then he drags her back into the kitchen by her left arm.

"Is this," he pants, "is this what you have waiting for me at the end of the day?" Barely able to contain his fury, he points at the overturned pot with his free hand. "Who did you think was going to eat the mess you have cooked up? Were you expecting me to eat it?" He yells deafeningly close to her left ear. "Maybe in your house they used to eat like this, but not in mine. This is my house and here you will do as I tell you."

Towering over her like demented jinn, he continues to rain down blows on the top of her head as she tries feebly to protect her face. As his fury and frustration mounts, he raises his clenched fists to work them like a boxer, pivoting sideways from his waist upwards. He strikes the softness of flesh and the hardness of bone and nail with equal force, completely oblivious to her passivity.

"Just because your parents called you Guddhi," he pants, "don't expect everyone else to treat you like a doll. Guddho, Guddho! When will you learn to stop wasting your day in play and start attending to your duties as a housewife?" He spits the bitter torrent of words out in between waves of blind and breathless activity.

"How many times must I . . . " He pulls her head back so that she can look up at him, and senses her growing limp in his vice-like grip. "How many times must I come home from work and find you lost in your play world of rag dolls and clay toys? Is this all your parents ever taught you, huh? Answer me, or I'll break every bone in your body!"

But by now there is nothing left to offer up resistance to the blows or the taunts.

"Guddho, Guddho! When will you grow up?" he yells to the crumpled mess sprawled before him, staggering to position himself better, and noticing for the first time in the dim light the streak of blood oozing from her cut lips. Enmeshed in the dark trickle he has noticed the pale half-chewed grains of rice.

The sight has an immediate and confusing effect on him; the blazing embers behind his eyelids are suddenly doused, and his entire body drained of all energy and will. Just as swiftly as it is broken, the storm now passes. Bewildered by his own outburst, he looks down as if suddenly aware for the first time of the presence of this jumbled pile of flesh and clothes. Now that she faces him with her arms no longer arced in self-defense over her head, he notices the grimace on the face of the child who dares not look up into his eyes. The only sounds are that of his laboured breathing and her feeble whimpering.

After a long pause he reaches down to lift her up, and finds himself unable to do so, for his body, too, has suddenly grown heavy with exhaustion. He settles down on the floor next to her.

The couple lie limply on the floor as the house darkens. Words of the Maghrib adhan fill the air, dogs bark in the quiet deserted street outside, and the unfed brood of pigeons flutters down from the rooftop onto the courtyard floor. Eventually, Guddho drags herself up, and after carefully bypassing the somnolent body beside her, limps over to the nalka to wash her face and gingerly explore its tenderness. By the time she has dragged herself into her bed, her body is in the grip of an uncontrollable trembling. Clutching her legs close to her body for warmth, she lulls herself into a fitful sleep.

During the night she awakens several times to clear the blood clogging her throat, and each time finds herself under the stifling snugness of a heavy quilt. In her delirium, she half-hears the desperation of his faint and faltering comfort, the warm breath fanning her face and caressing its tenderness. She is also dimly aware of something light as a feather brushing her face; his fingers skimming the sore contours of her closed eyelids, her ears still ringing from the blows, her cheeks and lips all puffed up and desensitized; and finally of a moist ball of cotton wool sliding gently over her inflamed skin.

For Guddho at twenty, four years of marriage and a shared bed have come to this. Khalda, or Guddho as she had been nicknamed by everyone she knew at her parents' home, her actual name all but forgotten until the formalities of the wedding day, had been the second youngest of five eligible sisters when she was married at sixteen.

As she had told Pino, her neighbour Khala Fatima's daughter, a few days after the newlyweds had moved into their new rented home: "In my parents' crowded household I was either pampered or ignored outright, and never had the slightest inclination to learn the most basic of household chores. The kitchen in our home was always a claustrophobic, crowded place, and I was glad to be left alone with the cleaning and washing, unpleasant tasks that my elder sisters deigned not to bother themselves with. Since I love rice so much, it is the only dish I ever learned to cook with any skill."

"Then what do you two survive on?" Pino had asked, incredulous at what she was gradually beginning to uncover of the personal lives of her oddly paired new neighbours. "If you cannot cook and your husband does not either, then what do you two eat?"

"Probably each other!" Guddho had offered wanly, her childish grin in sharp contrast to her withdrawn eyes and hollowed cheeks. "I wish I had listened to my ammiji more than my stupid sisters, and had learned to cook when I had the opportunity. But it's not as if I had much of a warning of what was to follow, when his mother showed up one day at our house with the proposal asking for my rishta."

The proposal had come as a great shock to everyone, and when Guddho's mother first heard of it, she could only stammer: "But, paenji, the child is barely fifteen. Why don't you consider Azra, Nadira or even Akhtar, my elder daughters? I believe either one of them would make a better match."

"You see, Ammiji was also playing at matchmaking, just like me when I am playing with my rag dolls, but in a more earnest manner. As a mother of five, she was desperate in her desire to see her elder daughters married off before they were too old. She expected that she would only be able to turn her attention to me after the elder ones were happily settled down. However, at the back of her mind, there was always the nagging fear that no further proposals might ever come for her elder girls. Moreover, with me married off, would my youngest sister, Mano, be next in line?

"Nevertheless, his mother had been adamant in rebuffing all my ammiji's objections. 'No,' she had haughtily announced. 'My son wants Khalda, and no one else will do!'"

And Pino had asked her: "Who is this Khalda?"

"That would be me," Guddho had beamed back at her. "Everyone at home called me Guddhi all the time so the name just stuck."

"So, Gud-dhi! Didn't your father oppose this match, seeing how you were still a child?" Pino was unable to disguise how appalled she was that any parent would let a child into marriage at so young an age.

"Yes, Pino, he did, initially. Abbaji was equally baffled by this proposal but these matters have always been the domains of mothers. And Ammiji, being whom she is, rose above his protests and immediately set about arranging for the wedding. So here I am, five years later."

Pino had been tempted to quote her mother, who offered the same advice to everyone who would listen to her on such matters: "In order to judge the prospective girl's character, always see her mother's mother; and to judge a potential bridegroom, examine the character of his father." As Guddho further delved into her husband's troubled past, Pino realized that had Guddho's mother heeded her own sound advice, at least in Azam's case she would have had an accurate foreboding of what was sure to follow.

Now, looking down at Guddho's trusting face with a renewed awe and admiration at her fortitude, and seeing that faraway look in her eyes whenever she spoke of her parents' home, Pino is reminded of the child wedding she had once witnessed from her rooftop. The children whom she had watched being hitched had been barely five or six years of age. She found out later their mothers had betrothed the two first cousins shortly after their birth. And what she remembered more poignantly was that the bride and the bridegroom had slept through most of the ceremonies in the arms of their respective mothers.

The two girls now stand on the rooftop looking down into the court-yard. A razor-sharp edge of sunlight is racing across the fresh layer of mud. Guddho has spent the better part of her morning skillfully applying crushed clay over the cracked surface. On an impulse, she now unknots a corner of her chunni and, taking Pino's hand, pours into her palm some uncooked grains of pale Basmati rice. The polished grains glisten in Pino's palm.

"This is one of the few things I can cook really well, but I prefer to chew it this way. As far back as I can remember I have been chomping on uncooked rice grains. I especially like the aroma of the fresh crop that we normally have to put away for ageing till next year. In fact, I sometimes eat so much of this stuff that I begin to feel nauseous. I even hide a few grains under my pillow to munch on at night, and the sound really drives him crazy. You know, on our wedding night he kept chiding me on my habit of grinding my teeth."

They shriek loudly over the shared intimacy, grinding their teeth in unison on the hard grains of rice. Then they happen to notice the crowd of men gathered at the tea stall opposite their house, becoming aware of their gaze for the first time. Instinctively, Guddho covers her head with her chunni, smoothing her dress and shyly averting her eyes.

By early dawn, with his wife finally asleep, Azam prepares to leave for the city for work. He discovers that in the confusion of the previous night he has completely forgotten to take care of his prized flock of pigeons. Set free from the rooftop coop the previous dawn, so that they can spend their day foraging or in idle preening on bamboo roosts, the courtyard is now littered with hundreds of mangled and bloodstained feathers. Apparently, during the night, their pet cat, Mano, who had also not been fed, had climbed into the open coop and killed all but three of his two dozen prized birds. He discovers the survivors flat on their backs with their matchstick legs twitching feebly in the air.

Azam cautiously descends the stairs and spies the cat sprawled underneath his bike, sleeping off the night's feast, its fur stained with flecks of dried blood and feathers. He cradles the purring animal in its sleep as it instinctively moulds its back into the crook of his arms. He carries the cat out into the street. Finding the street deserted, he turns to the brick wall opposite him and with a sudden vigorous motion slams the cat's warm furry body against it.

The mass of fur crumbles in a shrill screech of wails, coming to lie in the gutter that runs the length of the street. Satisfied with his efforts, he now returns to the house for his bike, and after latching the door securely from the outside, hastily pedals off in the direction of the city.

But the cat does not die quite so easily.

Late that night it is still alive and producing long sustained low-pitched shrieks that make the hair on his arms stand on edge; the sound, like that of a child in pain, makes his wife want to jump up from the bed and rush out of the house to comfort the poor animal. Finally, unable to bear the creature's pathetic wailing or his wife's compulsive sobs, he steps into the dark street, a lantern in one hand and a heavy brick in the other. He discovers the feeble creature flailing helplessly inside a street drain that is not deep enough for it to drown or shallow enough for it crawl out of.

He raises the brick.

The cat had once been a stray kitten that had tumbled one night into their courtyard from a neighbour's roof banister. After several unsuccessful attempts to return it, Guddho had adopted the scrawny, terrified creature. She named it Mano, after her younger sister, and not because all local pet cats are called by this name. Guddho had learned to feed it with a cloth dipped in milk, and later supplemented its diet with scraps of leftover food. Occasionally, over her husband's protests, she even allowed it to sleep in her bed. Every evening, when Azam would return from work, it would be waiting for him at the door. During the day, the cat would dutifully follow Guddho everywhere, like a shadow.

Guddho is now beside herself with grief over the loss of her pet, the mourning somehow overshadowing her own traumatic row with Azam.

Almost thirty years old, Azam wonders how four years of marriage and a shared bed could possibly have come to this. It had begun differently, as most marriages do, with him as an ardent and considerate suitor, insecure in her company yet able to unselfconsciously revel in the comfort of their bodies. He had once been all bluff and bluster, unwilling to admit that he had any weakness or vulnerabilities; and she for her part had not yet quite been intimidated by his presence, or aware of the menace that lay sleeping behind his rituals of formal attentiveness.

During the first few months of living in his family home, she continued to flounder at the even the most basic of kitchen chores. She had quickly learned to disguise her limitations by taking on the chores of washing and cleaning in the extended household. But by then the whispering and the recriminations and resentments had begun, eventually building up to a shrill crescendo, with him struggling to remain impartial in not siding with either his three brothers and their conspiring brides, or his embattled new wife. His parents had been reluctant to intervene or offer counsel of any sort, his father too domineering to accept that something was not quite right in his household, and his mother too cowed from years of bullying by her husband.

After one too many such nasty confrontations in the crowded household, Azam had taken the bold step of leaving his family home and finding a place to rent that was as far away as he could find. As it happened, he settled upon the portion of the house that Fatima had recently partitioned off from her own, to rent out and make ends meet. She had had a wall built the length of her own courtyard so that a third of her house consisting of one room, a tiny kitchen, a veranda and the partitioned courtyard now ran parallel to hers. A short, rickety ladder allowed the owners of the two-story house to descend onto their tenets' single roof.

Guddho had been excited at the prospect of finally setting up her own doll's house so far away from her nagging in-laws and their wagging tongues, and Azam had been equally eager to enjoy some relief from the tyranny of his father and the derision of his three brothers. By making the bold move he had finally become the master of his very own household, and in setting it up he had felt a confidence in his own potential that he had never before known. The newlyweds had eagerly set about arranging and rearranging their meager belongings, excited as children playing house and under the spell of their belief that they were the first married couple to find such a heaven on earth.

This initial naiveté and euphoria had lasted for the first couple of months before finally wearing off, when they reluctantly discovered how meager were the initial resources available to them. They reminded each other that with Azam's salary no longer being squandered on the upkeep of a large household of a dozen individuals they would be able to live quite comfortably by themselves.

Their neighbours' nosy daughter, Pino, leaning over the banisters of her rooftop to peer down into their new adjoining yard that first day, had been curious to see what her new neighbours would be like. She watched bemusedly as a frail teenage girl in a floral dress moved frantically in and out of the single room and kitchen, unpacking and rearranging the collected belongings that were heaped in the middle of the courtyard. A slim but much older man, who seemed to tower over her from such distance, appeared to be issuing orders about where each item should go. He was also doing all the heavy lifting by himself. Pino had known that a young couple were supposed to have rented the property from her mother, and now she was suddenly curious to see when the wife would emerge. She wondered whether the wife was incapacitated in some way and the husband and daughter had no choice but to do all the heavy lifting. She had even considered climbing down her bamboo ladder and offering help, but she had been unwilling to intrude without finding out more about whom she would be dealing with.

On descending into the upper story of her own side of the house, Pino now began searching for her mother. If there were anything to find out about her new neighbours, surely her ammiji should be the one to ask. After all, wasn't it she who had chosen to rent out the property to them?

"Ammiji?" she called.

She found her mother squinting at her embroidery of chikan-karai. "Ammiji, you told me that a young couple has rented the new portion of our house. Yet all I can see is a tall man and his daughter who is helping him set up the house. There is no sign of his wife!"

Fatima chuckled loudly to herself at her daughter's observation.

"Ay, budhu, you silly girl! That is Azam and his wife Guddho. They have been married a year now and have decided to live here with us, and as far as possible from his own family. Her family lives in Sherpur."

She stared at her daughter in amazement, seemingly enjoying her obvious discomfort. "Whatever made you think that Azam was her father?"

"I don't know." Pino says, looking away. "The girl appears so young to me. She is even younger than I am."

However, Fatima was not yet fully done with her. "Now listen, I want you to go down there and ask them if they need anything. They will probably not have their kitchen set up by nightfall. Go and see to them and I will add some more water to the stew. And do be careful in descending that precarious ladder. Do you have to climb it in such a hurry each time?"

When Pino finally managed to overcome her nervousness and decided their new tenants for the first time, she took an immediate liking to her eager hostess. It would be years before she would get over her initial impression that here was a young girl who seemed merely to be playing at housekeeping, rather than a grown adult fulfilling a marital role. She is only a child, a part of her mind kept reminding her. How can she possibly comprehend the responsibilities placed in her of maintaining an entire household and take care of her husband?

With her overbearing husband now lurking nervously in the background, Guddho gave Pino a grand tour of the house and all her proud possessions. Along the walls of their single room were two beds arranged end to end and facing each other. Pino noticed that Azam had installed two wooden shelves that ran the length of the room on opposite walls. So that would explain the sounds of hammering that she could recall from the last few days. One of these shelves, set within an arm's reach, was completely lined with horses made of baked clay, the earthen handiworks of the ghughu korhay collection that Guddho claimed she had acquired from the local carnivals. Pino also noticed that the parallel shelf on the opposite wall was also lined with a odd and colourful rag dolls. This, Guddho pointed out, was her precious patola collection.

The only other items in the room were a copy of the Quran bundled in a flowery cloth wrap, and Guddho's copy of *Baheshti Zewar, The*

Jewels of Paradise, a manual of ideal and pious domesticity that is traditionally presented to all newlyweds.

With Guddho chattering on animatedly, Pino noted that some of the dolls appeared to be the worse wear. Yet they all seemed to have a personal name and history for their owner, and they were creatively arranged, the newer ones resting against the wall while the favoured, older ones dangled their feet off the shelf. "Some of them date back to my early childhood," Guddho explained, eager to show off all her treasured companions at once.

One elaborately dressed doll was larger than the others and towered above them.

"This is Guddhi," she beamed, lifting it up. The doll was clothed in a bright tinsel-edged dress that trailed all the way from the neck down to the feet. It even had a luxuriant dark head of hair that was plaited neatly into an abundant single braid.

Picking up on Pino's piqued curiosity, Guddho elaborated breathlessly, lisping some of the words: "Each hair on this doll has come from my own scalp. After all, Guddhi is a miniature me, isn't she? I even had her dress made from the same materials used to make my wedding joras. However, unlike me she has already been remarried more than fifteen times." She crinkled her eyes mischievously and then hastily looked away.

When they ventured out of the room into the bright light, Pino noticed that Guddho had brought the doll out with her, dangling it limply by one arm.

A year after their move, Azam's father suddenly fell ill, complaining of acute chest pains. Within the space of a week his heart gave out on him.

After the requisite forty days of mourning, his brothers made polite noises about family reunification, nudging Azam to return to the family fold once again. However, Azam was fully aware that with additional work at the press, he was making more than the combined incomes of his siblings. Surely, the motivating factor behind their offer could not have been pure filial love.

Azam and Guddho's domestic contentment gradually soured. First came the unexpected revelation of her total ineptitude in the kitchen. He then reluctantly took on the responsibility of hastily cooked crude meals that they often ended up eating for days on end. Then he began bringing in prepared meals on his way back from the city, but when the novelty wore off they realized how tasteless and expensive the food really was. The responsibility for the preparation of meals finally fell on Guddho's inexperienced hands. And when Azam began coming home to half-cooked or burnt meals, he began to suspect that his young wife spent her entire day in his absence in playing with her dolls and gossiping with her neighbour. He gradually began to resent returning home at the end of each day.

The first time that he raised his hand to her, it had not been easy. Allaying his guilt was the feeble complacency that he had done the right thing and taught her a valuable lesson. After all, he thought, she was but a child who needed to be disciplined and taught what was important and what was not. However, when he caught her sulking the next day, reluctant to meet his gaze, her face swollen and her upper lip gashed badly, he had barely any recollection of beating her.

When next he found her playing shattapu in the middle of the courtyard and the dinner once again uncooked, the violence had actually come more naturally. The next morning when he set out to work, he had simply locked her inside the house. From there his method of discipline had progressed to locking her inside their single room, making sure to latch the window from the outside. By evening, when he returned from work, he was surprised to find that a dinner had been prepared and she was sulking in the kitchen, reluctant to venture out into the courtyard and greet him, as had been her habit. He was, however, still unsure how she had managed to escape from inside the room, unless her neighbour had let her out.

These confrontations would usually be followed by days and nights during which they would exchange barely a word. Azam's life became a routine of waking up and biking to work, toiling all day at the machinery, and then biking back home and sleeping till dawn. No one else seemed to exist for him in his state of limbo. She watched him from a distance, always wary of his presence.

"Khalaji, he doesn't really mean to hit me," Guddho had one day finally blurted out to Pino and her mother. Living in such close proximity to each other, she was sure they were aware of the state of affairs in her home.

"It's just that we somehow end up fighting each other over the most trivial things. Just last week he lost his temper when he could not find a clean handkerchief. It was right there under his nose, but not in its usual place. What can I do with a man who thinks everything else in the world has to be perfectly in place but will not make the slightest effort to adjust to me? I am only a child. Shouldn't he take better care of me instead of beating me on every trivial excuse?"

Fatima had clucked sympathetically: "Unless they can have what they want, all men are basically the same. Even though Pino's father never lifted a hand on me, I know that the Chuddhas, Azam's clan, has always been known to be especially harsh masters."

In saying this she was relying as her daughter had done earlier, on the timeless, shared pool of local wisdom that one dipped into when there was no other way of confirming one's gut instincts or suspicions. Truisms like the views that the Billas are callous as companions, and the Lammas are big talkers, and you should never marry a Jinn or let a Kamiar into a secret.

Finally, it was Pino who came to Guddho's rescue.

"Well, Guddho, maybe you can learn to cook by watching Ammiji and me. See this daal I am washing to cook today; it is the most simple of dishes to make. Why don't you stay over for a while and watch how I prepare it so that bhai Azam will not only want to eat it, but will want to eat it directly out of your hands."

"Shhh, besharamo!" Fatima had swiftly admonished. "Maybe all those dogs intently watching Rasheed's every move will one day become butchers! You two girls stop gossiping. The only way you will ever learn, tiye Guddho, is to actually cook the daal on your own."

This was to be the beginning of Guddho's domestic training. It would transform her relationship with her irascible husband. Since cooking was the most challenging of all household chores for her, she would yet show him the stuff she was made of. Under the daily tutelage of Fatima and occasionally Pino, Guddho learns among other skills the economy of daily household chores: how to thoroughly wash the soil from spinach before cooking it and diligently pick out the pebbles from daal; how to temper each type of daal after cooking; how to soak the chickpeas overnight and pickle wind-plucked, unripe mangoes in early summer, and use nimh leaves as a pesticide in her wheat and rice storage bins.

Since rice is the only dish she can already make all by herself, Fatima now shows her how to transform it into khitchri, pillau or biryani, and also how to enrich it with meat or vegetables to make it wholesome and satisfying. Guddho tries a new combination of available ingredients each week, serving them in silent anticipation to Azam, who plows through her efforts in total silence.

However, for Guddho, with the eagerly anticipated words of approval not having yet materialized, this minor setback is resourcefully tucked away to the back of her mind. Three months later, she has moved on to basic cooking of the seven types of lentils, first as dishes on their own and then as medleys with various vegetables.

After having watched her eager pupil roll out rotis in every imaginable shape but round, Fatima shows her how to produce rotis that are always geometrically perfect. With a knowing smile, and Pino and Guddho eagerly watching her, Fatima presses an inverted metal pot on top of the uneven patch of uncooked roti, and lifting it reveals how the jagged edges have all been sliced off before the roti is cooked over the skillet.

The next very morning, as he eyes the symmetrical paratha proudly placed before him, Azam's face lights up with amazement. Fingering the perfect edges, he voices his grudging appreciation: "Not even my mother could have cooked such perfectly shaped paratha as this! What did you do, cut off the edges with scissors?"

Hearing such high praise, Guddho begins to tell him how, but then thinks better of it and merely smiles back contentedly, suddenly bashful.

As each season jealously offers up its own particular bounty, she is fast to pick up on every variation in the theme of lentils, legumes and chickpeas. Then there is also the learning of the complementary combinations of potatoes, spinach, turnips and yams, and by year's end she has graduated to the meats: the chhota and wadha gosht of mutton and beef, and finally the princely chicken dishes. With each proffered dish the conversation at mealtimes grows longer and deeper, becoming more and more personal and intimate. He begins recounting the trivial details of his day, waxing eloquently about his pet obsessions and projects.

"The cardboard box that I am designing for the halvai's sweetmeats will have a cutout window so that you can actually see what's in it," he recounts in between bites. "And each set of boxes will have a different coloured kite paper glued inside the lid. I will have to get Chacha Rashid to design the die to make the cutouts. No one else can do the job even half as well as he does." He looks up from his food, as if aware of her presence for the first time, before gulping down a glass of buttermilk and proceeding, unsure that she is following the narrative of his future plans.

"Anyway, I was thinking that if I could design a new kind of a box for the owner of the Simla Sweet House, you know, the one that is between the tanga stand and the Trunk Bazaar, and if I could get a contract — I know the halvai well — then I could bring the supplies home and we could both work on the boxes here inside the house, and then once a week I could go out and deliver the order. We could easily make about five dozen of these boxes a week."

"Who is Chacha Rashid?" she interjects.

"Chachaji is this old man who works from his home in the city. He designs the entire supply of cutout dies for our press. Even though his eyesight is deteriorating rapidly, he can still build the most precise cutout dies in all of Sialkot. One day when I have my own press . . ."

Guddho interrupts him once again: "Hold on a minute, what are 'cutout dies'?"

Azam looks up, exasperated.

"A cutout die is what we use at the press to cut a card or box from a cardboard or paper sheet. It also creates the creases for the folding to be later done by hand." Seeing the blank look on her face, he gestures with his hands, drawing a rectangle in the air and punching a window into it: "You know the Eid cards that come with those fancy cut edges and have holes cut in them so that you can see the inside of the card from the outside? Well, a cutout die makes that possible."

Azam gesticulates wildly in the air, his hands shaping his thoughts. Guddho nods her head in acknowledgment, as if all this is finally beginning to make sense to her, and that it is the most natural of subjects for him to be discussing with her. She is amazed at the transformation she is witnessing in her normally recalcitrant partner.

"Well, Chacha Rashid first has to make a die for each cut or fold. Then I load these onto the press cutter and feed it one sheet at a time. By applying just the right amount of pressure, I can cut right through the paper. However, the cut only takes place where it is required. And where you need just a fold, the pressure and clearance has to be less in order to . . ."

"Clearance?" she blurts out. "What is clearance?" She is trying her best to keep up with his torrential flow of words and images but this time he is less forgiving at having his train of thought derailed yet again, and he moves petulantly to get up and leave. She is swift to respond by placing her hand gently on his shoulder.

"Sit down, sit down. It's all right. I will figure it all out later. For now just sit and talk to me about your work." She heaps his plate with another generous helping of the mutton and spinach curry, conveniently overlooking the fact that there will now be barely enough left over for her.

This is as close to marital bliss as they will ever come.

The matrimonial harmony doesn't last long. One chilly December evening, Azam returns home to discover that the remains of another burnt aloo gobi dish have been hastily tucked away behind the garbage. He is livid in his frustration with her, immediately abandoning his resolve to be more tolerant with her. Guddho, having anticipated his anger and the storm of recriminations that is sure to follow, has locked herself inside their room.

However, in her haste Guddho has forgotten to lock the window. Azam climbs in through it and lunges at her, but she swiftly unlocks the door and leaps nimbly out of his reach. Thwarted in his attempt, he searches for something to vent his rage on. He sees the rag dolls neatly lining the length of the opposite wall and with one sweep of his hand sends them tumbling to his feet.

As Guddho watches in through a film of bitter tears, Azam heaps her treasured possessions in the middle of the courtyard. The he takes a match from his pocket and sets the pile alight.

The heap of faded organzas, satins and velvets with detailed tinsel edging burns readily, and in an instant the smoky flame becomes a raging bonfire filling the air with the stench of singed hair. As she watches in mounting distress, her favourite piece flares and is the last to be consumed. Each of its wavy cinnamon strands of hair had been plucked from her own scalp from the ages of six to twelve and woven skillfully into two pliable pigtails, which begin to curl and then dissolve in the heat. This doll had been the one doll to accompany her in her wedding palanquin as she left her parents' home for the last time for that of Azam, and it was now a pile of ash.

For days the house reeks of the acrid, vinegary residue of burnt hair, keeping alive the memory the catastrophe.

Guddho's mourning, however, does not last that long. By the end of the first week, she has lugged home a mound of pliable clay from an open field close to their home. The clay has been brought in ostensibly to lay down a new layer of mud over the roof and the courtyard. But she has already decided to put the clay to better use.

Over the next several afternoons, with Azam away at work, Guddho patiently begins to fashion the first of the four clay figures, the mitti de baway. By the end of the week, satisfied with the result of her efforts, she begins the firing process. Each figure goes into the hearth fire with the day's meal. At the end of the firing process, with her handiwork safely tucked away in the rice bin, she stitches the first of the several dresses she will need to assemble from patches of left-over cloth, discarded muslin chunnis and torn bedsheets.

It is nearly summer before Azam stumbles upon the first of the set of fired clay figures, hidden deep beneath a winter quilt. The assembled doll family consists of a large central lump that is so indistinct and blurry as to be almost featureless. It towers over a spare female figure with lovingly detailed eyes and mouth, the hair tied into two neat pigtails, the details of which have been lovingly etched into the clay with a fine comb or nail. This smaller figure appears to be clutching a miniscule lump in the manner of an adult carrying an infant. Resting at the feet of three lumped human figures is what appears to be a crude miniature cat that Azam recognizes as the wretched, ill-fated Mano.

As an act of reconciliation and consolation, Azam brings home a large plastic doll with golden hair, blue eyes with eyelids that actually close, and a bright frock of gold and green painted directly onto the hollow plastic body. The gift remains wrapped in its brown paper bag a week later, discarded under her bed.

Their life somehow returns to their set routine. Late one night, while nibbling on her earlobe, he stumbles on the discovery that in spite of their mutual recriminations, her youth has priorities that only he can satisfy. After their first prolonged bout of lovemaking since the debacle, Azam rises from the bed and steps out of the house, carefully latching the outer door shut from the outside.

The night is crisp. As he steps out of the shadow of his doorstep, he finds the street before him completely deserted; even the mongrels are gone. Light from the lone streetlamp carves an arc over the cobblestones and makes the water flowing in the drains glisten in the dark. He pauses for a moment to enjoy his solitude, the dull, languorous ache in his joints receding, and his mind beginning to detach itself from the surrounding walls and soar overhead. A rushing of air makes him duck his head involuntarily. The lone bat living beneath the gargoyles of Dr. Aziz's house is busy out sweeping the night air, its wings humming in the silence.

Through the dark comes the erratic sound of the hollow tapping of the night watchman, the pehredar's stick rattling on the cobblestones, and this is is followed by the call to vigilance: "Hoshyar, jagte raho!"

In the silence that follows the retreating sound, a fluted train whistle rides the wind, the sound subdued enough during the day to go undetected, buried as it is beneath the ubiquitous metronome beat of the chakki mill.

Azam pauses to light a cigarette. The first two matches sputter reluctantly to life but then die before he can inhale. He curses under his breath, fumbling with the matchbox in the dark. The third match finally flares to life, briefly lighting up his face and the dingy corner of the street. He inhales deeply, the smoke infusing his body like the lukewarm liquid. He exhales, grateful for this moment of quiet contentment, the faint glow of the ember tip glowing and receding with the brief puffing of his cheeks.

He tosses the sputtering match into the drain, watching it flash briefly like a firefly before it is completely extinguished. For some vague reason, the sight of the doused matchstick causes a wave of anxiety to pool at the pit of his belly.

Strolling into the welcoming anonymity of the night, his step is light in its fall, his arms swinging rhythmically as he winds his way northward in deliberately slow, measured steps, the tip of his cigarette flaring regularly in the dark. He traces his familiar route by following the matching quilt patchwork of opalescent starlit sky outlined above him by the jagged rooftops. Following the layout of the street overhead and feeling its familiar texture beneath him, he turns corners mechanically; a vague feeling of anticipation sweeps through his limbs and loosens the tightly wound ball at the pit of his stomach. With a warm meal under his belt and the day's labours falling away, his mind conjures up the beteljuice-stained cards at the dhera. He can already taste the bitter hooch awaiting him.

Upon reaching his destination at the northern end of Kotli, he ducks into the thatched hut without knocking. The room is brightly lit to his dark-accustomed eyes and already crammed with half a dozen men his age, each one lounging on the floor durries and the puffed pillows. For the ensuing card game it is common knowledge that the aces have been surreptitiously scuffed at the upper left corners, yet easy camaraderie swirls about the room, softening the edges of rough male egos.

A couple of hours later, he is stumbling back onto the cobbled streets, his mind struggling to recall the familiar irregularities in the street patterns ahead. He searches for the elusive pieces of information that will complete the jigsaw and head him in the right direction. Yet, this time, nothing emerges out of the dark to guide him and he clings to the single most lucid thought he has had all night: that the blended aroma of wine and musk is exactly that of the king among flowers, the magnolia champa blossom.

Meanwhile, there are abutments, recesses and niches, arched doorways jutting into the street, or raised above the street level and accessed by stairways; ornate plaster décors on outer windows, even low wooden gargoyles extending from balcony beams, each of which he must negotiate, step over, duck under or maneuver around. In addition, he must also be constantly mindful of the obstacle extending outward from his own door.

After he first moved into his new home, Azam built a palm-wide bike ramp up the steps over the doorsill and then down into the courtyard. Viewed from the outside, the cemented slope looked as if the house had extended a leg over the staircase and into the middle of the street. Initially, it had even baffled their neighbour Babaji Feroze, who, being partially blind, kept tripping over it every time he set out for the masjid, before learning to negotiate the hazard with the tapping of his cane.

Luckily for Azam, a half-crescent moon has inched its way up into the eastern sky so that the angular features of the houses now gleam brightly for his benefit. He strolls aimlessly down the curving streets, dragging his feet and pressing down on their slight curvature, so that he appears to glide over the grating joints between the interlocked crisscross of the bricks, the convex middle bulge keeping him centered and safe from straying too close to the gutters. For a moment he even wonders if these really are his own two feet touching the ground or that of another person, alien to his own yet anchored to the same ground. The faint, milky sky is now a river flowing ahead of him, and his body slips with ease around the dark corners stretching out of the unlit alleys. More than once in a single night he has circled the entire village thrice before stumbling home, all emotion drained out of him.

He fumbles with the latch to let himself in the house, the unfastened chain rattling as it strikes the wooden door frame. The sound awakens Guddho from her restless dreams, her jaw clenching and grinding rhythmically, bits of half-chewed rice sticking to her pillow. On such nights, Azam will eventually crawl into bed beside her to cradle himself into her warmth, arching himself around her back and cupping her breasts in his free hands before falling asleep, then snoring loudly in her ear. And she, still half-asleep, will in time disentangle herself and move over to his bed, turning back to gently cover him with the sheet.

Sometimes he awakens in the early morning to the sound of the Fajr adhan, surprised to find himself curled up into a fetal ball and all alone in his bed.

Late one Sunday in morning spring, with the sunlight spilling out over the encrusted courtyard mud that is beginning to chip away beneath his feet, Azam, freshly shaven and bathed, and clad in a starched white shalwar kurta, steps outside to check if the chai khokha is open and occupied.

His eyes, casually skimming over the features in the middle distance, are drawn to the lurid text that completely covers the square wooden tea stall before him. The newly applied cladding of recycled tin sheets facing him reads: OLD FLAKE GOLD FLAKE GOLD FLAKE GOLD FLAK, in a repeating pattern of six horizontal rows. The bottom corners of the front flap, now propped open with two slim bamboo sticks, are lowered at night, but not locked, by its corpulent owner, Ghaffar.

Azam, possessing the trained eye of a detail technician, has never been able to turn away from any such distraction displayed before him in bold text. Furthermore, having to keep a close professional eye on the characteristics of text all day at work, too, the khokha now appears to him only as a garish splatter of off-centered text in black, red and orange. With the print registers having shifted, the effect is that of three similar but differently coloured stamps overlapping randomly.

When he first began to work at the press in Sialkot, Azam had not been aware of how repeated exposure to such a visual overload would affect him. He would return home at the end of those lengthy and exhausting early days, and his head would be reeling so that he would have to pull over and stop several times before he had even reached the outskirts of the city. It was only much later, in hindsight, that he was able to figure out the reason for this. As soon as he approached the city bazaars, he subconsciously began reading every piece of text that flashed before his eyes, from traffic signs and film billboards to commercial advertisements and signboards. It got even worse at the press by the end of the day. Even now that there is nothing to shield his view of the exposed chai khokha from his doorway, each time he steps out of his new home, the sensory overload overwhelms him.

Seeing Azam heading his way, Ghaffar, the squat chaiwallah, rises reluctantly from his perch at the open edge of the khokha to shoo away the row of squabbling crows lining an unoccupied wooden bench. He also makes a half-hearted stab at brushing away the swarms of flies crowding the spilled chai. By the time he returns to his perch he is already panting, his chubby fingers ineffectually priming the kerosene-fired Primus stove, and sliding a needle into the flame to clear the build-up of slag.

"Ao, Azamji, ao," he says in formal greeting, all the while emptying an open pan of used tea leaves onto the heaped mush directly beneath him, banging the battered metal utensil against the open side of the khokha. He fills the emptied pan with a cup of fresh water, tosses in two teaspoons of sugar and places the mixture to brew over the sputtering stove flame. By then, Azam has settled down directly in front of the fire. He turns his attention to the two men seated opposite him on the benches, each noisily slurping from a glass of chai. He knows them as local electricians, and cannot but help eavesdrop on of their loud argument over some film trivia. They are bickering over whether the popular Indian film star Dilip Kumar actually has a twin brother in real life.

"I say that if there is no twin brother then how can there be two Dilip Kumars onscreen at the same time in *Do Bhai*," one of them asserts. He is speaking of a film plot involving two brothers, the evil one making the life of the saintly one miserable until the very last reel. The speaker, now fully aware of his growing audience, continues in an even louder tone of voice: "And if there really is a twin brother somewhere, then what is his real name and how is it that he is never mentioned in the newspapers?"

His partner has also noticed Azam settle down close to them, and he now pointedly remarks: "Well, never mind that. What I really want to know is, when we see the two brothers together in a film, how can you ever tell them apart?"

Azam intervenes, unable to suppress a snicker: "Oy, that is easy! The real Dilip Kumar does not have a mustache. And the other one is already known to everyone as Yusuf Khan."

Seeing that the befuddled listeners have not yet caught on to the actor's use of a stage name, he turns to them in disgust: "Salay! You people! Where do you come up with these ideas? Doesn't your supervisor give you enough work to keep your heads busy?"

He now turns his attention to Ghaffar, who is sprinkling a miserly pinch of dried tea leaves into the boiling water. The floating flecks instantly stain the sweetened solution, and Azam has to raise his voice over the hissing of the stove in order to be heard.

"Ghaffarji, do I have a weird tale to tell you about my adventure last night. You are not going to believe what happened to me."

Azam watches attentively to see if his words have had the desired affect. He notices the cocky electricians around him suddenly fall silent and feign a sudden interest in a stone that is lying before them in the dust. Ghaffar only manages a surly look of reluctant encouragement, anticipating yet another tall tale, but knowing Azam well enough to know it will be worth listening to.

"Well, the story I have to tell you begins when I was returning home after a late-night card game at the dhera with my friends. Tonight, mere yaar Azam, I kept reminding myself . . ." He pauses dramatically, glancing through the corner of his eyes at the electricians. "To you, mere yaar Ghaffar, I am finally going to reveal how I encountered the bride of the morning mists."

Azam spends a moment in contemplation of his distant doorstep before loudly clearing his throat and proceeding with the narration.

"You see, I had already lost a fortune during the night at the card game. As I stepped out I saw this woman moving about at some distance ahead of me in the bushes. My reasoning was that since I had already lost so much in one night, maybe here was an opportunity for me to make up for some of it."

Polite snickers from the seated men egg him on.

"As I began my journey home . . . I suppose you all know where Midhe's dhera is located, don't you?"

Once again a few polite grunts prod him to get on with the story.

"Well, as I left the dhera in the early dawn and headed home, I found myself stumbling over a very unsteady path through dense vegetation. You see, I had taken a shortcut through the cemetery, and it was then that I saw her shrouded figure moving only a few feet ahead of me."

"Why were you stumbling about?" asks one of the men seated opposite him, a knowing smile stretching across his broad, oafish face.

"Well, partly because it was so late and still quite dark, and partly because I was . . ."

It is now Ghaffar's turn to interrupt the narration by loudly clearing his throat, while swirling the brewing tea around the pan with a practised motion. He pours some milk into the brew and, looking up at Azam, sets the pan down to come to a boil once again.

"Anyway, I became so intrigued to find another human being out all alone so late in the night that I began to give chase by maintaining a short distance. I noticed that the figure appeared to be wearing a red dress, and even in the dim light I could catch the glint off the tassels of a chuddar and embroidered dress. With the discovery that it really was a woman out all alone so late at the night, I was even more intrigued.

"However, as I continued to pursue her, I was only partially aware that she had begun to lead me further and further away from where I was supposed to be headed. However, by then I was past caring, my initial stupour having completely vanished with the brisk pace I had to maintain. Occasionally she would pause to adjust her chuddar, and it seemed as if she were teasing me and merely waiting for me to catch up to her."

Azam pauses dramatically in the middle of his story once again to sip some water. In the background the stove sputters back to life and the chai hissing to a boil.

"Just when I thought I had finally gained on her, I noticed that her dress appeared to have been ripped open at several places. Her midriff showed through one of these cuts and one shoulder was also partially bare. Moreover, as she moved through the dense vegetation, the nettles and thorns seemed to be ripping off further bits and pieces of her clothing. Part of me now wanted to stop and take stock of the situation, but my excitement kept urging me on, so I began to quicken my pace. A moment later, I tripped over a large twig and tumbled into her."

"And then you woke up, right?" someone nearby asks.

However, the question does not register on Azam for some time. A rope lighter strung from the side of the khokha diverts his attention. Ghaffar is now using the short length of rope to light a cigarette for one of his customers. One end of this spiral has been left smouldering. It is the faint glow from this ember that has suddenly caught his attention.

While the rest of the gathered audience waits the conclusion to his story, Ghaffar notices the look of unease that has crept into Azam's face. He inquires: "Ki ay, pai Azam?"

However, Azam is evasive and, turning his gaze away, quickly changes the subject. He points to the mound of mushed tea leaves piled underneath the khokha and asks: "Ghaffar, why don't you ever think of tidying this place up and getting rid of this stinking mess underneath your khokha?"

"Oh, that! I am saving it for the science teacher at the high school. You know Masterji? He uses it for his compost heap. He claims it is good for his orchard, his Baghe Firdaus!"

"His Baghe Firdaus?"

Ghaffar's brow is ruffled in concentration as he repeats: "Baghe Firdaus! That is what he calls it. What is that verse he keeps repeating, you know, the one about heaven being right here beneath our feet?"

Azam, coming to his rescue, offers: "You mean Amir Khusrau's verse:
Agar firdaus bar roo-e zameen ast,
Hameen ast-o hameen ast-o hameen ast.

142

If there is a paradise on earth,
It is this, it is this, it is this."

"Yes, yes. That is the one. He calls his orchard his heavenly garden. Do you know he is able to grow all those exotic leeches and out-of-season mangoes and oranges in that measly walled garden of his? Once a season he comes by here to collect all of this garbage that I have managed to save for him. Can you believe it, he even pays me for it!"

As the speaks, it dawns on Ghaffar that Azam's query has not been made out of mere curiosity. Somewhere in it there lingers the menace of an implied threat. Accordingly, his own tone of voice also begins to sour: "Azam, don't you go around complaining about the mess under my khokha. At least I know what it is doing there! Why don't you clean up the mess under your own khokha?"

Noticing the first signs of a spat, the other customers have abandon their perch on the benches and, grabbing their chai, step away from the khokha.

"What are you talking about, Ghaffar? What mess under my khokha?"

"Don't ask me; go and ask your wife and her girlfriend. They spend the entire day chattering and laughing on top of that rooftop of yours, shamelessly parading out there in full view of everyone. Throughout the day, I have a hard time getting my customers to vacate these front-row benches, so absorbed are they in the show."

Azam has heard enough. He has always disliked this shifty, lecherous creature before him. On an impulse, Azam reaches a hand out and seizes Ghaffar by the collar, dragging him from his precarious perch at the edge of the stall. Before Ghaffar can recover, Azam deposits him directly on top of the pile of tea leaves. When the heavyset man tries to stand up or fight back, Azam rains down further blows onto his head.

In his desperate attempts to rise, Ghaffar seizes upon the collar of Azam's kameez, ripping it loose in his fist. Their limbs continue to flay about as they tumble over one another in the dust of the open ground. Blood oozes from Azam's nose when Ghaffar's elbow inadvertently finds a target. The tussle lasts for barely two minutes before Ghaffar manages to tear himself away from Azam's grasp, and, finding himself standing upright again, races for home, abandoning his unattended khokha.

His heart still racing, Azam brushes his clothes and settles on the nearest bench, his breath emerging in spasm. An unsteady hand reaches out to pick up a discarded glass of chai. Alternately wincing in pain and sipping at the chai, he notices the stove sputtering as it runs out of compressed air. He reaches out an unsteady hand and turns off the supply of kerosene. Then acting once again on an impulse, he removes the lighted rope dangling from the side of the khokha, and dips the smouldering end into his chai, an idiotic grin settling across his face when he hears the satisfying hiss. He feels calm and lucid, the blinkers of familiarity falling off for once from his comprehension of the world around him.

Oh, the tyranny of these open courtyards of our crammed houses . . . his mind gropes through the newfound pathways of self-awareness. These extended households knotted together beneath exposed rooftops, and the open book lives of all our families, all huddled together in tiny rooms, forever peering over the banisters and walls into each other's lives. Where all privacy is an illusion and the lecherous among us, even within the confines of strict purdah, commit adultery with every glance. Where the misery of one is carried from mouth to mouth across barriers of brick.

What intimacies could possibly remain private or personal for any duration of time out here, he muses solemnly, before noticing the crowd of people now hurrying towards him. Word of his outburst has spread as rapidly a rumour.

Azam watches them in a detached manner. The first to reach him is his wife, who, with her face fully exposed for once to the public, has never looked so ravishing to him. As she unselfconsciously marches straight up to him, he notices that she has rolled up her sleeves, bound her chunni tightly around her hair, and has on her angelic face the determined look of one who will take on anyone who dares to cross her path. She rapidly tears a strip of her chunni, and uses it as a bandage to staunch the blood still flowing from his lip onto the ripped open collar of his kameez.

For almost nine years, Azam's daily routine on weekdays has involved biking seven miles to work in the morning and then heading back late in the evening. Rain or shine, he has disciplined himself to follow this one routine, six days a week. Only floods will keep him home, and that only because he has been on more than one such occasion swept partially away by the floodwaters, and once almost lost his bike while crossing a flooded depression in the road. These twenty-feet-long dips in the road were built in as an economy of cost and design; forming a reverse image of the bridge, they allowed the seasonal floodwaters to spare the main road by flowing over sections of it. On approaching one of the four such locations on the road to the city, each of the male passengers would have to alight from the tanga and wade across, while the tangawallah led the horse across the water on foot. Bikers also learned from experience what depth of water could be forged. On two occasions, Azam underestimated the ferocity of the undercurrent during a time of flood and had to turn back and head for home.

The road he takes daily to work has perennially been in a state of disrepair, even though it is Kotli's sole link to the nearest metropolitan area, the city of Sialkot, and from there the outside world. Somewhere at the back of Azam's mind there exists an impromptu and regularly updated map, locating each of the major potholes and puddles of mud that mark this road. Two-thirds of the way to the city, the neglected roadway merges into the sturdy, well-maintained and tree-lined tarmac of the cantonment. Even the diligent Lohars of Kotli, obsessively preoccupied with the strict maintenance of their village's streets and drains, have somehow historically lacked the required political and economic clout to alter this fact of their daily life.

Azam leaves for work earlier in the cool breeze of summer mornings, and returns later when the sun has nearly set and the road is in partial shade. He is thus able to evade the worst of the noonday heat. Sometimes a sudden late summer afternoon downpour will surprise him, and he will continue to glide through the moist curtains of air until the raindrops bead to form twin rivulets and seek out his eyelids. He will then pull over to the side of the road and lean beneath the umbrella of one of the massive tahlis, leaving his bike lying prone in the rain. Rolling his head from side to side like a soaked mutt, he sloshes the rain out of his hair. And once the shower passes, he will resume his journey, with the sun now peeking through the backlit clouds. He will skillfully maneuver the bike's front wheel on inch-wide bridges of dry road between pools of mud, his body cooling, the muscles beginning to cramp, and his clothes steaming.

In overtaking a tanga, he notices the moisture steaming off the beast of burden.

With the onset of the monsoon later in the summer, and jamnu, mangoes, and amrud ripening in the orchards surrounding the road, the unsettled weather disrupts all well-laid human plans. With the road now snaking through the cloying humidity of rice paddies, Azam's shirt will cling tightly to his chest, a second skin he is equally uncomfortable in, blinking his eyes to keep the bugs out, and lifting one hand to sweep the sweat off his brow. At such times, each leaf of the tahlis is stilled with not a rumour of breeze during the entire hour of his ride; the sun is blinding in its interrupted staccato of reflections off the roadside pools and fields. Crossing the arced back of the narrow bridge over the seasonal stream of Aik and traversing the expanse of the cantonment parade grounds, he rides past soldiers parading stiffly or slouching around roadside toilets.

Eventually, in crossing the river Palkhu, he approaches the outskirts of the city. His bike rattles in passing over railway tracks, and he has to dodge the web of pointed bamboo beams of the several tanga carriages heading towards him. A chaotic river of pedestrians challenges him at every push of his pedal. Ruminating oxen sit in the middle of the busy road, herds of goats wander aimlessly in and out of traffic, and remarkably, a blind man is traversing the hectic confusion of the street, all alone.

With his personal dreams of one day owning his own press, a press he will call Mughal-e-Azam after the popular Indian film, nudged aside once again for the duration of the day, he enters a narrow back alley where his place of work is located. This is Medina Press, and Azam

146

Karighar is the senior printing technician. As Azam steps into the clammy interior of the print shop, his mounting surliness makes it difficult for him to concentrate on his assignments for the day. His attitude is not helped by the tone of despondency that has descended upon all at the moribund business. All the employees have noticed that with newer and better-equipped presses opening for business all around them, there has been less work left over for them to survive on.

The walls of Azam's workplace are decorated with colourful samples of past jobs, proof runs, fancy Eid greeting cards and wedding invitations, religious posters, unfolded halvai sweetmeat boxes, pages of Urdu textbooks, political manifestoes, and posters and such. There is even an early copy of the weekly Urdu paper, the *Sialkot Nama*, with a circulation of 246, that Medina Press still somehow puts out each Friday. All these artifacts attest to the fact that this press has seen better days. Chaudhri Saab, the owner and manager, could once have easily reeled in all the juicy and, more importantly, prestigious contracts available in the city. One such contract had led to meeting the unending demand for religious texts; a demand that was perennial enough to require the full-time hiring of three Arabic calligraphers in its heyday. These katibs spent their entire workday crouched in corners peering over their scripts with their ink pens in hand. Sadly, with its dated print and typesetting machinery, the press today is a relic dating back more than half a century, and is in as derelict a state as its sedate owner. New business has been reduced to a trickle.

However, because of the industrious skills of technicians like Azam who perform daily miracles with their limited tools the press has so far survived. With the floor littered with sawdust and ink-smudged newsprint, the roof leaking during steady downpours, and on stifling summer afternoons the stench of curing leather from the neighbouring shop turning everyone's stomach, they have had to learn to cut corners and improvise with less each day. The photo plates are now routinely exposed using only sunlight, and on overcast days the crew has been known to sit idly by rather than risk timing the exposure by manual overcompensation. It is now only on rush jobs that the mechanism, consisting of a series of coils and exposed wires that are screwed onto an inner wall, is pressed into service to power the light source so that every other light in the room flickers and dims. Cheaper inks are substituted wherever possible. And, in spite of these cost-cutting measures, the finished product is always far superior to their better-equipped competitors. A younger, more dynamic Chaudhri Saab would proudly have pointed out to his workers and customers that fine printing, like the other arts, is achieved through attention to detail.

The three ceiling fans and two pedestals stir up the muggy interior of the shop with its residue of oil and ink. For Azam, the only difference in pace between working indoors and the routine pedaling of his bike is that now he has to exert less effort. With his disposition progressively more disgruntled each day, he is becoming less and less focused on the operation of the machinery before him and increasingly obsessed with the wayward behaviour of his colleagues.

During the four daily cigarette breaks that he allows himself in addition to his lunch break, he squats in the inner open courtyard and leans against the shaded wall. He has always been unwilling to risk smoking inside the print shop, fearing sending the whole place up in smoke as one carelessly flicked ash could ignite the oil-soaked papers and the sawdust underfoot. He is especially edgy around Shaukat Ali, the other machinist, a chain-smoking lout whose ubiquitous cigarette butt is always hidden behind a shriveled snakeskin of ash, an overhead plume of pale smoke identifying his workplace.

"One of these days this place will burn down and then where will we be?" he complains to Chaudhri Saab on a routine basis. "You know the risks of letting Shaukat smoke so close to the machines, so why do you always let him get away with it?"

His complaint elicits an unchanging response. Chaudhri Saab silently rolls his eyes and puffs away busily at his hookah, his breath rasping noisily in his throat. He glares back silently at Azam with that look of pained suffering that he reserves for employees who ask him for a day off or permission to leave work early.

As it turns out, it is not a carelessly discarded cigarette butt that becomes their undoing, but something far more insidious; something that they could, with a little foresight, have foreseen if not prevented, instead of being so completely blindsided by it.

A month before Ramzan, Chaudhri Saab slips a metal lid onto the clay cap of his hookah and tucks some spare tobacco into his waistcoat pocket. He catches the first bus for his seasonal visit to Lahore's Urdu Bazaar. Almost five hours later, he is busy wandering through the narrow warren of back alleys that forms the heart of Punjab's print industry, scrounging up some form of sustenance for his ailing business.

He returns the next day, beaming with excitement, telling everyone that he has finally managed to bag a really plum contract: forty-five hundred hand-printed, three-colour Eid greeting cards. The client is a prominent national bank and the cards are to be delivered to select customers during Ramzan, a week before Eid-ul-Fitr. To the printer's trained eye, the catchy design is as exquisite as it is complicated, and printing it will be as groundbreaking as it will be challenging: six gold lotus flowers with red accents floating in a black background. A white crescent is breaking through the dark upper-right corner of the sky.

This is an important milestone in the illustrious history of their press, and the moment deserves to be savoured. Chaudhri Saab, realizing the full enormity of the challenge that awaits them, offers a bonus of ten rupees to each of the technicians, on the condition that the task is completed satisfactorily, and, more importantly, on time. After allowing them to bask in a rare moment of buoyant celebration, he hustles them all back to work and sets about taking delivery of the costly paper stock. A katib has already been dispatched to Chacha Rashid for the preparation of a customised cutting die.

Their problems, however, begin to mount from the minute they approach their first task. The colour separations from Lahore arrive a week later than promised. The delivery of the card paper is also delayed by yet another critical week, and by mid-Ramzan, a week from the delivery date, they have still not begun the actual laborious task of printing. When the printing does finally begin, Azam discovers that the gold colour he has so carefully chosen through numerous print tests will not behave exactly as expected.

Once it is on the cards, it does not dry fast enough, and Azam spends two sleepless nights trying out various combinations of solvent and paint to arrive at a working compromise. He even begins staying at the press during the nights, fasting and breaking his fast with the rest of the local crew, and sending out word to his worried wife that he will definitely be home before Eid.

Once the cards are fully printed, the wet paint glues them fast together, so the paint stains the backside of each card and the fingers of anyone who handles them. In desperation they try spreading all the cards out onto the floor in order to dry them faster, and even rent four additional pedestal fans to run day and night. But all this proves to be in vain.

Once the paint has partially dried, Azam begins hand-correcting the gaps that have been left by the shifted register of the faulty printing plates. The deadline for delivery approaches and then passes, and in their frustration they begin to blame the colour separator and the poor quality of the printing plates for the delay; the glossiness of the card paper and the moisture in the air, the delayed printing schedule, and their failure to estimate the time required to correct errors and omissions are all desperately held up as accountable.

By late afternoon, days before Eid, the fate of the workshop, and its eight workers and its owner, is sealed. The restive crew hired to manually fold and then place each card in an envelope is sent away.

The debacle of the Eid greeting cards eventually results in the final closure of the press. Azam shows up for work one cold winter morning and watches in bitter frustration as the the shop's equipment is carted off, suddenly aware of his need to find other work. He discovers that each one of Chaudhri Saab's old rivals are wary of anyone who has ever been loyal or associated with him.

For days after the press shuts down, Azam pretends to leave for work in the city. Once he has ventured far outside Kotli, he heads instead for Maralla to spend the day fishing. At the end of the day he sometimes returns home loaded with his catch, pretending he has bought the fish on his way from work.

In evading the inevitable confession, he is once again following family tradition. In addition to being known for other, less savoury traits, the Chuddhas were also famous for their predisposition to walk off everything unpleasant. Over the generations, they had learned to deal with every major crisis in their lives by setting off on foot. The excuse before meals was that they were working up an appetite; afterwards, digestion. The local midwife had often told Azam how on the day he was born she had emerged with the auspicious news, and Azam's father had been nowhere to be found. He only returned at the end of the day, having walked all the way to the cantonment grounds and then back.

How long Azam could keep the news of his unemployment from his wife became a matter of speculation when Raheem Kingar, Kotli's peripatetic angler, caught the big one. As fate would have it, on that particular day Azam happened to be fishing right next to him, and ended up helping Kingar lug the shifty mass of fins and scales all the way home on the back of his bike. On proudly showing off his catch, Raheem Kingar let slip that it was none other than Azam who had helped him reel in the monster and load it onto his bike, and then followed behind him all the way home just in case he needed further assistance.

What was Azam doing at Maralla, a curious neighbour asked, when he was supposed to be out at work in the city? And that is how, when word finally filtered down to Guddho, Azam had no choice but to sheepishly confess. But she now has a secret of her own to acknowledge to him.

As he looks on in surprise, she sweeps her entire clay collection of mute horses onto the floor, excitedly picking each one and cracking it open. He is tempted to interrupt her madness, concluding that this may be her way of taunting him and taking revenge for the earlier insult. But, miraculously, onto the earthen floor of their room spill folded rupee notes and fistfuls of silver currency. She sorts through the broken pottery, excitedly piling the money to one side. Each paisa of these savings has been salvaged from measly housekeeping expenses, a skill that no one needed to teach her. But their euphoria quickly evaporates when they realize that the sum of all her clandestine efforts at squirreling away bits and pieces from her kitchen money will barely tide them over for a single week. Seven days and nights. Seven meals!

A week later, relying on cover of night to hide the blow to his personal dignity, Azam approaches the local goldsmith with his dowry gold bundled in a handkerchief. A few months later, it is his prized watch that he is forced to sell in the city.

Unable to muster enough humility to approach his brothers for help, Azam squirrels into his home the discounted and damaged foodstuffs from the city, where no one knows him personally or of his predicament. He is also unwilling to go to any of the local merchants, proudly maintaining an outwardly respectful self-sufficiency.

The couple now switch from the daily luxury of ghee to cooking with oil, rediscovering economies of a simpler lifestyle and the shunned delicacies of ox tails, wild tubers, and half-spoilt fruits and vegetables. They even convert a section of their courtyard into a vegetable patch.

After an absence of over two weeks, Pino looks down from her rooftop and wonders why Azam's bike still leans against the wall. She distinguishes a dark stubble covering the neat mounds and furrows that stretch half of her neighbour's yard. About a dozen chickens are already busy scratching into the mud and pecking at the new shoots.

Still debating whether to drop in on her tenants, she watches as Guddho, dressed in the same flowery voile Pino has seen her in the entire summer, emerges from her kitchen. Unaware of Pino's gaze, she hops, skips and then jumps in passing over the shattapu pattern coal-etched into the veranda clay, and then plucks a few leaves of fresh coriander after shooing the birds out into the street.

"So, what do you have planted in the yard?" Pino shouts, startling Guddho into looking upwards and shading her eyes, one hand still clutching the dark leaves.

"Oh, just some dhania, and thom and . . . payaz over here. I even planted some palak but the chickens got at it before we could. I find payaz is the easiest to grow. No bird will touch it. Do you want to come down here? Azam will be out for some time."

"Maybe later. And Guddho, I have been meaning to ask you for some time now. Why does your husband not go to work anymore?"

There are evenings when Azam has had enough of his thoughts chasing themselves in endless circles inside his head. He constantly reminds himself to keep in mind the Quranic passage about Allah providing sustenance to the lowliest of creatures, even those with a heart of stone. Surely he deserves better and will one day see better times. Better days, better days, I will see better days, he comforts himself.

Glad for once at not having to bike to work on a daily basis, he takes Guddho for a ride over the unpaved roads used only by local farmers. However, before they can leave the house he must first service the bike. Now that he is not obligated to maintain it in working order for daily service, the tread-bare tires need to be topped with air. Guddho watches in amusement as Azam doubles over the air pump, comic in his sighing as he pushes the pump handle down below his knees and then pulls it up waist high. His comic, awkward motion at the task reminds her of a frog hopping across a field.

Seated sideways behind him on the carrier frame, the unevenly patched tire tubes wobbling beneath her, she holds onto the frame for balance. Once they are past the last row of houses, she leans forward into his tense, hard body, their warmth passing freely through the intervening layers of clothing, their bodies in a silent shared flight. The foreshortened path before them zigzags through the fields; the cool, speckled shade of foliage flowing smoothly over their united bodies like the play of light across a stream flowing over pebbles and stones. Their mutual bliss lasts beyond the first bump in the road that jars the bike frame and briefly interrupts their rhythm.

This time is reminiscent of when they had first moved into their new house, so far from the constantly prying eyes of the rest of his extended family. They discover in each other a newly uninhibited and unselfconscious physicality. Late one night, with no wind to stir the leaves of the jamnu trees in her courtyard, Pino is unable to sleep in the oppressive heat. Rising from her bed, she happens to glance down from her rooftop into her neighbour's courtyard where she can see two adjacent manjis. She notices that only one of these is occupied. As her eyes become accustomed to the dark and she wills herself back from the banister, she notices Azam's dark body sprawled out diagonally across that of

Guddho. Even from such a distance, Pino can see their bedsheet ripple as if by a gentle breeze.

Eventually, as the trauma of being unemployed wears off, Azam ventures back to the city to seek whatever work he can find. For the first few months he works as a typesetter in a small print shop. During the dull hours of repetitive work, his mind is busy analyzing the rapidly changing world around him and formulating plans for digging his way out of the ditch he has tumbled into. He begins dreaming once again of the illusive and ersatz Mughal-e-Azam Press, and of an apprenticeship to Chacha Rashid, the dying master craftsman. Surely the growing number of packagers in Sialkot's burgeoning sports and surgical tools industry would truly appreciate a piece of equipment that allows a cardboard sheet to be cut to a hair's breadth of specifications.

The nation, he notes wryly, is growing rapidly, and signs of prosperity are everywhere. To be healthy, Mashallah, now means to be plump and rosy-cheeked with rolling layers of fat. This unfettered indulgence in newfound freedoms is gradually turning a mainly agrarian people towards an urban sophistication, or failing that, a metropolitan pretense. Nowhere are these new tastes more apparent than in the increasing sales of sweetmeats called mathai. The consumption of these has been associated with carnivals, holidays and weddings, and much happier times. Now anyone can tap into this pool of pleasant memories at any time. A new sweetmeat shop, aptly titled Happy Times, has just opened its doors in the Trunk Bazaar market, and is already doing a brisk business.

Noting the insatiable seasonal demand for the colourful triangular flags that are made out of kite paper for the Eid Milad-ul-Nabi parades that mark the Prophet's birthday, all the streets and stalls are festooned with the humble filamentous paper. Azam examines it with a new respect.

Three months after of returning to work, Azam has arrived at the final design of a prototype cardboard box that will hold one seer of sweetmeats. It has a three-square-inch window punched into the lid. This cutout was originally to be backed by kite paper of various shades, but he has discovered that this paper is easily stained by the oily contents of the box and switches to the more expensive and resilient gloss of transparencies. He works out the economics of manufacturing these boxes on a larger scale. If he sells twenty boxes a day for about twelve paisas each, and working from home could churn out a hundred boxes a day, he should make over three hundred rupees a month. He would purchase the paper in the city, have it cut there and then lug it back home on his bike.

One day he hawks the prototype to Happy Times Sweetmeats and is surprised when they take him up on his offer with an initial order of a dozen boxes a day. Thus begins his new career, which will see him claw his way out of the ditch.

Another early evening in late spring as Azam arrives at his doorstep he can once again smell the burnt food waiting for him. This time, however, he is too weary for another open confrontation and decides instead to withdraw and return an hour later. Hopefully, Guddho will by then have had enough time to prepare a replacement meal, so instead of alighting from his bike, he sets out on a circuitous route of the streets that will take him through the entire village and out to the western boundary of houses. From there, he will take a border path and end up back home again.

Traversing the open ground before his house, he encounters Manni Tangawallah's mare at the end of its homebound journey. With the empty tanga carriage now deserted for the night and tilted to rest diagonally in the mud, and the beast finally unfettered and its blinds removed, it stumbles groggily homewards guided by instinct and habit alone. With sweat steaming off its coat into the dense surrounding air and its nostrils flaring, the horse is to Azam like a living bellows on legs. It cleaves through the herd of buffalos returning from the fields, and without a flick of the mare's tail to bother them, the flies that swarm it are lured away by more enticing aromas. Their desertion is only momentary, before they return to the moving feast of dried sweat, lather and salt. The cobblestones rattle with the clink of a loosened horseshoe and passersby seeing the half-sleeping beast heading towards them hastily step aside. In one narrow winding alley, a nervously giggling boy on a dare holds his ground, cheekily waving his hand before the animal's glazed eyes, then darts swiftly to safety, his heart racing. The somnolent creature blindly plods on home unaware of all the surrounding activity.

On such a day as today, Azam would normally have encountered Mohammed Din, the kulfi-wallah, returning from the city with the wheels of his empty cart rattling over the cobblestones. Mohammed Din, the ice cream seller, lanky and taller even than Azam, had walked just like him with drooping shoulders so that his arms hung down to his thighs and almost seemed to touch his knees. He would walk seven miles to the city and then back, seven days a week, twenty-six summers of stooping low over a flimsy ice cream cart with delicate wooden handles, a child's plaything in his outsized hands. In winter he would switch to selling vegetables and fresh fruit from an open cart. Mohammed Din had lived all his life next door to them, and as a child Azam had eagerly waited each evening for the mushy unsold icicles that sometimes remained in the cart upon its return from the city. Sadly, the gentle giant dropped dead at forty and left behind a family of six children, and his wife has continued to work as a servant at Azam's family home.

More accustomed to the freedom of an open road on his bike, Azam is clumsy in this tight street, narrowly missing a determined looking Kittu as he scurries away from home, his mind probably preoccupied with some new prank.

Further down the street, Azam has to maneuver around Malhaara's ladder, which is leaning midway into the street. Malhaara himself is perched on his stepladder, kerosene can in hand, his attendant mutt wandering off after Kittu. Here, too, buffalo dung patties are splattered at intervals across the street attesting to the recent passage of the herd. In dodging these hazards, Azam brushes past Malhaara, narrowly avoiding the handmade lighter he is holding up to a lamp's wick. The rope lighter is similar to the one that had triggered the earlier violence at Ghaffar's chai khokha.

As the youngest male in his family home, and the youngest apprentice in their family workshop, it had been Azam's sole responsibility on pain of humiliation to keep his father's hookah alight at all times during the day. This was no easy task, and it had to be diligently completed in all kinds of weather, so that in some protected corner of their house, some coals or cow dung cakes were always kept smouldering. These would then be kept smothered by just the right amount of ash to conserve the heat through the foulest of weather. It was also his responsibility to keep the hookah cap filled with the right mixture of tobacco and molasses and to replace the stale water in the reservoir at the end of each day. He could still remember as a young boy taking the first few perfunctory puffs to get the whole process going and then respectfully passing the hookah over to the master of the shop.

These thankless chores he would have to perform each and every day that he was in the workshop, come rain, floods or sunshine. But what he remembers now most of all are the times he was not able to carry out his assigned job and the fire died, and all the beatings that always followed this. Even well into his adulthood his cantankerous, overbearing brothers continued to punish him. They had all thought him to be dull and incapable of carrying out a simple appointed task with any consistency or dependability, and in their ribald company he had always been treated as something of a dimwit.

Since the entire extended family of fifteen had lived in the same six-room, two-story house, these simmering tensions would sometimes spill over into their domestic lives. Their arguments would always begin innocently enough before acquiring a life all of their own, erupting like a wall of fire.

Early one morning during the Ramzan, with the entire family awake for saheri keeping of the fast, Kaneez, the wife of the eldest son, had innocently asked her mother-in-law if she was ready for her meal. Somehow, Kaneez had addressed her mother-in-law as Ammiji in keeping with the local tradition. In the past every time she had done this, the whole household had erupted in a round of recriminations.

"Nu meriye, sunn!" her mother-in-law had softly lectured her several times, in a gentler tone than her words implied. "You have only one ammi and she will forever be your ammiji. Never forget that I am your elder uncle's wife, hence your tayi; so always remember to call me Tayiji, and nothing one else."

As Azam now recalled the incident, this encounter between the two women had somehow triggered a series of bitter exchanges between his elder brother and his father. Before anyone could take stock of the situation, the father had abruptly slapped his eldest son with such force that it had knocked him onto the ground, the sound of the slap echoing throughout the house and bringing everyone rushing into the room.

However, this had not been an isolated incident. Ever since Azam could recall, there had been in the relationship between men of the house a similar pattern of abuse and humiliation. Sometimes his father would raise his hand against his sons right in front of the entire family, their humiliation written in their wives' concerned faces, for once the bond of blood not mattering as much as the threat to their shared dignity, the simmering rivalries and resentments between them briefly overcome. Azam had grown up seeing his father beat their mother in front of all her children, and had felt powerless to intervene. And later, as she became the matriarch to an extended household of four daughters-in-law, it would also be the three grandchildren who would whimper at the sight of the jinn who had possessed their easygoing and adoring grandfather.

Out in the darkening street, long after Malhaara has moved away, Azam remains lost in thought. Something similar had occurred in the kitchen of his own home when he had for the very first time raised his hand to his own wife. That first breakdown had taken place around the similarly glowing embers of a hastily extinguished hearth fire.

In the apparent chaos of this moment in the street, Azam comes to a sudden realization. The world spins around him like a dizzying whirlpool. His abusive father is long since dead and buried, he is once again gainfully employed, and waiting back at home for him is his life's companion. He is tempted to turn his bike around and head for home, but loiters on, not yet quite ready to abandon his current train of thought.

In the preoccupied busyness and single-minded pursuit of the lone bat outside his doorway, the mute half-asleep horse heading homewards, the tragic circumstances of the late Mohammed Din's life, the industrious Malhaara at his self-appointed chores, and even little Kittu's innocent distraction, Azam realizes how each one of them, like wind-up toys playing out their latent energy, are set on a personal path and focused in on their destinies. And in the midst of this spiraling blur of human activity, he himself, assiduous and dynamic as any individual, has come to a grinding standstill.

He can, for the first time now, say it aloud to himself: The bastard is dead! Plucked in mid-sentence, his foul mouth opens to pour forth more invective on his hapless family; plucked, as it were, in vituperative mid-sentence. Azam is as alarmed as those around him by the vehemence of these congealing thoughts, emerging at last as irrepressible words from his mouth.

The bastard is dead! He says it out aloud as a self-affirmation. And Azam has somehow survived to see his father's head outlined beneath the shroud, a white gauze bandage clamping his jaw shut forever; the face turned in reverence towards Makkah to await his maker, and his entire life now parodied in the act of dying.

With the menace removed forever from his life, what was he, Azam, husband and lover, now doing out here all alone in the chilling dark of dusk, wandering aimlessly on a bike, reluctant to ease into the warmth and comfort of his own home? Somewhere, somehow, he must find the strength within himself to douse the embers that so unpredictably unleash the beast within him.

Once, at the local mela, he had seen her gums exposed in biting the crisp winter air in the pure thrill of the rides, as her squealing wooden carriage had lurched higher and faster into the sky on protesting axles; she, breathless in the rush, the checkered slicing of sunlight and shadows spinning faster and faster. In swirling past him, he had seen her teeth tear into a pomegranate, her stained lips slurping back the juice. He had felt his heart caught up in the exhilaration of the motion, his queasiness of tracking her in motion dispelled in the heady moment. He had been too timid to openly approach her or hitch a ride in the next carriage when it came time to pick up new riders, and she had paid to stay on. He had been content to just hang back in the shadows of the bare jamnu trees and observe.

That very same evening he had steered his ammiji's attention towards her, laying down the clues by which she would follow a week later to approach the parents of the girl. Guddho. His mother had initially tasted the word like a relish, hearing how its cadences fell gently on her son's ears. Guddho! Tasting the name for the first time on his own palate, he had squirmed in his nervousness and rushed out of the house, unable to bear his mother's teasing.

That was five years ago. Since then, he now wonders, what has been the sum of the days and nights of our married lives? And now that she was his, how had he been treating her? She, who has stood by him through all the abuse that has come to characterize their marriage, stoically sharing his misfortunes as she once had his early affluence and the sunshine of his undivided attention.

But she is only a child and needs to be disciplined, he reasons as the bike wobbles over the cobblestones, his inner turmoil heightened by the need for attentiveness to the path before him. In his hesitant progress, he is now approaching the point where the street narrows so that only a single person or a bike can pass through at any one time. Unwilling to encounter anyone else in the narrow space ahead of him, he finally decides to turn back, executing an awkward U-turn.

She is only a child, he thinks to himself, and I have treated her as only a child should be treated, his mind still shying away from the admission of reality to himself. Yet, in this newfound acceptance of his own culpability, he is now ready to gradually confront the guilt that has been growing in him.

She is only a child, he thinks, and I have treated her like a burr I casually picked up while walking through a field. Five years of learning to share a life, and here I am, indecisive and unsure of myself, wildly blundering about in an impractically narrow street. What am I doing here, awkwardly maneuvering my bike in clumsy half-circles?

Inside the house, Guddho is still busy in the kitchen, trying to salvage the day's dinner of mutton and potatoes that she left unattended for what must have been no longer than a minute, but which was long enough to sear the meat to a consistency of black leather. The pungent, lingering odour of the scorched mutton permeates every corner of the house. She realizes that it will also have drifted out into the street. Her first impulse is to get rid of the evidence by hiding it somewhere other than the kitchen. Perhaps she should tuck it under the bed, or spread it out on the roof so that the crows and house sparrows eat it up, and then run and hide herself from Azam's inevitable wrath.

Her dilemma lasts a mere heartbeat, the realization dawning on her suddenly of what she must do. As her mind races on ahead, her body trembles uncontrollably. As warm tears splash down the front of her kameez and onto the cluttered kitchen floor, she stands up determinedly and heads for the courtyard. Listening for the sound of the bike pulling up outside the door, she knows that no one will ever come to her rescue, and that she has no other option left.

She returns to the kitchen and picks up the wooden rolling pin, feeling its heft against her palm, nervously swinging it back and forth, practising getting the swing just right for that critical moment. Several minutes later, having steadied her breathing and now more confident than ever in her resolution, she listens intently for the clink of the bike chain behind the thin barrier of wood.

Mitti da baawa naiyo bolda, naiyo chaalda, naiyo denda hungaara. Nhaun laggi da khur geya mera mitti da baawa.

Malhaara Moving to the Sound of Water

Muqam Faiz koi rah meiñ jacha hi nahiñ
My heart, Faiz, could not approve of any place en route

There are certain days when the river sits quietly in profound contemplation of itself with not a ripple to disturb its thoughts. And then there are other times when it becomes as restless as a bead of quicksilver, para, that I hold in the palm of my hand, its eddies restlessly unfurling into lines that slant through each of my sunlit and ordained days. The bead twitches and quivers, splinters abruptly before my disbelieving eyes, slithers through my clenched fingers and shatters onto the ground. A moment of distraction is all it has taken to displace the perfection of its mirror surface.

It seems almost a lifetime ago that an ash-smeared sadhu sitting by the banks of a holy river squinted into the creases on my forehead then averted his gaze. He offered only these words in consolation: "With the river you will never know its beginning or its end; in every moment will be its dying and its rebirth." Had he divined, so early in my life's journey, the fact that in the fidgety, impetuous rush of water with a destination on its mind, I would live to hear the gurgling laughter of my children and my wife's first murmurings to our unborn child? That the quicksilver, para, would never be stilled; and I, with my focus momentarily shifted, would never be able to reclaim what I seemed to have so casually misplaced?

I comfort myself with the thought that this is how the resonant notes are muffled by water, that it is in a hurry and has somewhere to go. And I realize that Allah Miañ, in all his wisdom, upon sitting down to inscribe my kismet, probably decided instead to set it afloat on the surface of life's flowing waters — a kismet that in the form of a paper amulet adorned with holy verse would be ritualistically administered in exactly three gulps. The burden of this kismet now sits like an unanswered prayer bearing down on my soul, and comes tumbling down on me like landslide. Through my acts of atonement, I have earned my sorrows. Briefly distracted from my immediate concerns, my life becomes, momentarily, bearable. Give thanks for these temporary lapses of memory, these numbed hours of the cessation of pain, these passages of transient fevers that have flown like shadows over the landscape of my daylit hours.

Nowadays, the burden of my past weighs so heavily on me that I sometimes fear that I am becoming waterlogged, and must expend a greater effort to keep from drifting into the mouth of a vast dark cavern. As I kick my feet outward to stay aloft, I watch a school of inquisitive catfish rau, their elongated feelers inspecting the floating ash from the hearth of my collapsed house. The doors and windows, which I clearly remember having once locked so securely, have come undone from their hinges and are now soundlessly swinging in the current. I try to shut them tight and lock them, without success. The kitchen pots have been launched into the middle of the living room; our clothes are afloat and have come to life. Kelp and slime continue to multiply in the corners, and a school of minnows darts in cloudlike formations like a flock of birds rising on the wing in unison. Schools of sticklebacks dart through the ventilation slats high above one wall, and families of turtles lumber all across the floor of our bedroom.

Somewhere a dog is barking out its urgent message.

Awake once again, I feel the grains of sand clinging to the roof of my mouth; bright spears of light flash through the chinks in the door. The choking red dust storm is finally here, informs the part of my mind that is not quite numbed by lack of sleep.

Malhaara awakens from his restless siesta to the abrasive irritation of fine dust in his nostrils. However, it is late in the afternoon, and he knows from the pale hue of light that the storm has not yet fully expended its momentum. He has heard the wind rattling the loose windowpanes of the brick houses towering over his lean-to hovel. Soon it will be time for the prayer of Asr.

Seeing how subdued the natural light is, he considers stepping out to light the lamps somewhat earlier in the day, but then a part of him is already worrying about having to face Baba Feroze, who is going to be furious with him for having been so wasteful. He finally decides to slip back into his rumpled bed until the lilt of the adhan awakens him, and drifts back into an uneasy slumber.

Malhaara thinks: Once upon a distant sunlit afternoon, I awoke from a deep slumber to the bubbling sound of my infant daughter's laughter. I once heard my wife hum to herself idly at a domestic chore. I was once a father. I was once a husband. The sound of that laughter now sometimes slips through the azure sky and the blinding light. Disjointed phrases from that whispered lullaby resonate over the rushing waters. Yet there are other times when all I hear in the mumbled susurrus is the whimpering of these same children, and somewhere my wife is desperately calling out my name, somewhere a child is whimpering and his mother is crooning him to sleep, the lilt of her voice lost in the heedless rush outside her door.

And there, once again, is his wife's face hovering over him, shaking him awake: "The roof, the roof of our house is collapsing . . ."

He wakes to find his skin cold and clammy, and opening his eyes discovers that he is on his knees by his bedside, all the energy sapped out of him, the air sucked from his lungs. Malhaara hastily unfastens the flimsy door, flinging it wide open, and the room immediately fills up with an ochre powder. The tawny mutt that has been whimpering outside his door, slyly steps indoors, its tail busy in anticipation, delighted that Malhaara is finally awake and will now be heading out to make his usual rounds. As he trudges from door to door, handfuls of food will be offered to him, some of which will eventually find its way to the floor.

Instead of leaving the room, it watches Malhaara hastily shut the door and collapse onto the bed once again, his body racked by deep sobs. The beast lays its muzzle on the edge of the bed and whimpers, blinking its eyes. The door rattles in the onslaught of the cloud of red dust. The local neri, which had initially woken him with the hiss of a cobra, is urging him out of his bed again.

However, Malhaara's flow of memory drifts away from him and deposits him in another room by the banks of another river that has been overrun by the floodwaters. Barely audible over the drone of the dust storm, there now rides the plangent, plaintive singsong of the adhan, rising and falling like a banner in the wind.

A passing seller of glass bangles with his enticement of wangaN char-ra lo! is silenced for the duration of the call. The staccato tuk-tuk-tuk of the chakki continues uninterrupted, though, the beat punctuating the call from the masjid. Allah O Akbar, Allah O Akbar, the unwavering daily routine of calling out to one and all. A train on a schedule of five daily arrivals and departures, Malhaara notes sardonically.

Long before the onset of the seasonal monsoon, Malhaara has known that dust storms such as this one could last for days. During such times it would be sheer madness for anyone to venture out on their own, without taking the necessary precaution of telling someone else where they were headed. A person need only wander a few steps away from his own doorstep to become hopelessly lost forever.

Standing at his doorstep, he now watches a powerful gust of wind tear across the open ground. A restive wave of fine dust billows into wide swirls, a clumsy lumbering beast that deposits its load of alluvium in briefly settling on the ground, before hastily picking up its choli as an afterthought and whisking off to camp elsewhere. Through the murky, filtered sunlight, Malhaara watches the horizon dissolve into the haze. Now the dust storm swells itself into an even more colossal being, a jinn disturbed from its sleep, lifting its nimble fastidious fingers to seek out the secret recesses between the hinges and the door frames, the chinks in the wooden slats and matchstick blinds. The great leveler is seeking out the fault lines, redistributing its largesse generously yet unevenly over the land, blessing a nook here and a cranny there.

On a day such as this, Malhaara, itinerant fakir, resident folksinger, retired sitar player, and now the village's official lamplighter, will not wait for twilight to begin his chosen tasks. Having finally decided to descend into the prematurely darkened streets and light the twenty-odd oil lamps strategically mounted at street corners that are his domain, he is surprised to encounter the buffalo herd returning so early from the pasture. He must now press his body into the wall for it to pass. A somnolent horse that has been set free from its tether follows the herd. Even in the late afternoon's muted light, sparks fly wherever it's single loose horseshoe strikes.

Malhaara begins his circuitous route by first leaning his four-step ladder against a wall. He ascends it stiffly, gingerly reaching out for the lamp that is located closest to what for the time being he calls home. Stretched out before his eyes, his fingers move efficiently as he trims the burnt-out wick and tops up the oil reservoir, all the time cursing under his breath his back aching, his constantly having to reach out to remove stains from the smoke-mottled panes of glass. He discovers moths and other nocturnal insects have crawled through the ill-fitting glass frame of the lamp, slivers of their charred bodies fused around the wick. With the reach of the new electrical lines limited to the center of the village, Malhaara's work now stretches deep into the peripheral streets that must still rely on these ancient oil lamps. By the time he has completed his rounds, the unlit sections of the narrower side streets will be total darkness.

At the other end of his restive night, he lumbers once again half-asleep out of bed to return in the pre-dawn hours to retrace his footsteps and charily douse each lamp. Still busy at his task, he encounters Baba Feroze headed for the masjid, all bundled up in a woolen blanket, counting his rosary beads in one hand while the other holds a walking stick. They exchange perfunctory greetings. Malhaara's task will now take him past the outer periphery of the houses that are occupied by some of the shadier characters that continue to thrive on the fringes of this society: the insolent local entertainers called the pandis, the clandestine midwives, and the lean-tos where all newcomers unable to find any other housing are relegated. Here also is the dhera favoured by rogue males like some of Azam Karigar's nighttime comrades.

A week after the last of the dust has finally settled down and swept out of the clogged gutters, once again it is early dawn in the limpid light of a half-crescent moon. There is a lingering chill in the air as Malhaara emerges onto the streets, his mind this time focused on another one of his chosen tasks. Several of the mottled and scruffy mutts rise from the their individual perches on doorways to growl at him through bared fangs, and Malhaara, who carries a deep-seated fear of dogs since having once been bitten as a child, is wary of their presence. However, with the lamps all doused, he is intent on another mission and is not overtly threatened by their menace today. He encounters no other humans for the remainder of his trek, until turning a sharp corner near the outskirts, he almost runs over the slouched and slumbering figure of the night watchman. The Pathan awakens abruptly, blindly thrashing out his arms ahead of him, and spluttering verbal threats. Even in the dim light Malhaara can see the shiny green drool staining his chin.

Oy, its only you, Malhaara, he finally mutters in his accented Urdu, somewhat regaining his composure and reaching for the bejeweled snuffbox. See, I almost mistook you for a daku. You know, you cannot be too careful enough these days with all these robberies and Allah knows what going on. Only yesterday I encountered Sharifu at just about this time . . . sneaking his way out of Bhagga's courtyard, and when I reached out to grab him . . . but Malhaara has already torn away from his grasp and headed northward out of Kotli.

Walking briskly to warm himself, in a short while he is well beyond the furthest house of the Potters' mohallah. In the distance, he can barely distinguish the orchards of Chela, wreathed at this time in a blue haze of rising mist. This early in the day, the air is laden with so much moisture that layers of fine mist are beginning to peel off the ground, so that the distant trees and horizon all appear to be afloat. And towering over these even further in the northern background are the ghostly foothills of the Himalayas, also set adrift above the unsteady horizon.

More out of habit than necessity, Malhaara now amuses himself by counting out the five prominent peaks arrayed before him, now clearly distinguishable as they glow in catching the first light. However, he is immediately distracted from this diversion, as his destination has now come into view.

The surface of the body of water before him appears peaceful this morning. A wading bird is teasing up sustenance from the sludge along one receding shore, and a great white heron takes off in alarm at the unaccustomed sight of a human out so early in the day. Towards the middle of the expanse of the water that fills up his line of sight so that he must crane his neck to look away, the tiny lake appears to be exhaling in clusters of giant bubbles, the circular ripples stretching only a short distance from their source.

Malhaara scrutinises the margins of this natural pool carefully to get his bearings, this first sighting causing his eyes to blur with emotion. He is momentarily shaken by the sudden and profound sense of his own personal loss, and the aching void where there once resided love, and a fulfilled life of shared concerns. Whimsically discarding his open leather khusa at the edge of the water, he keeps on wading straight on until he is knee-deep, the slap of the cold water sending an involuntary shiver up his legs and backbone, even though his body, in its aroused state, appears to have barely registered the sensation. How many times has he relived this moment before, and yet he wavers before this important first step. Here, right before me, he realizes, is the final and vivid reality of my struggle to translate a wild dream into something concrete; this is how I shall subdue the daemon that possesses me in the early hours of the morning, and stymies me in mid-sentence, and chills my heart in the noon of a warm sunlit day. The mere concept of this is bigger, brighter, and more lucid than anything that I have ever dreamt or attempted. Does it really matter where the inspiration comes forth to possess me, this single-minded preoccupation that has kept me sane?

Until now, whatever Malhaara's fecund imagination had spun had become a reality for him. He had realized very early on in his journeys, that the most effective means of benefiting from his wild imagination was to in create a feasible situation, and then set out to achieve its reality. He would now need all his powers of personal motivation, for he had now set out to attempt was no less than the madness of a dream.

But no sooner has he voiced these thoughts that self-doubts begin to creep in to assail him once again. Where shall he begin his self-appointed mission?

The rapidly brightening sky, however, holds him enthralled, as he watches the faint blush of light race across the distantly illuminated snows of the mountain peaks. The first opulent glow seeps outward to define the horizon, and the night pads away on silent feet leaving the day to fill the vacated niche. The mellowed crescent is now clearly reflected in the pool, the glass surface continuing to gasp like a landed mudfish puffing empty air through its ineffectual gills. Swarms of swallows are already out feeding on wing, dimpling the mirror surface with their beaks. And Malhaara is surprised to discover that, out here too, wherever the dust has settled like a ghost, it has smothered all vegetation in its embrace. The fresh and gleaming waxen shoots of grasses that had until a few days risked slivers of themselves to the light are no longer distinguishable.

A number of opportune plovers and sandpipers dot the serenity of the opposite shore, and a resident titiri, a red-wattled lapwing, lands to perch on one leg within a stone's throw from where he stands, still knee-deep in water. Malhaara beams at the bird's peculiar roost, recalling how as a child he had learned that the titiri stands on only one of its legs because it fears the sky will fall, and by standing in this manner it can save itself and its chicks. In a sudden distracting flash of unexpected colour, a kingfisher swoops gracefully out of an overhanging acacia kikar branch, dips its wings, and homes in on the telltale ripples of the dappled skin of water. Now, with its meal secured between its bright emerald beak, and the wind ruffling its iridescent turquoise feathers, the kingfisher returns to its perch. As fish scales rain back onto the water, he wonders how something so utterly contrasting with its drab background and anomalous could have evaded his close scrutiny. The finger-long sticklers nervously return to feeding on the abundant mounds of dissipating cow dung, no longer wary of the menace of the singing light above them.

A sudden moist breath of air ruffles the water's edge, a wave of quiet sighing rolling over the hardy clumps of sedge grasses. This end of the pond is close to the ghats, the unused Hindu and Sikh funeral pyres, and has long been abandoned by humans as the dwelling of uneasy spirits. But then even a very cursory glance of the highly saline and fine clayey soil of the surrounding land would reveal to an untrained eye that it holds no potential for humans. And the only survivors to thrive here are the massive thickets of coarse crab and sedge grasses that have evaded the most persistent ungulates.

As the morning progresses, Malhaara has managed to retrieve the spade and pick axe he had hidden in these thickets, aware that here he is safe from all prying eyes and can work bareback, his salwar sleeves tucked knee-high, and his skin now glistening with sweat.

Unknown to him, though, word of his whereabouts has long since traveled the length of Kotli.

That crazy Malhaara, the entrepreneurial Bhagga conspiratorially proclaims to the men slurping glasses of chai at the khokha. I saw him yesterday in the morning on my way to Rana Saab's kothi. He was hacking away at the barren ground near the ghats as if a man possessed. I am sure he is somehow in collusion with that crazy Hafeez Tarkhan. In my opinion, both of them are seeking something buried near those siris. Maybe, all that single-minded singing about the promised but undelivered rains has finally affected into his head?

Though much later everyone was to remember exactly what he or she had been doing when Malhaara first set foot in their street, no one at the time knew exactly who he was or where he had actually come from. All they knew was that he had once been of a sound and educated mind and had had somehow landed in Kotli through circumstances of fate.

What they saw was a man who walked stiffly and yet behaved in a much more animated manner than anyone in his early fifties had a right to be; who was of average height, and always had an easy, ready smile that stretched lopsidedly across his mouth, so that under certain light he would appear to be snarling with the right side of his face. His short peppered beard was always kept neatly groomed and trim. Whatever turbulent life he may have lived before coming to us had drawn its history across the furrows of his forehead, the crow's feet framing his eyes, and yet his ready smile would linger long into the silence that followed the awkwardness of formal words. And, since he spoke a lot with his hands, there was one other feature that everyone noticed immediately: his right hand was badly scarred, with the thumb missing above the top knuckle.

In most of his truncated conversations, he appeared to have only a partial recollection of his own personal troubled past, revealing only that whatever it was that possessed him to abandon his home did not let him rest or sleep in peace. As a result of this affliction, he was also known to be an insomniac who managed to get by on barely two or three hours of fitful sleep each night. But these were traits of character he would only reluctantly reveal to anyone else, and though apparently voluble in his singing, he was otherwise a circumspect, silent man. He seldom trusted his own voice on emotional issues and other matters of the heart, choosing to leave unsaid that which mattered most; secure in the knowledge that what will endure will do so in spite of the heated exchange of words. And as a natural consequence of these personal traits, he had learned to trust in his own ability to quickly get to the very essence of things, seldom leaning on the crutches of formality.

These traits of character were also to ensure that he would remain friendless.

Since he always carried himself with such an easy and civilized grace, even when he was in the act of begging from street to street, his demeanour had been perplexing to those with idle time on their hands. They had seen him carry out odd jobs for whatever payment was offered. For one half of a harvest season he disappeared from Kotli, only to reappear, dark and tanned, and declaring that the persistent backache that had dogged him all his life was now completely cured. Another day, someone saw him bathing at a well and came back to report his amazement to anyone who would listen at how pale the rest of Malhaara's body was. There was also widespread speculation as to why Malhaara did not wear the loincloth tehmat or dhoti favoured by every fakir they had ever known, but was always seen in neat salwar kameez. Even the ease, with which he had managed to mingle with his patrons and bene-factors as equals, and without a hint of condescension or servility, had been duly noted and commented upon.

Just who does he really think he is, Bhagga had once demanded, while loudly slurping chai from another overflowing sauce, a Rajput Khokhar by birth, or another Rana Saab?

Emerging unexpectedly and erratically on the Kotli streets, Malhaara would begin by reciting the tried and true ancient verses of Sufi Sultan Bahu, and like the legendary poet of antiquity, in essence, a tangential figure, always blending into the shadows, and shunning the spotlight of all attention. Observing him in our midst, some of us who were sympa-thetic to his peculiar circumstances could readily divine that wherever fate had taken him, he had learned new tricks of trade to survive. His virtuosity at his chosen task would have assured him an edge over all his competitors. We also knew that at various times in his past he had suc-cessfully lived his days as a mendicant dervish, a spiritual leader, a music teacher, a lowly street beggar, and had once even posed as a gypsy. How long had he been wearing these masks, and perpetuating these myths before he became what he now was: Malhaara, a musical myth without a proper human name. We fondly recalled the aching in his songs about the rain and would thus learn to call him Malhaar, or Malhaara accord-ing to our local custom.

The name Malhaar had originally been the inspiration of Miañ Tan Sen, a musician of legendary fame during the Indian cultural renaissance of the sixteenth century, and one of the "nine gems" in the court of the Mughal emperor, Akbar. It was Tan Sen who, inspired by the turmoil of the elements during the monsoons, had created the raga Malhaar, also known as Miañ-ki-Malhaar. Legends of this serendipitous discovery abound. It is purported that with the aid of this raga alone, Tan Sen was able to summon the skies to douse the flames his rendition of Deepak Raga had ignited. Though Malhaara's efforts would have fallen far short of his guru's standards, there was to pour forth, from his equally prodigious mouth, a series of such evocative rainsongs, the likes of which, we the Kotli-wallahs, had never heard or would ever hear again.

During the period of two years that he stayed with us in Kotli, he learned to slip with beguiling ease in and out of our consciousness, as transient in his passing as the seasons. He was the wind honing its songs in roaring through the streets, and depositing its residue into the crevices gouged by time. To some he even appeared to be the ghost of a man who had lived another life but now inhabited this same body.

He had quickly learned to align his first tentative and faltering tunes to Bhulle Shah's epic verse in questioning his identity:

Bhullya ki jaana mein kaun?

Much later, he learned to switch from these self-questionings to the equally dense and effervescent kalam of Sultan Bahu, all the time fully aware that his listeners were sufficiently steeped in local lore and classical literature to fully grasp at all his allusions and references:

Dil dariya samundaron doonge, kaun dilaan di jaane hu . . .

The river of the heart is deeper than the ocean, who knows what resides in its depths.

Most of his time, though, during that last year in Kotli, was to be spent in the company of ghosts that like him inhabited the abandoned funeral pyres. These were such places that were seldom if ever visited or disturbed by any one of us. And superstition and folklore ensured that his sheltered hideouts would continue to remain as mysteries. He could then be whole again and emerge to join any one of the several armies of dervishes at the four dargahs of the local Pirs of Kotli's rich antiquities. Each of these dargahs commemorated a miraculous and celebrated healing, or an unexplained last disappearance, and in the case of the holy spirit of Pir Ghaib himself, a disputed recent sighting.

For a while it was from these dargahs that he would venture before us with his begging bowl, once again reciting the resonating verse of ancient Punjabi poets. In doing this, he was merely following a long tradition of Kotli's resident fakirs. No one now remembers Fakira's deeply furrowed face or his heavy beaded necklaces; how he would disturb everyone from sleep by announcing the arrival of the morning with his patchwork of local soulful tunes.

His successful reaping of Kotli's largesse had lasted several seasons before he was caught sneaking into a neighbour's house during the night. Similarly, the colourful mendicant malang, Saghira, the goat horn blower, who followed Fakira, lasted an entire summer. Perennially high on ganja, and draped in multi-hued rags and cowry shells, he would silently appear on your doorstep before tooting his horn, his cheeks bulging and eyes popping like that of a bullfrog, setting the street mutts on a fresh howling spree. He had had an uncanny knack for appearing at your doorstep just when you were washing up before a meal. Few now remembered how his downfall had come about; how the drugs eventually so addled his body that he would be completely out of breath by the time he entered the streets and the horn would be completely useless.

Now it Malhaara's turn as our resident fakir to sort in separate containers the gathered meals, of rice, curries and rotis heaped on him at the doorsteps at either dawn or dusk. The munificence of his hosts had once amazed him to such an extant that he had felt urged to repay this bounty. This is how he had one day stumbled onto a latent talent: his vast background in music that allowed him to refine his songs so that they offered some form of relief to his long-suffering benefactors. In an era of prolonged droughts he learned to promise downpours; where the sky was blue he painted gray clouds. And he set these themes to a clash of thunder only he could see coming our way. He promised us the moisture of heavens; the Manna of nectars, and morning dew multiplied a thousandfold; of rivers overflowing their banks into a desiccated and dying land.

It was in this refrain of flowing waters that he appeared to have stumbled upon an ingenious scheme to repay Kotli for all its hospitality. From this day onwards, he had told himself, the revival of the unused local Nehr Mardan shall become the central theme of my existence. He had daubed out the salient points of his scheme in broad, bold strokes of a river heaving in the grip of its waves, gushing southward from the foothills to distant royal gardens, and in the process circumventing the village of Kotli Loharan. With slight modifications to its path, the pristine, life-giving water would then be channeled for domestic use. It would even irrigate the surrounding fields, and in times of flood, the river would harness the monsoon's brute force and safely conduct it away downstream.

Imagine a river stretching as far as the eye can see. Colour it blue, the reflection of the sky, and upon it giant ships the size of cities. He picked up these threads from an overheard conversation with Babaji Feroze and his fondly recalled voyage to distant shores. Malhaara now blended these bits and pieces into the fabric of his narrative.

At first, the response to his optimistic message had been tepid. There were even murmurings about the state of Malhaara's mental health. But as the drought tightened its grip in the forthcoming seasons and distant rumours of clouds appeared upon the horizon only to fade, his delusions became the collective cross-pollinated dreams of the entire village, and blossomed in the eager fertile soil of their parched minds. His themes began to resonate as he continued to sing of torrents of water and towering curtains of rain drenching the soil, falling with equanimity on the dwellings of the rich and the poor alike, the adobe, thatch and brick. And soon enough he began noticing that his daily collection had gradually become more appetizing. There were now pieces of mutton and beef and even chicken where there had once only been gravy and vegetables. Even the rice had begun to look different, with each grain standing out on its own instead of a gelatinous mess he had become accustomed to.

Then one day, his nemesis, stout Bhaggas who had been hounding him every time he stepped into the latter's street, had even called him indoors to present him with a used but still luxurious woolen chuddar. To ward off the chill of these nights, he had said, laying a comforting hand on Malhaara's shoulder. And as the offerings grew, his songs became more elaborate and celebratory. He introduced lyrics from other songs, inflections of other voices, and rhythms borrowed from musical instruments.

But this success did not come about in the course of a single final season alone. At first, he had to spend countless mornings and afternoons in testing the waters with his voice. In the early mornings, he learned to shift into a refrain of a soothing, mellower note. All the birds are out there singing and yet you remain asleep, he proclaims:

Chiryañ bhol payañ, tenu jaag na ayee!

He would repeat the single verse at every turn of the street, pausing here and there to collect a coin, cautiously grasping it before it could roll into the side gutters. At this time in the morning, his singing sometimes also gleaned curses: Oy, Malhaara, shut up and let the cursed birds chirp for all they care! And undeterred, he would hasten on, somewhat chastened, the begging bowl now hastily tucked beneath an armpit. His remorse would last until the next street corner and seeing a new row of houses before him, he would regain his confidence and resume his song:

Chiryañ bhol paiyañ . . .

It was only much later in that first year that his singing began to come into its own, the torrent of his message delivered in an easy, undemanding manner:

Kotli-walyo, it does not rain anymore because we have forgotten our old ways, and the list of all our sins has grown long. The burden of these sins has grown such that the creator has decided to turn his benevolent face away from us, like a child who is bored with his all too predictable toys . . . and why does no one celebrate the rhythms of the earth any more, the change of the seasons, the days of planting and the days of harvest; why do mothers no longer sing to their unborn children, or people rely on healing themselves merely by prayer. I sing only of the promise of rains, and promise only the tidings of floods on the wings of monsoon breezes that rustle the sleeping seeds. I sing of the farmer scurrying to bring indoors his harvest scorched by the sun; I am the harbinger of thunderstorms that will turn your afternoons into night, and even the birds will hurry back to their nests thinking the day has ended. And the ants will return to the bosom of the earth, and the silken flags at Ronti and Mira Saab will flap noisily in the moist breezes. I sing of times still to come when the wheat stalks will rustle in endless waves as if swept by an invisible hand, and the sky fill with a descending haze, and the dust settle on the land before finally being washed away like all our sins.

This is my song, he would conclude, for once quiet and patiently awaiting the arrival of the odd child or servant or housewife bearing alms to seek him out at the doorstep, before proceeding to the next street.

It is only recently that his songs took a significant turn. They were now about the fleet bird of youth, the ephemerality of the hours allotted to humans, the transience of beauty, the cycle of wealth and poverty viewed as passages of sunlight and shadows playing over the land, and the conflict of purpose between man's well-laid plans and Allah's very own decree; of kismet, the rise and ebb in the tide of human fortunes. The songs were clothed in a stately verse that resonated in the breast even as it initially puzzled the listeners. They had heard these familiar themes before. Invisibly ensconced in the cool shade of their homes, behind closed doors, bamboo blinds and darkened balconies, or sprawled on sweat-soaked manjis, they would absentmindedly turn to swat flies, or cool themselves with woven cane fans. Malhaara's voice found the crevices and chinks in their barriers to heat to reach them. They had never been confronted before by a fakir who could beguile them with such original content.

By now they were weary from the months of drought, and they finally began to heed what he had to offer.

But by then, Malhaara's focus had shifted to other topics. His refrains were now set to the familiar folk cadences of Heer. It was instantly recognizable to the listeners, the improvisations now speaking of how love was a terrible thing to behold and to be gripped by:

The hakeem has a cure for the bite of the cobra
an antidote for the scorpion's sting
There is an amulet for Kali's evil eye
and a balm for every physical wound
A mantar for whatever spell Hadija can cast
over wayward husband and bored housewife
A cure for the churail's spell
and every possession by the jinn
But there is no escape for one who has been smitten
by the sidelong glance of the beloved
From the arch of her brow
no one heals!

The winter months in Kotli restrict life during the daylight hours to the top stories and the rooftops of the houses, as humans seek out the warmth of the sun. But now that it is early summer, the inhabitants have all moved back to the lower stories for the coolness and shade. Out in the streets, the shadows this late in the afternoon are harsh in bleaching all colour and the distinctness of textures. Flies buzz in throngs over patches of evaporating moisture. Inch long dark and angry, the ants are like polished splinters of coal. They scamper erratically in between the legs of equally restless week-old chicks that are busy marking the street with their scraggly curlicues. Cheeky house sparrows, magpies and opportune crows steal the diced bits of stale roti being tossed to the chicks, and menacing scarlet wasps explore the fissures in the crumbling houses.

Under the swinging arch of the noonday sun and its unyielding light steps Malhaara once again. He immediately crosses over into the shaded side of the street and finds that an overflowing drain blocking his path. A massive dun-coloured spaniel has joyously planted its backside into the running water, the dog's tongue now flopping at odds with the panting torso. With the flush and momentum of the newly shaped lyrics that have carried him this far now threatening to desert him, Malhaara is only able to regain his confidence after he has moved further down the street.

He proceeds cautiously, his neck aching from the constant scanning of the overhanging balconies and the raised doorways, knowing only that above him there are some listeners for whom this particular verse carries a personal message. He begins with his lament of Kotli's tragic diaspora, his voice now high pitched and nearly stretched to its limit by the emotional resonance of the lyrics. Once again, his words have undergone a miraculous transformation. This time he addresses the legendary craftsmen of Kotli and those of their loved ones who have settled abroad: Africa, England, Arabia, Iran . . . wherever the seeds have landed they have blossomed, and hard work and sacrifice have paid off. But the price of this success has been terrible upon those left behind, who must tirelessly wait for the footfall of a loved one at their doorstep. Shafiq, the sacrificial circuit, has been one such offering to Kuwait:

Hai ni maye kedi nazar lagi
Tera ladla Shafiq, koyet kha gaya!

And after this street, there are others with similar wounds to show and Malhaara will now pick at each of these, seemingly importune and perverse in his choice of subject of lyrical content.

When he comes to the recently built, three story, towering house of Saif Ullah of Nairobi, the verse has evolved into:

maye tera ladla afrika kha gaya!

and still further down the street it transforms into:

maye tera ladla valayet kha gaya!

Miañ Tan Sen may have seemed to be the original source of all his inspiration, but if you asked Malhaara to name a single person who was his hero, he would surely have named the Persian engineer Ali Mardan. A statesman, warrior, and more importantly for the Punjabis, an engineer, Shah Ali Mardan brought to the infrastructure of Northern India, the Persian genius of innovative water management. The introduction of the Persian wheel with its looped chain of buckets replacing the locally prevalent inclined slope and single bucket pulled by a draft animal had for centuries permitted extensive irrigation in Punjab. But without the engineering skills of Shah Ali Mardan at delivering pristine fresh water hundreds of miles far from its source, there would certainly have been no Mughal gardens in Punjab.

As the Governor of Kashmir and Punjab under the Mughal emperor Shah Jahan, it would be a testament to his skill and life's work as a water works engineer that would inspire Malhaara's final obsession and lead him to Kotli. And interestingly enough, he first heard of the man who was to influence the last two years of his life from a casual acquaintance in Lahore.

Late one spring, on a visit to Lahore's famous Mela Chiraghañ, which is held annually at the Shalimar Gardens, he had been admiring the efficiency of the water works inside the elaborately terraced facades. He had happened to express aloud his amazement at how these original engineering works had fared so well through the turmoil of the last three centuries. An elderly heavy-set man with a broad round face and drooping jowls, dressed impeccably in a light brown sherwani, who had been standing next to him, had instantly seized upon his sense of enthrallment, and guilefully introduced himself as Ibrahim. The man claimed he had been a former guide during the British Raj and said he knew all there was to know about the Mughal antiquities in and around Lahore. As they shook hands, Malhaara was struck by the similarity between the man ardently pumping his hand and our former late Prime Minister, Liaqat Ali Khan. At the time, Malhaara had no inkling of how drastically this chance meeting with Ibrahim Bhai was to influence the remaining course of his life.

Casually making their way over the length of the three garden terraces, Malhaara had been subjected to an impromptu but informative tour of the entire garden and its history. He had hung on to every word the guide uttered.

From the terrace, with unbridled, childish wonder, they followed the path of the water as it cascaded down a waterfall and into an elaborately carved marble slab called the Sawan Bhadon, the Season of Monsoons. Here the curtain of water poured out over the exquisitely carved scalloped niches that created a sound reminiscent of gently falling rain. Oil lamps had been placed in some of the sheltered niches behind the flowing water, and though it was still fairly bright, the overflow sparkled with an inner light as if it were itself the source of light.

At the end of an hour, with the tour finally over and Malhaara contemplating his journey back, Ibrahim Bhai had somehow let slip the fact that the water supply to these conduits inside the Shalimar gardens had originally been brought here by means of a canal that had been designed and dug up specifically for this purpose.

Wouldn't it have been simpler to pipe the water in from the nearby river Ravi? he had inquired, thinking that perhaps here again was another one of those elaborate myths that professional guides fabricated to lure unsuspecting tourists.

Oh, no! You see the Ravi water was even at the time of the Mughals so heavily silted and seasonally variable that it would have been impractical to run it through to these gardens. And even if there was an appropriate filtration system in place that could meet all the needs of these gardens, and you have to remember that initially there were five terraces instead of the current three, it would have been overwhelmed very quickly.

By then they were both standing outside the garden gates, and Malhaara was looking for a tanga to take him back, suddenly very conscious of the fact that if he stayed here any longer he would miss the last one available. However, Ibrahim Bhai was not yet ready to let his fascinating conversation end just here. Clambering aboard with Malhaara, and his tone of voice indicating imperiously that the tour was not yet over, he gave directions to the tangawallah to head for the monuments at Shahdara located on the outskirts of Lahore.

You see, continued Ibrahim, maintaining the unbroken thread of his conversation, the ideal terrestrial garden to Mughals was meant to be a representation of heavenly paradise with all its lush foliage, sumptuous waterfalls and gently bubbling fountains. And the most important ingredient of this vision was obviously water in its inseparable relationship with eternity.

This dilemma was resolved by a man who was also the emperor Shah Jahan's Governor of Lahore at the time. The Persian engineer, Shah Ali Mardan Khan, is also well known for his work on other Mughal buildings, especially at the Kashmiri Shalimar Gardens at Gulmarg. He was also responsible for the Delhi canal that runs between the Red Fort and the old city. To meet the demands of the emperor's beloved gardens at Lahore, the only solution was to bring the water in from river Ravi. And in order to do this, the prescient engineer chose a spot hundreds of miles upstream where it was still clear and pristine. The Nehr Mardan, or Mardan's canal that he designed for this purpose, would bring crystalline, unpolluted, potable water using a three-tier lift irrigation system. At places thirty feet higher than the surrounding terrain, this canal once stretched from the foothills of the Himalayas at Madhopur near Gurdaspur, and delivered the water directly to the Mughal palaces and gardens in and around Lahore. Filtration systems at Shalimar further purified the supply before introduction into the gardens.

As they alighted from their tanga outside a dilapidated but imposing octagonal mazar overrun by weeds, Ibrahim pointed out that this location was actually the burial site of the former Governor of Kashmir, Shah Ali Mardan Khan himself, who died in 1657 and was buried at the site alongside the graves of his mother and her maidservant. The grandly imposing, crumbling structure before them was in a state of total neglect. Malhaara noted that the area directly surrounding the grave appeared to have been heavily frequented. Soot covered one of the walls where an oil lamp had been left burning, and devotees had piled dry petals on top of the marble grave and lit incense around it. However, his lasting impression of the tomb was to remain forever linked to the sight of countless trilling swallows that nested inside the overhead crevices, as they tirelessly swooped in and out of the ruins in the late evening damp. The rush of air from their wings stirred memories of other such sites from Malhaara's past.

The two men offered their fateha prayers, and as they parted company, Malhaara promised to look Ibrahim Bhai up the next time he was in Lahore. Perhaps the next time they met, they would get to explore other similar Mughal antiquities. Only when he was heading back into the city did he realize that he had been left with the distinct feeling that he had somehow insulted Ibrahim Bhai by offering to pay for his services, which the old man had obligingly pocketed.

When it came time to leave Lahore, Malhaara felt once again sufficiently compelled to alight at Shahdara and revisit Mardan's tomb. Something in the decadent grandeur of that pitted architecture and the lovingly polished grave had motivated him to dedicate his life to chasing the dreams of a dead man, and once again trace the vanished manmade riverbed back to its source. He had been vaguely aware on that very first day, when he piled his belongings onto his back, that the pursuit of this illusive riverbed would only lead him upstream, and that perhaps, if he followed it long enough, it would eventually lead him home.

In the following weeks as he pursues his newfound obsession, he becomes the waters flowing over a vanished bed. In carefully surveying the terrain ahead of him, he anticipates the route of the Nehr Mardan. Malhaara's prodigious imagination channels its misplaced path, tenaciously extracting cues from the lay of the land, and seeking out any recognizable signs of the water's low pooling in the course of its flow. Becoming a snake, he slithers close to the ground, sacrificing every short route for the ease of flow. He holds the bead of para, quicksilver, in his hands and watches it creeping along the folds of his palm, seeking the easiest and least challenging means of flow; now more than ever conscious of only one fact: that he must circumvent all obstacles rather than clamber over them. He knows that his path must head forever north by east, and the barrier of the distant soaring parallel outlines of mountains must always be arrayed to his left, and the land must always slope gently upwards.

He practices repeatedly asking himself: If it rains, how will the water flow?

Even though almost three centuries of alluvium has silted most traces of the original canal bed and human greed has assimilated the rest, he remains steadfast in its pursuit. His path leads him past small towns perched precariously on hillocks that rise out of the flats, and he surmises correctly that each of these dwellings is built on the detritus of numerous ancient civilizations beneath the feet of the present inhabitants. He notes how each of these dwellings is conveniently close enough to the water and yet at a safe distance from the nonexistent banks. Sometimes he stumbles onto hamlets where only the mosque is built of brick and cement and the rest of the dwellings are of humble adobe, the best apparently having been saved for loftier adulations. Further on, there will also be habitations where the only firm dwelling is that of the local landowner and even the mosque is a sorry lean-to affair.

In routinely pausing for namaz, he would remember the spiritual lesson that every true Muslim carries within himself a lodestone buried deep inside his heart, always pointing to his true north: the home of his soul, the black silk-draped square rock of the Kaaba in Makkah in the west. Without the benefit of any visual clues or the sun to guide him, he spreads his prayer mat out and finds himself unerringly pointing westwards.

Following the path of a vanished glory, his path today crosses modern-day canals, tree-lined barrages, immense concrete siphons and span bridges, and now becomes a series of narrow dotted lines following parallel paths that appears and disappears at erratically. It surfaces here and there before receding completely underground or merging into the banks of a newly dug canal. However, by traveling thus, always west to east and in his mind plotting out the original route, within the space of a month he has reached the lands that Raja Rasalu had adventured through more than a millennium ago. Here for the first time he completely loses sight of the original canal amidst its ruins and the dry beds of seasonal streams. He digs deep down into the hardened clay until encountering the reassurance of dried green scum deposited three centuries ago, and then confidently continues his chosen task.

Then one day he comes to a town that appears to be more prosperous than any of the villages and hamlets enroute. Surrounded by lush fields of ripening wheat in this season, he is intrigued to learn that the inhabitants here have totally rejected the land in taking up a trade that involves skillful crafting of metals.

The river channeling through his dreams had finally picked him up and deposited him at our doorstep, like alluvium left behind by a departing flood.

Today the gray bleak day has descended upon Malhaara like a burial shroud, awakening him once again from the dark portents of a vision where his horizon stretches not only the length and breadth of the sky but even maps out its depth.

Once again, he has stumbled upon a lingering dream in which a flock of elegant, streamlined shore birds appears suspended in mid-flight over an immense and still body of water. The part of his mind that is still half-asleep surrenders to the comforting lilt of a languorous, laid-back rolling of still bodies caught up in the sweep of the wind. Thus the natural world, he reasons, must forever have existed externally under these impersonal skies, long before humans would unburden into it their self-loneliness and suffering. I know, he reminds himself, I am not yet fully done wrestling with my personal demons, and the delirium of my fevers has yet to run its entire course. My work, on this sphere, is still unfinished.

The nagging sound that has brought him back to reality from his restive siesta is the drumbeat of the tandora. And the only brief snatches of words he is able to latch onto from the commotion in the street is the name of Alam Lohar. He is instantly awake.

It seems that there is to be a musical stage play at Ronti grounds after the Maghrib namaz. Waris Shah's timeless classic *Heer te Ranjha* is to star the very talented legendary folksinger of singers: Alam Lohar! And accompanying him is his gaudy troupe and the female lead, Soraiya Khanum, posing as Heer to Alam's Ranjha.

Alam Lohar! Alam Lohar, the lohar who does not work with metal, except of course if you consider his trademark chimta a metal tool, is here for the first time visiting the world of master metal craftsmen. He has brought his personal brand of metal craft to Kotli for the total of five nights only, and his attendant retinue is now camped in the vacant space between the sterile mango trees of Ronti and the graveyard of jamnus of Mira Saab. Hurry now, for the paltry sum of only one rupee per ticket, one and all can watch the legendary lohar play the lead as Ranjha, the villains Kaido and Varisha, and even some of the other minor roles as well. Opposite him, Soraiya Khanum will star as the sultry heroine, Heer! And, yes, she too gets to join the chorus, as a jealous sister-in-law, and then as Heer's very own mother.

Malhaara snickers at the thought of all the hurried makeup and costume changes. He wonders who in his right mind could possibly keep Alam Lohar from donning the costumes of the entire cast, one on top of the other, and attempt the entire show as a solo effort.

When the show finally opens at dusk, the stage lit up by Coleman hurricane lamps, Malhaara, unwilling to part with price of the ticket, moves as far away from the curtained main stage as he can, to squat on an elevated platform beneath a giant pipal. From this distance, the star appears to him as a comical round figure in a ridiculously gaudy silk costume, as he openly flirts with his co-star to wolf whistles from the audience, a caricature of his own legend, the chimta held diagonally across the body like a weapon.

Alam opens the show with a Jugni; the wave of applause drowning out the human voice. The assembled audience knows exactly what to expect from this combination of chimta, dholak, ghunghroo, ektar, bansuri and voice. Stepping frontstage, Alam Lohar recites the opening few verses and then steps back briefly, to let the dholak and bansuri dominate. Then he reemerges with the next verses. As the show progresses, his limitless repertoire of folklore and local tunes puts the vulgar mirasis and even Malhaara to shame. The voice and the accompanying chimta beat soar into the overhanging branches of the pipal. A sudden shake of his oily locks marks each punctuated bow of the head and the end of a stanza:

Bol mitti diya baawya, tere dukha ne maar muka ya . . .

The singer's inventory is still unexhausted a full hour later, when, after having wowed and eventually fatigued all the fickle frontline thrill-seekers with his line-up of proven favourites, Alam launches into the the epic adventures of the local Robin Hood, Dhulla Bhatti. This is followed by the classical verse of Miañ Mohammad, Bhulle Shah and Baba Farid. Each heavily nuanced word of the venerated poets is passionately held up on display, tirelessly tapped out on the chimta, and eagerly lapped up by the audience. A few stragglers seated at the backbenches groan and leave to crouch behind the cloth-wall barriers and light their bidis.

It is at this point, with his audience now more receptive, that Alam Lohar is ready to launch into Waris Shah's perennial tragedy of the showpiece for this night: *Heer te Ranjha*. And a full two hours into the show, with the entire cast assembled onstage, it becomes obvious that the seasoned and astute performer has saved his energy and the best for this very moment. At the end of it, the deafening applause rises up from the dust into the vacant night sky, and fades.

After that first night's virtuoso performance, a part of Malhaara had even been tempted to join up with this ragged troupe in whatever capacity he could, and leave Kotli forever behind. However, he had felt sufficiently repelled by the sycophantic retinue of hangers-on and the constant feigning of predictable audiences to stay behind and continue with his unfinished mission.

A week later, in the final parting, Malhaara was left with a vague image of Alam Lohar toiling as a majestic beast and casting a colossal liquid shadow across its chosen horizons, and lumbering fluidly on, uncaring and unmindful, of the undergrowth of leeches that are siphoning off its vital lifeblood.

By then Malhaara had also moved out of his hovel and was now living amongst the dervishes at the tomb of Mira Saab. Throughout this final chapter of his life, he gravitated as far as he could from the stratified hierarchy, the obfuscation and obscurantism of the cult of piri muridi prevalent at these local dargahs. Perhaps it was the result of a residual memory of once having overheard a malang address another as seli or girlfriend, unwilling to accept that most supplicants approached their creator as a beloved. Among the ingratiating pseudopirs, the ash-smeared fakirs and the tilak-bearing adherents of the uneasy fusion of Bakti culture assimilated into the ascetic Sufism, he always stood out as too modest in his ambitions. No one was convinced that he was ready to forsake the world of other humans just yet, and as a result, he was to remain restricted to the fringes of each such group.

In staying with the dervishes at the tomb, he would begin to emerge before them only at the time of the langar being opened, seemingly reluctant to linger or mingle with anyone else. Oftentimes, on a Thursday or Friday evening, the offerings would consist of a small degh half full of the sweet concoction of molasses and rice that was served to everyone on a pipal leaf. He shared in none of the dervishes' anxiety and fervent hopes that the faithful, who had brought them the offerings of new clothing, had also brought along another degh of sweet saffron fried rice or zarda. This one would be horded for distribution later on only to the truly faithful.

To one side of the entrance of this tomb are the living quarters, and there is a small raised circular platform of brick. This serves as an impromptu stage for the qawwali performances that mark the annual Urs, literally in its celebration of the marriage of the Pir to his creator, and the two local melas that held at the nearby orchard. During these few celebratory days, there is always a tumultuous rush of human bodies as they pass through the narrow pathway to the tomb. The devotees offer lighted incense; and sometimes, in the rush of compacted bodies, they are merely content to caress the outside wall, or kiss the ground close to the main gate and return home. The air is filled with the pungent decay of marigolds, drying rose petals, and the decay of the wedding saheras offered in dedication.

On these auspicious evenings, the fakirs, malangs and other mendicants, viewed by many as pagans in their rituals, and not permitted inside the shrine alongside the pious dervishes, are content merely to be able to perform their adulations outside the main entrance gate. They too gather beneath the pipal. Bowls of milky concoctions of ganja and bhang make the rounds and add to the revelry and the carnival atmosphere. A desiccated man dressed head to toe in green, his face flushed from the pipe he has been puffing, extracts a coiled goat horn from the voluminous folds of his dress, and blows the smoke in a hoarse strangled croak that drowns out the tumult.

A carpet has been spread out on the platform and a band of qawwals arrives to squat in a semicircle before the restive gathering audience. The first punctuated clapping echoes up into the hollow dust-choked interior of the overhead pipal branches. The rattle alarms the monolith's single nocturnal occupant; the lone bat hurriedly beats an early departure. Refrains patched from the words of the saints are passed from hand to hand throughout the chorus. Subtleties of Sufi mysticism, the sonorous naats to the last prophet of Allah, the profanities of popular romance; all intermingle, as the qawwals switch freely from the classical to folk and then to the secular, and end with the profoundly mystical. By midnight, the resonant Sufi chants are replaced by other staples at such gatherings: words of Nizamuddin Aulia and Hazrat Datta Gunj Bakhsh merge and blend, until finally fetching up with the perennial favourite, the verses of the father of the qawwali, and India's venerated renaissance man, Amir Khusro.

Perched on a tree limb above the motley crew of seven qawwals, Malhaara notes that only one of them is bearded.

Gradually, the frenzied and gyrating devotees all drift away into stupor or fall asleep. A listener swaying to the music in the front row collapses in the dust in the grip of an inner ecstasy, the state of spiritual bliss, the wajjad. He is gently lifted and carried away to lie on the string manjis until his fit passes. With the night beginning to cool, fires are lit in front of the unstinting qawwals and the flames now leap in unison with their clapping. The chants weave complex rhythmic patterns, each stanza held up for examination before the still unsated appetite of the audience, and repeated to the accolades of Wah! Wah!

Finally, an hour before dawn, on an unseen signal, perhaps an inflection of the leader's chant or a slowing of the beat, the exhausted qawwals wind up their act. They hastily bundle up their instruments and, brushing their clothes, gather up the coins tossed before them in the dust. They troupe now heads for home in the dark. Malhaara, too, awakens to find the area around him completely deserted, except for a stray dog eyeing him with its head rolled sideways.

Later in the day, on his way out to the lakeside to check up on his previous day's handiwork, he encounters a scrum of vultures. The ungainly squabbling birds are gathered around the carcass of a dead calf that the chamar has discarded in a low depression of land that was once a part of the Nehr Mardan. High overhead, the vortex continues deep into the sky, with one bird dropping out of formation and triggering a shower of others for miles. He averts his eyes from the scimitars of claws and beaks tearing into the tender hide.

The time for him to move on is once again close at hand.

Malhaara had been in Kotli for nearly three months before realizing that he had not yet seen it rain even once. And the only time he had actually seen a clouded sky had been on the day Labha had received his letter and a mist had descended from the sky and left the ground completely dry. He had never seen such an amazing natural phenomenon before in his entire life.

As the months of drought wore on, they brought the wild boar out to raid the unripe and wilting wheat crop. One day, Azam Karigar, on his way to the fishing waters of the old canal, discovered his path blocked by a family of cobras heading for the cool moistness of the diverted riverbed. Jackals, emboldened by their desperation, had also become less flighty at the sight of man, and the pehredar reported witnessing a truly rare sight: a pair of hedgehogs scuttling across the street cobblestones at night. To the weary watchers of the sky, these were surely signs that life as they knew it, was nearing its end, and surely the Day of Judgment was now drawing close.

By common consensus among Kotli's elderly males, a Friday afternoon was selected as the most auspicious day to offer a special prayer for rain after the Jumma namaz. Now, with all the men gathered at the masjid, Baba Sultan opened up a path down memory lane in recalling that he had attended such special prayers only twice in his entire life. The last time had been when he was still a burly youth of about fifteen.

We were still in the masjid, he recounted, when the first raindrops began to fall. And then it had continued to rain for sixteen straight days and nights. I even managed to swim in the pond where Bhagga's new haveli stands today. We had to later on peel off dozens of leeches that had glued themselves all over our legs and feet, and were able to continue fishing for kingar and dholis for months in all the local pools. In the chaos of the ensuing floods, my cousin Sohail passed away, Ina lila he . . . and we could not dig a grave deep or dry enough to bury him before it would flood with water. We finally ended up wrapping his body tightly in chuddars and kept it stored in our kotri till the waters receded. That season, the floodwater actually touched the doorsill to Shah Halvai's sweetmeat shop, and we . . .

It had been difficult to put a stop to this torrent of memories from an old man who could remember every trivial detail of his childhood fishing trips, yet would often fail to recognize his very own children. And Maulvi Saab, in drawing the congregation's attention back to their current predicament, had loudly declared that after pondering over the strange phenomenon of last week's mirage of dry rain, which Subhan Allah we had all been witnesses to, he had concluded that this was Allah

Kareem's way of further testing the resolve of us mortals. We aligned our rows facing the west and began our fervent prayer for rain.

Emerging from the masjid under the harsh bright noon sky, we immediately began scanning the skies for signs of cloud cover. And during that first night, some of us took to climbing atop our rooftops to gaze longingly at the faint distant flicker of lightning as it flashed tantalizingly at the base of the foothills to the north. Sometimes, a moist teasing breeze would even carry the faint drum roll of a thundercloud.

The tantalizing glimpse of that distant rainstorm now began to percolate into the landscape of all our shared dreams. But our patience was to be tempted for one more week. And then we would awaken one final dawn to the searing crackle and sizzle of overhead lightning, and the sight of our sky smeared gray as if by a dirty cotton rag. And on this day, the muezzin ascending the rickety ladder to the top of the masjid to sound the adhan would lose his voice and end up instead beating in his excitement the tambura with both his bare hands. And the Kotli folks, still half-awake, would not know whether to begin their fast or end it, since the tambura had only been known to be sounded during the month of Ramzan. And this was definitely not the month of Ramzan.

Our world now to be rudely shaken and rearranged by forces we believed we had unleashed upon ourselves.

The first signs of the coming turbulence are the rustling of the grasses. Overhead static jumps from charge to charge, a flickering quivering flame that leapfrogs from one density to another of condensed vapor, alive and restless, fickle, favouring a node here, a spark there; the mass of clouds collide like giant brimstones. The resounding crackle and its reverberations fade away gradually. The prayed-for maelstrom that had percolated through our collective dreams, and of which Malhaara had had us dream for so long, had finally arrived!

Standing idly for once at the periphery of the pool and anxiously contemplating the effectiveness of his recently completed task, Malhaara also welcomes the approaching storm. The humid wind has picked up the scent of the wilting transplanted rice shoots. In the shade of the bulrushes and reeds, the famished catfish wriggle deeper into the oozing mud. A solitary stork alights from the shade of the poolside kikar with

191

barely a wing beat and briefly chases its reflection across the reflected sky of the shriveled pool. Malhaara recalls a dream of floating shorebirds.

The blades of grass stir underfoot and shed some of their powdery coating of dust. By now, the horizon in the distance is a blur of motion that is rapidly sweeping forward. Craning his neck to get a better view of the ragged layers of clouds racing overhead, Malhaara feels a dizzying disorientation, a sensation one gets when looking down from a boat or a bridge and the rushing waters below seem to be standing still while you race over them. The commotion around him is momentarily hushed, the moistness of mud smelled and tasted before the first signs of the darkening earth are actually seen. Then the onslaught begins in earnest. The first splotches of dark tan mark the ground at his feet. Instead of turning around and hurrying to take shelter, he eases himself out of his clothes. Uninhibited for once, he plants his feet firmly against the wind, and reaches upwards with his raised arms as if tempting the distantly crackling flashes to find him. He is greeted by a deafening roar that makes his statically charged hair stand on end, as droplets the size of fingernails pelt his weathered, upturned face, his pale shoulders, the tanned skin of his forearms, his sun-bleached hair.

Wherever the droplets crash into the powdered dry earth, they send up miniature mushrooms of dust that rapidly lose their individuality in the uniformity of mud. In a short while, the crackled texture of slush has merged completely into a smoothly churned and homogeneous layer that has the consistency of butter. The rain now descends as sheets of glass, and wherever there was air, there is now only water. A million bejeweled crowns erupt to dimple the surfaces of impromptu lakes that have become seething cauldrons. Rivulets pool and overflow their natural barriers, and with the sluice gates set fully open, the brick walls of houses are stained a deep ochre and the mildew left in sharp contrast; the overflow overwhelms the drains.

At times such as these, Malhaara had listened to the rain and wondered what it would remember. The path of past downpours, the rainsongs of the muddy rooftops, the overflowing drains and gutters, the remembered flow of street rivulets and streams, the heady rush for union in the pooling of individual torrents? Whatever it remembers seeps into its character and in its sighing and susurring the rivulet streaks down remembered pathways.

Malhaara had sung to us of the shape of the word "Paani" and how it rearranges our internal landscapes. For the next several days, it would also shape the reality of our dreams, making this land possible, and also making life on this land impossible. Out on the road, the oxcart's wheels spin ineffectively, unable to secure a firm footing in the yielding ground. And no one is willing to risk racing their charges during this soggy time. Even the tangawallahs' workhorse must stand by idly fettered.

In the brief glimpses of sunlight offered in between the pounding showers, mists rise and peal off the earth and its vegetation in blanketed layers. Opportune lichens and slime moulds saturate the air by spraying clouds of multiple spores. A hardy jamnu seed that had been washed down a narrow drain almost a season ago has now lodged inside a wall crevice and sprouted a mini waxen miniature of its parent. Orchard fruit trees topple over. Water from the local wells tastes of fish and forests of adiantums send their heart-shaped leaves out from the well interiors and thrive in eking out nourishment from the filtered light.

In the absence of light mushrooms continue to thrive. Suffocating tendrils of moss promptly line anything left unmoved for long. Amorous, peripatetic bullfrogs throb in hormonal rivalries, emerge into the fields to drone bubbles of belly-deep love calls. Late into the sultry nights, their tireless roguish booms echo as they flop from one new pool to another, raggedly persistent in their quest for mates, maddened by an orgiastic celebration that once again reaffirms life. Mudfish slither out of the ooze and gasp mouthfuls of moist air. Panicked grass snakes emerge to slink deep into dry hollow tree trunks. Slugs thick as fingers seek out the undersides of sturdy broadleaves, the ubiquitous ants disappear underground and the chorus of crickets and cicadas are for once completely silenced.

And no birdsong is heard, except for the koel that will now mate and lay its eggs in an unsuspecting host's nest.

The pooling rainwater that had initially been clear and crystalline for the first week of rains begins to cloud over. It is now blended with the floodwaters that have overflowed the banks of seasonal streams and rivers and reshaped the surrounding miles of landscape. The muddy water roils in bursts of cauliflower heads, the suspended sandlike folds of silk that mushroom and dip, form and re-form; tirelessly in a state of flux, lapping and exploring the edges of a softly jagged world.

The rise in the water level, which had been imperceptible at first, creeps higher each passing day as the banks of larger river are breached. Churning ceaselessly, the floodwaters are deceptive in their depth, tyrannical and willful as a ruler redrawing the map of its domain; conquering or reclaiming lost territory, fortifying its many conquests. Word seeps in that further upstream the river Tawi has breached through the final defences of its fortified five-story-high embankments. This is emulated by the Aik, and then the Palkhu, as both these seasonal streams openly pour into the fields, the rising waters sweeping everything in their path. Malhaara's deserted lean-to collapses under the constant onslaught, as do several other mud houses with rain-weakened foundations. The entire top three stories of the mildewed house left deserted on Hakeem Shakeel's street collapses during one night, the abrupt collapse sending a shockwave through the neighboring walls so that Shakeel wades out to the end of the flooded street to see if anyone is hurt. The entrenched inhabitants of neighbouring houses move to the higher stories.

With school out for the summer, Kittu, who at the time is still living with his mother, has long been anticipating the coming of this selaab. As soon as the belated monsoon had begun in earnest, the roof of their single room house had begun to leak, and he had excitedly helped his mother move the bed closer to the door, placing a bucket and several rusted pots and pans under the multiple drips. Watching the drains at the end of his gully begin to backup and inch closer to their doorstep, it now becomes his daily chore to keep his mother informed of the daily march of the water level. And today, it has finally reached the pakore-wali shop at the mouth of their street, and now the goldsmith's, he informs her, often too excited at the prospect of the selaab so close at hand to hold still a moment longer.

In spite of the havoc the floodwaters have wreaked, they have restocked the local ponds with fresh fish, and Kittu and his friends are kept fully preoccupied during the lazy rain-filled afternoons. The four major pools adjacent to the Eidgah are teeming with stickleback kingars and multi-mustached catfish called dholis. A seemingly endless supply of sluggish turtles keep grabbing onto the earthworms dangled before them, and Kittu keeps cutting them loose and tossing them back into the water with the hooks still sticking out of their mouths. Sometimes he manages to sneak his mother's muslin chunni out of the house, and with the help of a few friends is able to fill a small bucket full of hundreds of brightly darting fry. His mother then deep-fries these in batter to make his favourite dish of poong pakoras that Kittu gulps down while still piping hot and dripping with oil.

On such days as these, he will warily accompany his mother as she sets off to work, proudly offering to guard her from all the grass snakes that may threaten her along the way. Hugging the edges of solid dry ground, he now clings nervously to the hem of her dress. She will eventually dislodge his grip and gently nudge him back to the house, while she wades into the open water and heads for Rana Saab's Peacock House.

On the fifth day of the floods, the river Mardan comes back to life, flowing freely and washing away whatever human obstacles it finds placed in its path.

Kittu and his mother awaken to find that the muddy water has finally stepped over their doorsill and poured into their entire courtyard, and in the process has demolished their clay hearth. The house sparrows that nest under the roof and have somehow survived the onslaught of Kittu's target practices now descend to splash noisily in the water. He watches them raptly for an hour as they fluff up their feathers and roll beads of water off their backs. Before he can tire of this distraction, his friends gleefully wade into the house, not a word being exchanged as they drag him off.

Even though it is still very early in the day, a newly formed playground awaits them where the open Dara-tul-Aman grounds had been until yesterday. Kittu and his friends notice that loose wood planks are floating out from Hafeez Tarkhan's workshop and are being washed away in the water flow. They salvage as many of these as they can to hoard until it is dark for what they have planned. Then they all strip down, giggling at each other's nakedness, and in their nervousness toppling each other into the muddy water. They push away from the submerged staircases and float off towards open water, swimming and diving with total abandon. Suddenly aware of the increasing tug of the rising tide, they rush back to where the water is shallower. Their distrust of this fast rushing water is ingrained, and they have learned to keep out a wary eye for snakes that are skimming over the water surface or clustered on floating tree trunks. Unseen to them, leeches anchor onto their ankles or shins and have to be later teased off by the application of a lighted cigarette.

The boys leave only when they are totally exhausted and their limbs have begun to wrinkle like prunes. Extracting the dresses they had tucked into dry, overhead niches, they giggle and point at each other's shriveled organs. Chawaray! Chawaray! Shahid hollers, alluding to the dried dates served at weddings.

It is completely dark when they return to the water's edge once again, intent on a rare mission. The clay oil lamps that have been stolen from the walls of the local shrines are now lit one by one. And once all the lamps are lit, these are crowded onto planks and gently nudged afloat, one at a time, to sail into the dark with the only sound that of the rushing water. The flickering flames fade into the night as the planks overturn or are swept out of view.

At the end of the week, with the water's havoc having played itself out with all the schemes, hopes and machinations of men, there is a guarded optimism that the tide is finally beginning to turn in their favour. There is also renewed respect for the foresight of ancestors who placed the masjid at the highest point of the reach of the floodwaters, and not merely for it to tower over all the houses and be visible for miles around.

But we were soon to discover this was to be an unusually prolonged monsoon for us, and one that we would not so easily recover from. With the Nehr Mardan now flowing freely, it brought even larger volumes of water in close proximity to the center of the village then it had ever been known to. And after ten days of flooding the water level was still rising. As we surveyed the surrounding villages, we realized that although the water had already begun to drop elsewhere, it was still pouring into the Nehr from all the surrounding fields. With more and more water pouring into the Kotli streets and houses, there was now no available means of egress as the Nehr Mardan had been shored up and reclaimed for land use further downstream. Something had been drastically altered in the surrounding landscape without our having been aware of it.

It would be much later that we would discover telltale signs of Malhaara's digging and subsequent weakening of the intervening barriers of earth between the surviving sections of the Nehr Mardan. And how he had managed to revive the canal of his dreams, even if for the short period of two weeks, and in the process nearly destroy Kotli forever.

During this time, the foundations of many of Kotli's original houses gave way and the clay roofs and walls collapsed. However, this may have been partially due to a design fault in the buildings itself. Each of these houses had walls that had originally been built by sharing the wall next door, so that only half of each roof rested on its own slim outer brick walls. Thus, in crashing to the ground, each of these roofs brought the neighbouring ones down. In the ensuing chain reaction, about twenty families were made homeless and were temporarily moved to the masjid. Fortunately, no one was known to have been caught unaware in the destruction. And it would be another week before the waters would begin to recede and leave behind a village in total chaos. The heaps of slush and mud that had clogged all the drains now littered the streets, and the stench of dead fish lingered everywhere.

A month later, with Malhaara's disappearance still an oft-pondered mystery, the weekly sabzi mandi is once again in full swing. A vegetable vendor from the border town of Chaprar overhears Malhaara's name repeatedly mentioned in the local gossip.

Was this missing Malhaara ever known to play the sitar? he inquires from the owner of the neighbouring stall. You see, there once used to be a very peculiar man by that name in our village . . .

A sitar player? No, no! Malhaara could only play the tabla and badly at that, given his deformed right hand. He could sing, though. Subhan Allah, what a voice! You could hear him all the way across the Kotli rooftops. He was here for about two seasons only before, he left our town of Chaprar, such a long time ago, for the city of Sialkot to learn to play his sitar. I can recall his name so clearly now because of a cruel twist of fate that so completely shattered his life that he was never whole again. Soon after he returned from his training at Sialkot, his entire family perished within a single night of floods while he was away shoring up a breach on the flooded river Tawi . . .

His account of that fateful night is now interrupted by the first widely spaced raindrops of the day that crash into the caked soil.

In those days the river used to wipe out whole swaths of our village each year, before we relocated to higher ground. I remember it all clearly now. The poor man's wife and children, I think he had two or three children, I forget now how many, were all swept away when their house collapsed on top of them. After the tragedy, Malhaara sort of drifted away from all his relatives and friends.

The scattered shower begins to drench the ground, and the narrator pulls up a gunnysack to cover his head, before continuing with his recollection.

This must have been about seven or eight seasons ago. Do you think this man you call Malhaara could have been the same person? The name Malhaara is unusual as it is . . .

At this moment the downpour intervenes in earnest and the vendors hastily cover up their produce with woven mats, and in dispersing take shelter under jute sacks or huddle close together at the foot of the pipal tree.

Nearly two hours later when it is late afternoon and the sun returns to peek through the clouds, the market is hastily broken up and the uneven grounds left deserted for the day. Rainwater seeps underfoot, the top layer of mud beginning to harden and cake once again. A fresh breeze rustles the pipal leaves stripping them clean of beads of water.

Gradually the evening blends to dusk.

In the streets, where the oil lamps have long been left unattended, awaiting their replacement during the next phase of the expansion of the electric lines, darkness descends. The steady *tuk tuk tuk* of the flourmill is finally silenced, and wreaths of hushed blue smoke arise from hearth fires and are whipped up by the wind.

In a darkening portion of the nearby Nehr Mardan, a flash of lightning becomes a silvery rau the size of an angler's forearm, as it leaps clear out of the water, rapidly receding from its own reflection, writhing and hovering in midair. The sky becomes an even dark cerulean bowl inverted above the earth, and the earth is a dark cerulean sapphire bowl placed below the sky; the water's reflection of itself, a dialogue, a bright flash of indigo light. The dimpled surface tests its elasticity, finds its equilibrium, and in seeking its level once again becomes once again a mirror. With the burnished fish suspended at the zenith of its flight, time is also suspended. And as the brief flash of silver collapses, it is immediately enveloped into the warm waiting embrace of its own perfect reflection.

Far away in the foothills of a mighty mountain range, whose faint outline of snow-capped peaks floats ethereally in midair, a distant thundercloud rumbles, the waves of sound surging over the land that is already quivering in its anticipation.

Once the floodwaters had crested and then receded, this time the body of water left trapped inside the Nehr Mardan was greater than it had ever been before. In fact, this reservoir would last well into the next season of floods when it would be further replenished. The fickle town folk had by then gone back to feeding the fish with their prayers kneaded into flour pellets, and Shafiq and Malhaara were becoming distant myths.

The schools of illusive rau, brought in by the floods and trapped by the embankments, would grow to legendary proportions to taunt the local anglers. Their reprise, however, would eventually come to an end five years later, when a passing column of soldiers would end it all with the casual toss of a hand grenade.

The tragedy of that distant flooding of Kotli would be diluted over time and enter into the stuff of legend. And so would Malhaara, who had known like all similarly inclined men before him, the local concept of Parya mela chadh jaana—that one must depart the carnival of life when it is at its peak.

After all is said and done, what else is the sum of a man in the final reckoning but the essence of all his aspirations and his actions, an effervescence of all his fevers and evaporating humidities?

For those of us who are left behind, Malhaara's story remains suspended between the two notes that only time shall conjoin: the paa' and the ni.

Maqaam Faiz koi raah mein jacha hi nahin,
Jo kue yaar se nikle to sue daar chale.
My heart, Faiz, could not approve any place en route,
Forced out of my love's street, I made for the gallows straight.

Selaab . . .

This inspired flood of memories could not have been put down on paper without the unstinting support and encouragement of my family: my beloved Nina and our children Salman and Farrah. Thank you all for your nurturing love, creative energy and radiance.

This book is a tribute to the spirit of my parents' enterprising generation that triumphed over adversity by sheer resilience and sacrifice; to those wise men and women who were able to fluently quote verbatim passages in Arabic from the Quran and follow these with elaborate translations in moments of moral rectitude, and, when moved to do so, would tearfully quote the classical Urdu and Farsi poets, and yet were unable to read or write a single word of their own mother tongue.

For their inspiration: Thanks to Mohammed Amin and Manzoor Sahib for their wit and wisdom and their help in retracing the culture and history of Kotli; to Khalid and Marit Mughal, who read the first tentative drafts of some of these stories, for their patient and invaluable criticism, guidance and encouragement; to my brother Arif Suleman Malik and sisters Saeeda, Tahira and Zahida; to my friends Fayyaz Zaffar and Ihsan Piracha; to Farooq and Tillat for memories of simpler times in a younger Kuwait; to SASIALIT for an online education no classroom can ever deliver; to the hallowed ground of Vancouver Public Library for the peace and quiet and a vacant desk on summer afternoons; to the invaluable online resource of the Academy of Punjab in North America (apnaorg.com) for the overseas revival and promotion of

Punjabi literature; to Bill Clive for his informative web page on SS *Dara*, and his help in locating a copy of PJ Abraham's excellent account of the Dara tragedy, *Last Hours on Dara*, and for his offer to personally locate the book's untraceable author; to the co-author, Peter Padfield, for permission to quote from the book; and to TR Aashi for material from his forthcoming book, *Birds of Pakistan*.

And last but not least, I am indebted to my editors and publishers Nurjehan Aziz and MG Vassanji for venturing out on a limb on behalf of unpublished authors, and for bringing first voices to print with such care and dedication.

June 2004, North Vancouver

Sources

Kotli Loharan and its mythology is not entirely a product of this book, even though I have taken some poetic liberties with its geography. In reality, there are two Kotlis, one known as the east (Chardi Kotli, or the Kotli where the sun rises) that is my hometown and the location of the book, and the other that is the adversarial one to the west. The two towns are situated about seven miles northwest of the city of Sialkot in Pakistani Punjab, and were once separated by a mile of what was at the time of the book an unbroken stretch of lush marshland and a patchwork of fields.

"... Paani": "Everyone lives downstream" is the ecologists' motto adopted by Windhorse Farm, Nova Scotia.

Partition: With currently every sixth person in the modern world tracing his or her roots to the Indo-Pakistani subcontinent, the impact of the partition of India by its British colonizer's in mid-1947 continues to loom compellingly large on a global scale.

The page 2 quote is from Ishtiaq Ahmed, Dept. of Political Science,

Stockholm University, *The 1947 Partition of India: A Paradigm for Pathological Politics in India and Pakistan.* He writes:

> The Partition of British India in 1947, which created the two independent states of India and Pakistan, was followed by one of the cruelest and bloodiest migrations and ethnic cleansings in history. The religious fury and violence that it unleashed caused the deaths of some 2 million Hindus, Muslims and Sikhs. An estimated 12 to 15 million people were forcibly transferred between the two countries. At least 75,000 women were raped. The trauma incurred in the process has been profound. Consequently, relations between the two states, between them and some of their people and between some of their groups have not normalised even after more than half a century; on the contrary, they have consistently worsened with each passing year. . . . The riots and pogroms, which accompanied Partition, were most harrowing in the Punjab and effectively led to the first successful post-war experiment in massive ethnic cleansing in the world.

"The Sacrificial Circuit": Shafiq, Chachaji Suleman and Babaji are the only real-life characters in the book. Shafiq Ahmed Malik was a cousin, a childhood hero and a larger-than-life big-brother figure in my life until his departure for Kuwait. His premature death devastated everyone who knew him personally. Chachaji Suleman's character is partially based on my father's early years in Kuwait. Babaji Feroze was my father's elder brother by nineteen years, my tayaji.

SS *Dara*: For the final part of this story, I have had to rely on PJ Abraham's excellent first-person account of the Dara tragedy: *Last Hours on Dara*, 1963 ©PJ Abraham and Peter Padfield, printed by Peter Davis Ltd. In his introduction to the book, the author writes: "In the number of lives lost and the terror on board, this was one of the worst peacetime maritime disasters since the loss of the Titanic."

The following quote is taken from Bill Clive's online page on SS *Dara*: "There is some conjecture that, due to the circumstances, the perpetrator of the crime may also have been on board at the time of the explosion … there was a total of 819 on board, including 19 officers and 113 crew; 238 died from burns or drowning … It was never clearly established who planted the bomb, or why, but there was a high loss of life attributed to the incident, despite the fact that no one was on board when it sank."

While searching for further records of the shipwreck, I have encountered several messages posted on the web, some as recent as spring 2004, by relatives and friends of the missing victims, who have yet to find closure on their personal loss, more than forty years after the tragedy.

"Mitti da Baawa" (The Clay Doll): The opening and closing quote is from a poignant, resonant Punjabi folksong in which a housewife creates a clay doll to represent the child she is unable to conceive. Transliteration is by Suman Kashyap.

Characters
(in order of appearance)

Or, Why the Drawing Master's Wife Is Called Drangani

Hafeez Tarkhan: Village carpenter. Tarkhan means carpenter.
Balwinder and Sukhinder: The two Sikh brothers Balwinder and
Sukhinder address each other informally as Balway and Sukhi, whereas
their sister Sardar addresses them more fondly as Balwa and Sukhiya.
Sardar: Balwinder and Sukhinder's sister. Sardar is a common name for
Sikhs of both gender, and Sardarni is a traditional female Sikh title.
There is also a tradition among the Sikhs by which women are given
male names with Kaur attached as a suffix or second name
Qulsoom Tarkhanan: Hafeez's wife. The title Tarkhanan means the car-
penter's wife. (By the same token, a female doctor or a doctor's wife is
known as daktarni, and a drawing master's wife becomes drangani.)
Malhaara: Traveling fakir, lamp lighter, sitar player.
Bhagga: General merchant, entrepreneur.
Kittu Karim Bukhsh: Nine-year-old son of Sughra.
Rana Saab: Called Ranaji by those close to him, or in veneration Rana
Saab. Kittu addresses him more fondly and informally as Ranaji when
he is reminiscing about his own earlier life, and only calls him Rana Saab
when he gets to know him better. (Usually the reverential prefix or suf-
fix is assimilated as part of the first name, e.g., Ranaji.)
Ranima: Rana Saab's wife
Sughra: Pronounced Sughrañ, also called intimately called Sughi or
Sugho. In reality, a person named Sughra will rarely be called Sughra
but will probably be addressed more familiarly as Sughi or Sugho by
those who know her.

205

Mammu: Maternal uncle, also known as mammuji.

Hashim: Muezzin, Quran teacher.

Maulvi Saab: A Muslim trained in the doctrine and law of Islam; the head of the Jamiya masjid or central mosque.

Afzal: Rana Saab's son.

Rafiq: Shafiq's younger brother.

Jamila: Shafiq's fiancée.

Azam Karighar: Azam the technician; Guddho's husband.

Guddho: Azam's child bride. Guddho, also referred to as Guddhi, means a doll.

Ghaffar: Name of the chai stall owner.